Julie Wassmer is a professional television drama writer who has worked on various series including ITV's *London's Burning*, C5's *Family Affairs* and BBC's *Eastenders* – which she wrote for 20 years.

Her autobiography, *More Than Just Coincidence*, was Mumsnet Book of the Year 2011.

Also by Julie Wassmer

The Whitstable Pearl Mystery
Murder-on-Sea
May Day Murder
Murder on the Pilgrims Way

DISAPPEARANCE At OARE

A Whitstable Pearl Mystery

JULIE WASSMER

Constable • London

CONSTABLE

First published in Great Britain in 2018 by Constable

ISBN: 978-1-47212-494-4

Typeset in Adobe Caslon Pro by SX Composing DTP, Rayleigh, Essex
Printed and bound in Great Britain by CPI Group (UK) Ltd, Croydon CRO 4YY

Papers used by Constable are from well-managed forests
and other responsible sources.

Constable
An imprint of
Little, Brown Book Group
Carmelite House
50 Victoria Embankment
London EC4Y 0DZ

An Hachette UK Company
www.hachette.co.uk

www.littlebrown.co.uk

For Kas

Feel you behind me on the stair,
I look around and you're not there.
Seems like you vanished in thin air …

The Sinceros, 'Disappearing'
Lyrics by Mark Kjeldsen

PART ONE

Chapter One

It was late afternoon on a sunny Wednesday in August and the view from Whitstable's prom showed plenty of holidaymakers on the beach – even though the tide was retreating. Brave kids and determined swimmers had headed out with it, hoping to find sufficient depth to float a lilo or to manage a few last strokes before giving up and plodding back across a great plain of estuary mud towards the pebbled shore. Pearl Nolan watched them. She was seated on a wooden bench at the foot of some grassy slopes which were dotted with rows of colourful beach huts, their porches slung with pastel shades of bunting swaying in the warm breeze. The pale grey vintage dress she wore perfectly matched the colour of her moonstone eyes, and a few sheets of paper rested on her lap, though what was written on them had failed to hold her attention. Instead, she had slipped off her reading glasses and propped them high on her head, in front of a hair clip which barely tamed her long dark curls, as she gazed straight ahead, realising that the concrete prom before her appeared almost like a symbolic frontier separating the Whitstable natives from the tourists on the beach.

The acronym DFLs, commonly used by local people for Down From Londoners, was appropriate, as the majority of Whitstable's summer visitors consisted of day-trippers keen to exchange the stifling city for a stretch of airy coastline. For those who remained immune to the pleasures of Whitstable's pebble beach, there were always the delights of the two main thoroughfares of the High Street and Harbour Street, where an eclectic mix of quirky independent shops offered all manner of items from connoisseur cheese to vintage vinyl. A morning spent shopping in Whitstable generated hearty appetites, and by lunchtime visitors could be found huddling outside the town's various eateries to peruse the menus on offer. Many would be seduced by the panoramic views of the beach-facing establishments, but there were plenty who fell for the more informal charms of Pearl Nolan's own restaurant, The Whitstable Pearl, especially since it served the best seafood in town.

Over the past twenty years, Pearl had developed a menu to satisfy both locals and visitors, with a selection of signature dishes that included squid encased in a light chilli tempura batter, marinated sashimi of tuna, mackerel and wild salmon, and a popular staple of sardines with garlic and chilli *ajillo*; but one thing always remained in popular demand, the single item that defined this little north Kent town, which might have gone quite unnoticed without it – its native oyster.

Every year, the weekend closest to 25 July signalled the start of the town's Oyster Festival, the date marking the Feast of St James, when a veritable tsunami of visitors descended from all over the world to celebrate the famous bivalve with a series of events that included an eye-catching parade, a tug of war, concerts, fringe theatre, and the inevitable oyster-eating 'Shuck', during which a dozen of Whitstable's finest molluscs would be downed in record time. So popular had the festival become that every hotel, guesthouse, holiday apartment and campsite space was booked throughout the entire period, leading some to complain that the festival had now outgrown its location and should be limited so it could once again return to being a low-key event for the enjoyment of local families. But the genie was out of the bottle, and while the pages of Sunday colour supplements continued to be splashed with glowing reports about this eccentric little fishing town that had managed to retain its character in spite of being only an hour and a half's travel time from London, Whitstable would continue to draw its summer visitors like wasps to an open pot of jam.

Now that the Oyster Festival had come and gone, Pearl was reminded that the next significant date on the town's calendar was the summer carnival. Bearing little in common with its counterparts in Rio or Notting Hill, Whitstable's charity parade was a far more parochial affair consisting of a procession of floats, walking groups and comic cars – all presided over by a local 'royal family' consisting of a Carnival Queen and two Carnival Princesses.

Pearl usually contributed a trade float for The Whitstable Pearl, designed by her mother, Dolly, who was threatening to use her artistic skills this year to create a stunning aquatic scene featuring Pearl's young waitress, Ruby, as an appropriate marine creature – though what that might be was still undecided.

As one of the last events on the town's summer itinerary, the carnival took place when the days were growing noticeably shorter, signalling a time of restive impatience among holidaymakers who were keen to wring the last pleasures out of the season before it faded into autumn. And the same was true for the shopkeepers and business owners in town, who continued to benefit from Whitstable's new-found popularity. But for Pearl, business was not everything, and the period following the height of summer was usually a time for some welcome respite – especially since she now had a young assistant chef in place who was not only capable of replicating her menu, but also wished to add some dishes of his own. Looking down at the print-outs in her hand, Pearl realised that the beach scene in front of her had been acting as a distraction from the new menu items that Dean Samson had asked Pearl to consider in the hiatus after lunch and before the evening restaurant service began. Recipes combining roast turbot, razor clams and sea purslane displayed the young chef's originality, but they also blended perfectly with the style Pearl had long ago chosen for her restaurant – one characterised not by grand culinary statements but a clear respect for simple dishes created with the very best ingredients.

Pearl had never become complacent about the restaurant's success, nor had she forgotten what a struggle it had been in the early days – especially while bringing up her son, Charlie, as a single parent. She had known, even then, that in order to gain a good reputation, she would need to be more than the 'good cook' she had already proved herself to be, and so she had dedicated herself to the task in hand, immersing herself in tastes and flavours, and learning how to marry ingredients together successfully, including various herbs and spices – and not just the familiar ones like rosemary, thyme and mint, but the more exotic seasonings and fragrances of Syrian oregano, Moroccan saffron, Middle Eastern sumac and sticky Turkish *urfa* pepper.

How many oysters had she served to her customers over the last two decades? Certainly not as many as the twenty million that had been dredged from the town's oyster beds in past years but, nevertheless, in those early days, she had finished her services bearing the battle scars of cooker burns on her forearms and the smell of seafood and sautéed garlic clinging to her hair and clothes, to head home and take care of her son. In doing so, she had exchanged the thick humid air of her restaurant kitchen for the fresh salt tang of the expansive sea as a walk on the beach revived her. It still did so, but these days she no longer had to slave in the same kitchen over her dishes because she now had Dean to do that for her. Nevertheless, it was true that the young chef's keenness to contribute was serving to underscore a certain sense of redundancy for his boss. Pearl's presence was no longer deemed essential on the restaurant floor either, because a small group of dedicated staff now managed quite well without her – as did Charlie.

At twenty-one, Pearl's son rented a flat of his own in Canterbury, where he was studying graphic design at university and, after a gap year in Berlin spent designing and selling T-shirts, he was showing a fair amount of independence, though the odd session working at the family restaurant always provided a welcome boost to his finances.

Charlie's very existence had been the whole reason for The Whitstable Pearl, and for his mother giving up on the police training she had once embarked upon, and as she stared out towards the beach again, she allowed her mind to wander back to that summer romance with Charlie's father. She could almost see him again on the beach: blond, lean, like Charlie himself – a young man who had been merely passing through a small town on his way to explore the world. He had pressed her to join him, but Pearl had stayed behind, feeling sometimes like the small marine creatures left stranded on the beach at low tide, unable to leave the estuary waters for wider oceans . . . A simple pregnancy test had convinced her that she had no choice but to remain in Whitstable, forgetting all dreams of becoming a police detective and instead bringing up her child. And so she had thrown herself into a hectic world of food and cooking until, as her fortieth birthday approached, those dreams had resurfaced and she had felt the urge to respond to a new sense of purpose by starting up Nolan's Detective Agency . . .

Pearl was ultimately proud of having solved several local cases, including the high-profile murders which had set her on a collision course with DCI Mike McGuire of Canterbury CID. The police detective had arrived in Whitstable while on a temporary transfer from London, but had decided to stay on in the area and had made his home in a riverside apartment in Best Lane, Canterbury – just seven miles away from Pearl.

At the outset, there had been some conflict and competition between the two detectives, but a relationship had sprung up, based on mutual respect, physical attraction and a recognition that they complemented one another as much as yin and yang. Ultimately McGuire was proving to be an irresistible conundrum for Pearl, and the last summer months had proved frustrating for her as the police detective had been in London for a court case and Nolan's Detective Agency had received only the usual requests to locate lost dogs and stolen bikes – none of the real mysteries Pearl thrived upon. A few nights ago, during their last phone conversation, McGuire had promised Pearl that he would be back soon – but until then she had only the restaurant and Dean's new menu items to concentrate on. Slipping on her reading glasses once more, she took a deep breath and decided to do precisely that, when a passing cloud suddenly masked the sun and a sound began to fill the sky above her.

Looking up, she thought it might be the rotors of a noisy drone being operated from somewhere at the top of the slopes, but a silhouette soon became visible through hazy cloud, growing larger as the sound amplified from a helicopter sweeping in across the bay. For an instant she queried whether it could be the police scanning the area for a wanted criminal, or perhaps an escaped convict from one of the three prisons based on Sheppey, the island west of Whitstable behind which the sun set every evening, and the thought prompted Pearl to wonder whether it might even be McGuire, himself, in the helicopter. She hadn't seen him for several weeks, but if he had managed to return from London earlier than expected surely he would have contacted her? The helicopter hovered for a while, appearing almost stationary, as though scanning the retreating tide, but the lifeboat was still in place at its harbour station and a young beach attendant sat relaxed on his elevated platform, suggesting to Pearl that the chopper wasn't following up a coastal emergency. She got to her feet and took off her glasses, shielding her eyes from the sun to stare up – but the helicopter began to descend and seemed to head straight in her direction before swooping up and away at the very last moment to trace the entire length of Marine Parade, the residential road that ran along the top of the grassy slopes. With disappointment, Pearl realised that the chopper's appearance signalled nothing more than a local radio station's search for traffic news for rush-hour commuters.

Turning back to the bench, Pearl was just about to sit down again when her mobile rang from the depths of her basket – not the familiar tone of the phone she used for personal calls, but the dedicated line for Nolan's Detective Agency. It was a sound she hadn't heard for some time and she answered the call quickly, straining to hear above a sudden blast of music from a noisy beach radio. The woman on the end of the phone line was softly spoken. Giving her name as Christina Scott, she hesitated for only a moment before explaining with some urgency: 'I need your help.'

Fifteen minutes later, Pearl approached the gate to her sea-facing garden to note that Christina Scott was already there, waiting for her. Tall and with an angular frame and shoulder-length blonde hair, she appeared to be in her early thirties and was dressed in a pale pink cotton blazer and matching linen trousers, an outfit which seemed overly formal for the sultry afternoon. With the disappearance of the tide, the air had become muggy and the briny smell of seaweed clung to it, but Christina was leaning against the promenade wall and staring out towards the horizon, as though she might have been gazing at something infinitely more interesting than wind-farm sails waiting for a freshening breeze. Something seemed to tell her she was being observed, and she glanced quickly back along the prom just in time to see Pearl, who came forward, offering a smile as she asked: 'Mrs Scott?'

The woman shook Pearl's outstretched hand. 'Yes,' she said. 'But please call me Christina.' Pearl noted that the woman's deep-set eyes were the colour of topaz, and seemed burdened with a stifled sadness. She quickly indicated the way through her garden gate, and away from the revellers on the shore who were heading off to freshen up for the evening, perhaps before returning to the beach and to the old Neptune pub, where a band would be playing later.

The two women moved through Pearl's tiny, well-kept garden, brushing past huge banks of fragrant lavender until reaching the converted wooden beach hut that Pearl now used as an office. Once inside, she moved to open a window and invited Christina Scott to take a seat. Taking her own place behind her desk, Pearl saw that her prospective client was fishing for something in her handbag, finally taking out a small packet of cologne-soaked tissues. She used one to moisten her throat, then wiped her hands with it in such a thorough way that Pearl was reminded to give attention to a few dusty surfaces, until Christina produced a small bag into which she placed the used tissue, signalling she had come prepared.

'Can I get you something?' Pearl asked. 'Tea? Coffee?'

Christina shook her head and explained in a faltering voice: 'I'm ... afraid I don't have much time. I have to get back for my son.' She offered a tense smile before explaining: 'My mother's taken him out for the afternoon. She's staying with us for the summer holidays.'

Before Pearl could comment, a rabble of teenagers raced past on the beach outside and their screams caused Christina to flinch. Laughter followed and the voices finally trailed away, but still Christina Scott stared towards the window until Pearl gently prompted: 'How can I help?'

Christina looked back, allowing Pearl to note that she was an attractive woman, though her complexion was pale in spite of the good weather and her features were drawn, as though she might be experiencing some low-level pain. 'It's my husband ...' she began.

On hearing those three words, Pearl's heart sank. The stalking of errant spouses and partners was bread-and-butter work for most private detectives, but Pearl was never keen on spending her time searching for evidence of cheating. She braced herself, fully expecting to hear a catalogue of marital abuse or infidelity, but instead Christina simply stated: 'He's missing.'

The words came almost as a whispered secret, and a silence fell before Pearl responded. 'I take it you've notified the police?'

Christina nodded and Pearl continued: 'Then they should file a Missing Persons report, and—'

'They have.' Christina had broken in quickly, betraying some impatience, before she looked away again to the window, seemingly in an effort to calm herself. 'They haven't found him. And I don't believe they will,' she said determinedly. 'That's the reason I'm here.' Looking back, she held Pearl's gaze as she explained further: 'Steven and I met at university in London – though he dropped out to become an artist. It was really all he ever wanted to do.' She gave a sad smile. 'We fell in love, got married and moved down here several years ago when house prices were rather more reasonable. My mother helped with a deposit on our home in Seasalter. I was teaching at a nearby school and Steven was still working on his paintings.' She broke off for a moment then went on. 'One morning, I woke to find he wasn't there. He'd disappeared – into thin air.' She fell silent again and Pearl waited, allowed her time to continue. 'I thought he might have gone for an early morning run, but his trainers were still in the porch and . . . he'd taken nothing with him but the car.' She paused again, this time as though trying to remember precisely. 'I tried his phone, but my call went straight through to voicemail so I rang some friends and then family. Steven's parents live out in Herne Bay,' she added. 'But no one had seen or heard from him.' She bit her lip, then composed herself again. 'We waited . . . until the evening. Then I reported him missing.'

Christina fumbled in her bag, this time for a paper handkerchief, and went on. 'The police detective who came to see me said that over two hundred thousand people go missing in this country every year. Did you know that?' Her question was purely rhetorical because she quickly added: 'He said that most missing people return within a few days – so I held on to that thought. It was all I had. And I convinced myself that Steven would be one of them . . . that he'd come home . . . so when the doorbell rang that night, I was sure it must be him.' She looked hopeful – then crestfallen. 'But it wasn't. It was the police, coming to tell me they had found the car.' Her voice trailed into silence as she nervously began to tear off tiny pieces of the paper tissue in her hand.

'Where?'

'On the old slipway at Oare.'

'Oare,' echoed Pearl softly. 'You mean on the marshes near Faversham?'

The area was some thirteen miles from Whitstable, a beautiful but isolated spot used mainly by walkers and bird-watchers attracted by the nearby nature reserve. Pearl knew that a now disused ferry service had once operated between two points across the Swale river, from the mainland at Oare to the Isle of Harty on the southeastern side of the Isle of Sheppey. A popular pub, the Ferry House Inn, lay on the island side, but Pearl now remembered it was some years since she had been there.

'The car had been abandoned,' said Christina, 'and there was no sign of Steven. Only his jacket on the passenger seat. And a note.'

'A note?' asked Pearl.

Christina nodded. 'It said: *I never thought what I did was of value – so I really can't go on like this any more.*' She paused for a moment then admitted: 'Those words have haunted me ever since.' She frowned suddenly as she looked down to see that she had torn the paper handkerchief in her hands into shreds. She stuffed the pieces of tissue into her bag and Pearl asked. 'The note – it was definitely in Steven's handwriting?'

Christina nodded. 'And a search was launched straight away. Police . . . lifeboats. They scoured the river – its banks and the marshes. The coastguard had warned that due to the tides it might be days before a body might be found …' As her voice trailed off, Pearl guessed the outcome. 'But it never was?'

Christina shook her head. 'No.'

Pearl took some time to compute this. 'And the police?'

Christina Scott shook her head again but this time offered no further reply.

'But they did investigate?'

Christina's reply was sharp: 'Of course. They're obliged to. But with no body ever found and the car abandoned …'

She broke off again, as if trying to calm her temper before continuing: 'They began to suggest that Steven might have staged his own suicide.'

Pearl looked away as she tried to assimilate this. Beyond the window the sun still shone but the room seemed suddenly chilled. She looked back at Christina. 'And what do *you* think?'

Christina failed to respond for a moment, then stated finally: 'I don't know any more, but . . . I don't believe my husband would ever have left us like that.'

'Us?'

'I was three months pregnant at the time.'

Pearl found herself leaning back in her chair as she took this in. Christina seemed to brace herself before admitting: 'I can't wait any longer. I need to know what happened. It's almost seven years since I last saw my husband . . .' As she broke off, Pearl came to a sudden realisation: 'Death in absentia . . .'

Christina Scott nodded. 'Yes. That's what they call it. Steven's about to be declared legally dead.' A bitter tone entered her voice as she continued: 'Everyone says this should help us to move on.'

'Everyone but you?' said Pearl sagely.

Reaching down into her bag, Christina Scott took out a wallet, and from it a small photograph, which Pearl instantly assumed would be of her missing husband, but instead she saw the image showed a small boy, dressed in school uniform: grey short trousers and a bright blue blazer that was slightly too large for him as the sleeves covered most of his hands. He was smiling, perhaps in an effort to please the photographer, and his eyes were the same topaz blue as Christina's, though his hair was the russet colour of autumn.

'My son,' she said softly. 'Martin's six years old,' she explained. 'And he's never known his father.' She frowned as she continued: 'Perhaps he never will. But he deserves to know what happened to him.'

In the next moment, as Pearl considered those words, the photo of young Martin Scott seemed to blend into an image Pearl carried in her mind of her own son at the same age. Charlie had now grown into a man without ever knowing his own father and, perhaps, like the boy in the photo, he never would . . .

'Will you help us?'

Christina Scott's stark question snapped Pearl back to the moment. She looked up from the photo in her hand, and back at the woman sitting in front of her, and knew instantly, without doubt, what her reply would be.

Chapter Two

Shortly before 9 a.m. the next day, Dolly Nolan was using a Whitstable Pearl tea towel to buff the last few items of a set of crockery she had brought with her to the restaurant. An arrangement existed whereby Dolly's handmade ceramics provided the perfect tableware for Pearl's food, and the restaurant thereby promoted her work, which she also sold in her Harbour Street shop, Dolly's Pots. This stood beneath Dolly's Attic, the little flat she rented out to holidaymakers. Guests often took home some of their landlady's dishes as a memento of their stay in Whitstable, along with some of the smaller items of eccentric driftwood artwork she created, but the oyster platters remained a firm favourite, their forms reflecting the wavy contours of the oyster itself. It was fitting for Dolly's 'shabby chic' style of pottery to allow for irregularities in shape because Dolly herself hated uniformity – not just in her art, but in life. In truth, Dolly Nolan was a rebel.

While Pearl took after her late father, Tommy, in appearance (both in height and with her slim, willowy frame), Dolly struggled with her weight and had tried every diet known to man. Standing at no more than five feet four (and a precious half-inch, as she always insisted), she looked as though she had been compressed – a short, stout battery, but one permanently charged with energy. The colourful highlights she wore in her hair, once magenta, now cerise, seemed as much intended to gain attention as her flamboyant dress sense, evident today in the pink kaftan she was wearing over crimson leggings. Dolly's loud style wasn't usual for most women in their mid-sixties, but it certainly wasn't out of place in a town like Whitstable, which had become the adopted home of many artists, attracted as much to its *laissez-faire* attitude as to its stunning sunsets and the clear northern light of its coastline.

Certainly it was true that – as a coastal town – Whitstable seemed more accepting of new ideas than the surrounding country villages, which remained far more insular in nature. But nevertheless, close-knit ties existed within Whitstable's own community, along with an inherent suspicion of strangers that harked back to the town's former smuggling history. Whitstable had embraced and assimilated individuals from elsewhere, but it had also resisted changes wrought upon it by an influx of DFLs. Locals, including Dolly and Pearl, had campaigned against the arrival of chain stores, and objected to large-scale building developments which threatened not only to ruin the quirky nature of the town but also to kill off the goose that was currently laying so many golden eggs.

As Dolly set down the last of her new oyster platters, she turned to Pearl and asked: 'Scott, you say?' Pearl saw that her mother was looking perplexed. As a native, Dolly was familiar with all the old local family names: the Ganns, the Rigdens and Rowdens, but the surname of Pearl's new client had failed to ring any bells, and she now shook her head ruefully. 'I can't say I know anyone of that name,' she admitted, then: 'But to be perfectly honest, I can't remember this man going missing either.' Her statement was delivered with the same scepticism Pearl imagined the police might have adopted during their investigation into Steven Scott's disappearance. According to Christina they had found evidence pointing to a potential suicide – a note and a jacket left in an abandoned car – but in the absence of a body and no signs of foul play, they had seemingly suspected that Steven Scott might have faked his own suicide – a pseudocide, as it was known.

'His car was left out near Oare Marshes,' said Pearl. 'On the old slipway near the Harty Ferry mooring?'

At this, Dolly looked further troubled, not because she was unfamiliar with the area, but because she was a mine of local information and a nugget of it appeared to be missing. She frowned to herself. 'All the same,' she mused. 'If he was a local man, the Whitstable newspapers would surely have covered this?'

'Not necessarily,' said Pearl. 'He lived out in Seasalter and his family are based in Herne Bay.'

'Ah,' Dolly nodded slowly as though everything had become clear. 'Well, that would explain it, because as far as the local papers are concerned, Seasalter and Herne Bay might just as well be in London. I don't know why they have to . . .' she broke off, searching for the right word: '*regionalise* us like they do. If you ask me, the papers take "local" too far.'

Pearl reflected on her mother's inimitable logic, and the fact that Whitstable's neighbouring towns were all considered to be quite distinct in spite of their proximity to one another. Dolly bit her lip thoughtfully. 'I really should go and visit Dee, you know.'

'Dee?' asked Pearl, confused by the *non sequitur*.

'Dee Poulton. That wonderful woman I met on my flamenco course. She's a tip-top book-keeper and formidably numerate, which was lucky for me as she helped no end with my accounts last year.' She gave a rueful sigh. 'But that was before she crossed to the other side.'

Pearl looked up to see her mother's doleful expression. 'Herne Bay,' Dolly explained, adding: 'Everyone seems to be doing it lately: clearing the mortgage by moving to a cheaper town down the road? But Herne Bay's not exactly "down the road", is it?'

Pearl opened her mouth to speak but Dolly continued on. 'Oh, it might be in distance, and they all say it, just before they go: '"See you soon. I'll only be down the road", but once they're gone – they're gone. You never see 'em again.' She stared down at the plate in her hand and settled it on the table.

'You *could* visit Dee,' said Pearl knowingly.

'And don't think I haven't wanted to,' Dolly said in her defence, 'but chance'd be a fine thing.'

As if on cue, her mobile sounded with an incoming text and she quickly viewed it, tapping out a brief response before slipping the phone back into her bag. 'Attic guests,' she huffed. 'Having trouble finding my parking space, so I'd better go and rescue them before they get themselves clamped.' She grabbed her 'coat of many colours', as she called it, so named because she had made it herself from numerous squares of vibrant paisley fabric, and looked back at her daughter as she slipped into it. 'And what makes you think you can solve this mystery?'

'I didn't say I could,' Pearl informed her. 'Only that I'd try.'

'Well,' said Dolly, pausing at the door. 'You know what I'm going to say, don't you?'

Pearl looked at her. 'Be careful?' Pearl had heard this a million times.

'That's right,' Dolly replied, but as she opened the door she hesitated for a moment and looked back. 'Though if you're off to Herne Bay any time soon, let me know. I'll come with you.'

With that she exited, leaving Pearl no chance to argue. Instead, she stacked the last of her new plates before glancing quickly up at the clock to see she had only a couple of hours to re-interview her client and be back before The Whitstable Pearl opened its doors.

*

Pearl decided to walk the mile or so to Christina Scott's home in Seasalter, but as the weather on this stretch of coastline was always capable of sudden change, she took a white plastic raincoat with her, and soon found herself passing the old tollgate cottage situated on an island in the centre of a busy road junction, a reminder that the route had once been a historic toll road when Whitstable had first been developing as a seaside resort. In fact, Whitstable had never adopted the more garish styles of nearby Margate or Herne Bay, remaining quintessentially a fishing town, which was still part of its abiding charm.

Pearl's decision to head off on foot was soon justified as she noted a fair amount of traffic congestion on the long residential road of Joy Lane that headed west towards Seasalter. On its southern side, large Edwardian houses stared across at newly extended properties on the sea-facing side, where a rash of estate agents' For Sale signs indicated they were increasingly changing hands – not so much homes as investment deals. Pearl reflected on what Dolly had told her about her friend, Dee Poulton, recognising the disappointment of many Whitstable families whose younger relatives were having to move out to other areas since they could no longer afford to buy – or even to rent – in their own home town. Charlie was one of them, though for the time being he was enjoying life in Canterbury, but the demand for new holiday apartments meant that even the smallest of flats were becoming increasingly unavailable to local people. Further out of town, a series of dream homes, on a stretch known as Preston Parade, commanded a superb view of the coastline, before the road finally segued into an area of modest bungalows and convenience stores. A large sprawling holiday park signalled to Pearl that her journey was almost over, but she duly noted that an old pub, once called the Blue Anchor, now sported a fashionably dull-grey façade as well as a new name, The Oyster Pearl, in what seemed to be an attempt to link it to Whitstable's new-found popularity, while reminding visitors that Seasalter had once been as much a home to oyster fishing as Whitstable itself.

The morning tide had ebbed, leaving the muddy estuary bed stretched out like a damp brown canvas littered with puddles. Compared to the busy coastline at Whitstable, which was always populated whatever the weather, the beach at Seasalter that day seemed strangely lifeless and deserted. In the far distance, a lone sailboat lay motionless at anchor, like the subject of a seascape painting, with the dark ragged outline of Sheppey behind it. A gull skimmed the estuary bed close to where an old oyster rack rose up from the mud like a rusting skeleton and, as Pearl moved further along the beach, a few sparrows appeared, only to take startled refuge among some sea kale and yellow horned poppy. Seasalter could be a welcome retreat from Whitstable's summer crowds and boasted a fine Michelin-starred restaurant in an old seaside pub, but with no local railway station and only a series of bus stops, it seemed less of a destination and more of a settlement between Whitstable to the east and the market town of Faversham to the west.

As Pearl made her way along the beach beside a curved

sea wall, numerous warning signs giving the coastguard's details for use in the event of emergency seemed to add to a sense of underlying danger. Mounting a set of wooden steps, she soon found herself back on the road and crossed to the land side, only to encounter more signage concerning obstructions in the stretches of water which sliced their way through a rural landscape of freshwater marsh. The Seasalter Levels on the land side of the road were the result of centuries-old drainage of the marshes, but they now formed a prime wetland site for wildfowl and wading birds like redshank, lapwing and teal, while anglers came in search of pike, tench, roach and bream, especially near to an old pumping station where fishing remained free.

Seasalter Pumping Station was always put to use when the water levels rose too high, but Pearl knew that it was, in fact, only a matter of time before the very land on which she stood would be reclaimed by the sea, because the appropriate authorities had decided that cost precluded further sea defences and so the area was to form part of a 'managed retreat'. In spite of this, the beach-side properties continued to be snapped up at high prices, and traditional seaside chalets on 'leisure plots' from the 1960s and 1970s now stood cheek-by-jowl with newly extended brickwork houses. Fashionable clapboard façades clashed with pebble-dash and latticed windows, while house numbers painted on kayak paddles vied with cheeky bungalow names picked out in cockleshell. Minimalist glass balconies overlooked hanging baskets of Technicolor petunia and, while the newer properties sported burglar alarms, the older chalet homes displayed stone horse heads on gateposts and front gardens still strung with dusty Christmas lanterns in the height of summer. What each of the properties shared in common, however, were gardens that backed directly on to the shingle beach – an attractive feature to their owners in spite of the ever-encroaching sea levels.

On the land side of the road, looking oddly out of place, even amongst an eclectic parade of residences, Pearl found Christina Scott's home. She took time to study the property, recognising that as a new-build with a gabled roof and large driveway it would have looked more at home on any residential London street – something that perhaps reflected Christina's own status as a DFL. On the front wall, a steel plaque was engraved with the words, The Retreat, seeming strangely appropriate in the light of Steven Scott's disappearance. Glancing through the glass door to the porch, Pearl spied a few items of footwear: a small pair of Wellington boots decorated with cartoon stickers propped tidily beside some women's deck shoes. Christina had mentioned seeing her husband's trainers here on the morning he had gone missing. Now there was no sign of them. Had she long disposed of them – or was she still keeping her husband's clothes and footwear in the hope that he would return? As Pearl asked herself that final question, the front door opened. 'I'm sorry,' Christina said, confused. 'I didn't hear you ring?'

Pearl smiled. 'I didn't have time to.'

Christina threw an anxious glance down the empty road before opening the porch door wider for Pearl to enter, and ushered her into a spacious square hallway from which a staircase led to a single upper floor.

'I was just in the kitchen,' she explained, indicating an open door off the hallway but, as Pearl moved towards it, a figure suddenly appeared at the top of the stairs. The woman looked to be in her late fifties, her fair hair streaked with silver. Tall, and with the same angular frame as Christina, she wore a stylish fawn-coloured coat, a leather bag slung across her shoulder as she stood perfectly still, observing Pearl. Christina began to offer an introduction but the woman marched quickly downstairs and introduced herself. 'Sally Ferguson,' she said crisply. 'I'm Christina's mother. And I take it you're the detective?'

Pearl was about to respond and offer her hand when Sally looked away, giving her attention instead to her daughter. 'I shan't be long,' she said, making a casual phrase sound more like a warning. Pulling a yellow silk scarf from her bag, she slipped it around her neck, and looked back again at Pearl, scanning her features for a moment, as if trying to glean more information. Then she moved to the front door and, without another word, was gone.

As the front door closed, Christina looked both embarrassed and relieved in equal measure. 'Sorry about that.' she said. 'I have to admit ... Mum wasn't exactly in favour of my doing this, but ...' She broke off and offered a weak smile before adding: 'She'll come round.' She then led the way for Pearl into a large open-plan dining room and kitchen area, the windows of which looked out on to flocks of sheep grazing on the marshes. A quick glance around the room showed Pearl it was immaculately tidy and furnished with clean, modern lines. A shelving unit housed some decorative items: a few shells, some hand-painted bowls and a trailing spider plant, but nothing appeared out of its place. Artwork hung on the walls of the dining room: pretty pastel seascapes of Seasalter and a larger study, in oils, of sailing boats in an area that looked familiar to Pearl, though not instantly recognisable at that moment.

'I'd just made some coffee,' said Christina, offering Pearl a seat at the dining table, on which a tray was already neatly set with some mugs and a cafetiere. Pearl sat down and watched Christina pour as she explained: 'Mum's had to go into town and Martin's at a play group.' She handed a mug of coffee to Pearl and added: 'I'm so grateful you've agreed to help.' Taking her own seat at the table, she now waited patiently as though for instruction. Pearl added some milk to her coffee then took a compact device from her bag. 'Would you mind if I recorded our conversation?'

Christina's gaze shifted to the digital recorder in Pearl's hand, then back at Pearl, who explained: 'I could take notes, but there's less room for error with a recording, and anything you tell me will remain confidential.'

Christina chewed on her lip for a second before replying, 'Of course.' Then: 'If you think it'll help, go ahead.'

Pearl set the recorder on the table and checked that it was working properly before she took a sip of her coffee and offered another smile to her client in an effort to put her at ease. 'Do you have a good photograph you could let me have of Steven?'

Christina opened a drawer in the dining table. 'I thought you'd ask.' She took out a slim plastic folder and added: 'So I got this ready for you.' She handed the folder to Pearl, who opened it to find a number of neatly stacked papers, on top of which lay a poster bearing the bold headline: MISSING. Beneath it was a large colour photograph of Steven Scott – a young man in his late twenties with chestnut brown hair and eyes. A scattering of fine freckles across his nose and cheeks gave him a boyish look, as did his open and innocent expression. Pearl noted that his tousled hair was quite long and reached down below his collar. It was the same russet colour as his son's – the child he never knew.

'It was taken just a few weeks before he went missing,' said Christina. 'On his twenty-eighth birthday. It was a lovely day. We spent it out there on the beach.' She paused briefly, becoming reflective before she finally handed a poster to Pearl. 'I put these up as widely as I could. All around Oare and Faversham . . .'

'Faversham?'

'Yes. Steven used to go there to paint.'

Pearl's gaze shifted to the oil painting on the wall as Christina continued to explain. 'Faversham Creek. It was my favourite of all Steven's paintings so I made sure he didn't sell it.' She looked back at Pearl. 'It's very good, don't you think? He worked on it for weeks.' Pearl took another look at the painting, this time with fresh eyes, recognising that the boats were in fact sailing barges, moored on the southern quay of Faversham Creek, their tall masts and furled ochre sails mirrored in the reflection of a lowering tide beneath a flaming summer sky.

'He never went to art school and had no formal training, but he took up painting again when we moved here, and was just beginning to have some luck selling his work. A businessman had offered an exhibition, but it never took place because Steven went missing.' She broke off, looking pained. 'I still have most of the paintings in the garage.'

'You . . . said Steven had started painting "again"?' said Pearl. 'Had he given it up?'

'Oh . . .' Christina frowned, as though confused, 'Well, he'd . . . actually begun painting as a child. Art therapy after his brother Mark died. They were twins, only twelve years old at the time, so losing Mark was very traumatic. They were very close. Twins often are.' She looked down at her mug and took a sip of coffee, then saw Pearl was looking at her, waiting for more information. 'Mark drowned,' she explained. 'A tragic accident. He and Steven had been swimming together off the Street – the stretch of shingle off Tankerton Slopes – when Mark got into difficulty with the current.' She broke off for a moment and looked back at Pearl. 'Steven was heartbroken. He had counselling for some time but it was the art therapy that helped most.'

'He told you that?'

Christina shook her head. 'No. Alan did. Steven's step-father.' She paused again. 'Steven never talked to me about Mark – though Linda talks about little else.' She looked up quickly and explained: 'That's Steven's mother. She's never really recovered from the loss. She'd tried for years to have children and was in an unhappy marriage at the time, but having the boys must have given her the courage to leave her first husband and she then met and married Alan.' She looked down thoughtfully at the poster again. 'When the police failed to find Steven, I went to a Missing Persons' charity. They suggested I should make these posters and put them up anywhere that Steven might be known. And in London, of course.'

'Did your husband have connections there?'

'No.' Christina looked down at the posters. 'But it's easier to get lost in a city, isn't it? That's what everyone said. So I put them up around all the main railway stations – at Victoria especially, because it's the main route for this part of the coast.' Her expression began to cloud. 'It was only then, when I began talking to the Transport Police, that I . . . realised Steven was just one of so many. So many posters. So many missing people.' She frowned. 'Mispers – that's what the police call them.'

Pearl took her time before asking: 'And I'm presuming the police monitored any subsequent payments made on Steven's credit card – and from his bank account?'

Christina nodded. 'He hadn't taken his credit card with him,' she explained. 'And there was no further activity on his bank account.'

'What about his mobile phone?'

'He'd left it here that morning.'

Pearl took a moment to absorb this.

'I know what you're thinking,' said Christina. 'Steven

must have driven out to that slipway, left the note and killed himself. But if that was the case, why was his body never found? I've told you, the police made a thorough search, they combed the whole area.' Her expression was resolute.

Pearl asked: 'And is there any reason you can think of, any reason at all, why Steven might have left that day?'

At this, Christina looked away, and Pearl spoke softly but emphatically. 'Look, if I'm to help,' she began, 'you have to trust me. Tell me the truth?'

Christina looked back. 'If you mean, did we have problems? The answer is yes. We did. But I don't believe they amounted to anything we couldn't have got over.' She frowned and then admitted: 'We'd been barely managing on my salary at the primary school.'

'And you mentioned your family had helped you to buy this house?'

Christina nodded. 'My mother. Dad died just before we moved here. I don't like being dependent on family but there was no other way.' She frowned. 'It was a difficult time. Then I found out I was pregnant. I . . . wasn't sure Steven was quite prepared for us to have a family, but I'm not saying he wouldn't have made a good father,' she added quickly. 'I'm sure he would. He even seemed to be happy about the news but . . .' She broke off.

'But?'

'We argued. A few days before he went missing.' She looked up at Pearl. 'It wasn't a huge row. I . . . just felt I had to make myself clear. Steven had been spending so much time painting and preparing for the exhibition.' She broke off, then: 'I can't believe what I said that day could have pushed him to consider abandoning us. But if it did, I have to know. That's the reason I came to you. The police have given up. It's been so long now, the officer who was in charge of the case has retired. And there's no one else I can turn to.'

Pearl considered this, together with the desperate look in Christina Scott's eyes.

'And you had no responses to these posters?' she asked.

Christina shook her head. 'There were some phone calls, in the beginning?'

'Phone calls?'

'Hoax calls. The police said I shouldn't have put our home number on the poster, but I wanted to be sure that if anyone had any information they could reach me – if only to leave a message on the answerphone.'

'And did they?'

Christina shook her head again. 'No. The phone would ring, but the caller wouldn't speak. I could hear them, on the other end of the line, and I'd tell myself it was Steven. I'd talk to him, apologise, beg him to come home or at least to speak to me? Then the receiver would go down.' She frowned, her voice becoming faint as she added: 'It happens. People can be cruel.'

Christina's anguished look prevented Pearl from asking her next question, and a ringing telephone suddenly broke into the silence. Christina got up quickly to answer it, but in doing so, she knocked over her coffee mug, and the hot liquid splashed on to the photo on the table. Pearl moved quickly and dried it with a napkin before mopping up the rest of the coffee, but then she registered the look of horror on Christina's face as she appeared frozen, staring down at the stains on her white dress. 'Are you all right?' Pearl asked.

Coming to her senses, Christina glanced over at the ringing phone and made a final move to answer it, but before she could do so, it suddenly stopped ringing. She hurried to the kitchen sink where she began dabbing at her dress with a wet sponge, as she apologised. 'I'm sorry . . . so sorry . . .'

Noting her alarm, Pearl tried to appease her. 'It's OK. There's no harm done.'

But as Christina turned to face her, the distress on her face was palpable.

'No,' she insisted. 'I . . .' She broke off and looked from the table to her stained dress. 'I'm sorry . . .' she continued. 'Please give me a moment. I . . . must change.'

With that, she hurried from the room, leaving Pearl looking back at the poster on the dining-room table before she hit the Pause button on her recorder.

Chapter Three

It was almost an hour later when Pearl finally finished the interview – long after Christina had returned to the dining room, having changed into another outfit and mopped up any hint of spilt coffee. Having done so, she seemed calmer, though Pearl was unsure why Christina had over-reacted to the accident in the first place, and in consideration of this she limited her questions to timings and logistics, taking careful note of all her client's answers. Then she took with her the file of posters, and the recorder which had accurately transcribed their conversation, and at the front door, she promised she would return soon.

'You don't mind if I make up some new posters using the same photograph?' Pearl asked, warning: 'You may well see some around town.'

'That's fine,' said Christina quickly. 'But be careful which contact number you use.'

'I will,' said Pearl.

After saying goodbye to her new client, Pearl waited for

the front door to close before she finally headed off, not in the direction of home, but across to the coastal side of the road, towards an old prefabricated chalet.

Viewed from the front, the building still appeared intact, but as Pearl walked along the side of it towards the sea, she soon discovered that the rear was completely destroyed, and laid open to the elements like a doll's house, but one that had been effectively disembowelled. Furniture and kitchen items lay strewn across a sea-facing garden overgrown with weeds: a child's high chair, a tea caddy, a broken peach-coloured toilet bowl were scattered across the beach, providing an eyesore for the next-door neighbours, whose teak-decked garden boasted a jade Buddha statue and stylish wicker furniture. A Union Jack hung limply from a flagpole in another garden, and Pearl looked away from it and back across the road to view the steep gabled roof and double-glazed windows of Christina Scott's home.

Though the house still looked as if it belonged in any quiet residential city road, it was nonetheless here – as if trying to seek refuge. Even its name, The Retreat, seemed a further clue. But a 'retreat' from what? Christina had indicated her husband might not be ready for fatherhood, but if he had decided to retreat from Life itself, why had he decided to drive thirteen miles to Oare Marshes on the morning he had disappeared? If he had intended to take his own life that day, why had he not chosen a much easier option and simply walked into the sea at this place? Pearl took out the poster from the file and reconsidered his photo – recognising that this image might be all that his wife had left of her husband, along with memories, blighted hopes for a happy future, and perhaps guilt about a final argument. Pearl's hand moved instinctively to a locket around her neck, her fingers stroking it, almost for comfort. It was a modest piece of jewellery, and yet precious for reasons other than its material value. Slipping a fingernail between the two sides of the silver case, she was about to prise open the 'heart' when, in that same moment, a cloud of tiny black storm bugs filled the still air. They settled on the white raincoat she clutched under her arm and, as she tried to brush them away, using the poster in her hand, she saw that they now clung to this too, attracted to the white page. The thick humid air carried a loud crack of thunder before large spots of rain began to fall.

Pearl turned quickly back towards the road, but was instantly brought up short to see a car parked there. The driver's face was almost obscured by the rain-splattered windscreen, but as she leaned forward and opened the passenger door, Pearl recognised Christina Scott's mother, Sally Ferguson. 'You'll be needing a lift home,' was all she said.

Once inside the car, the steady rhythm of the windscreen wipers seemed to emphasise an awkward silence. Sally's gaze remained fixed on the road ahead, so it was left to Pearl to try to break the ice: 'This is kind of you,' she began. 'I live just on Island Wall.'

'Seaspray Cottage,' said Sally, glancing sidelong at Pearl before adding: 'I made a point of finding out about you.' She slowed down at some temporary traffic lights then spoke again. 'You have a restaurant in the High Street, The Whitstable Pearl, but two years ago you started up a detective agency.' She paused. 'Why would you do that?'

'I once trained with the police.'

'And failed to make the grade?'

'I left the force.'

'Why?'

Pearl hesitated. 'Personal reasons.'

'I see.' Sally looked as though she might have checkmated an opponent in a game of chess, before she announced: 'My daughter doesn't need a private detective.'

Pearl framed her words carefully as she replied: 'Perhaps it's closure she needs.'

Sally quickly met Pearl's gaze. 'Christina has been through a great deal.'

'I can see that.'

'Can you?' Sally's tone remained measured and controlled but her eyes narrowed as she went on: 'I don't think you know what you're taking on here.'

The traffic lights ahead began to change and she shifted the car back into gear.

Pearl tried to read Sally's expression but her features remained impassive as she drove on. 'If you were a good detective, you'd have seen by now.'

'Seen what?' asked Pearl as they passed under the old railway bridge into town.

Traffic crawled again as a car in front of them, with French number plates, slowed down to offer its owners their first view of Whitstable. For a moment, it seemed that Sally might have said all she was willing to say, as her expression was still implacable, but finally she explained: 'My daughter suffers from a form of compulsive behaviour.' Her grip tightened on the steering wheel as she went on: 'An obsessive need for cleanliness. It became worse after her father died. But then Steven went missing. She's had a lot to contend with. She had treatment and it helped – for a time.' The traffic in front of them moved on and Sally changed gear, heading seawards towards Island Wall, but without saying another word until reaching Pearl's home. Drawing up outside Seaspray Cottage, she paused for a moment before adding: 'Christina's starting to relapse. Relying on old behaviour. It's her way of trying to control things. But the most important thing remains out of her control.'

'Knowing what happened to her husband?' asked Pearl.

At this, Sally pushed a hand through her hair, then shifted her body so that she was angled towards Pearl, as though trying to gain her full attention. She explained: 'All you really need to know is that Steven Scott walked out on my daughter and her unborn child. He got up one morning, took the car, and drove to that desolate spot where he disappeared without trace – and without a thought for Christina. Tell me,' she continued, 'what kind of man does that?' Her eyes scanned Pearl's for an answer.

'Why he would want to?'

'Why else?' said Sally, exasperated. 'Because he's totally selfish and immature. And consumed with his own problems.'

'Problems?'

'The past.'

'His brother's death, you mean?'

Sally seemed to consider this then agreed. 'Maybe it stemmed from that,' she said finally. 'But he's never worked properly and has always been an underachiever.'

Pearl considered this before countering: 'But he *was* painting . . .'

'Escaping,' said Sally dismissively. 'He would take off for whole days at a time, leaving Christina completely isolated. They were husband and wife, but after a while she became more like a mother to him.' She paused for a moment. 'The mother he never had,' she said ruefully. 'You've yet to meet Linda Scott but, when you do, you'll understand. *That's* if you continue with this investigation.' She spat the word derisively.

'And clearly you'd rather I didn't.'

Sally took her time to respond to Pearl, reining in some frustration before she said: 'My daughter isn't listening to me. The nature of her disorder means it's hard for me to have much influence over her when she's like this – though I wish I had.' She looked away to where an old restored yawl, the *Favourite*, lay permanently moored at the side of Pearl's cottage on Starboard Light Alley.

'When did you last see your son-in-law?' asked Pearl.

Sally hesitated for a moment before replying. 'The day before he disappeared. I asked him to meet me in Whitstable, on Reeves Beach. When he arrived, I told him how I thought he was neglecting Christina and that he

42

should start showing her more consideration. I reminded him that he was about to become a father and that with parenthood came responsibility. I told him I hoped he would live up to that.' She tilted her chin at Pearl, her face set unapologetically.

'And what did he say?'

Sally gave a small shrug. 'Not much. Another man might have fought back and defended himself against his mother-in-law. Told me it was none of my business? But he did none of that. Steven was always so passive. No,' she decided. 'Passive-aggressive. Certainly his lack of engagement could be infuriating.'

'And did you tell Christina about this meeting?'

Sally shook her head. 'No. I didn't. But I did tell the police.' She looked back at Pearl and admitted: 'I didn't feel guilty about what I said to Steven that day, but I saw no reason to further upset my daughter. Steven's desertion had done that enough.' She looked through the windscreen, cold and unyielding. Pearl asked: 'Do you think Steven could have committed suicide?'

Sally blinked, then turned to look back at Pearl as she replied: 'Honestly – no, I don't. And I say that not to absolve myself, because everything I said that day was warranted. And I believe he accepted it.'

In the pause that followed, Pearl framed another question but then resisted asking it. Instead, she said quickly: 'Thanks for the lift.' She had just started to open the passenger door when Sally spoke again.

'Wait . . .'

Sally laid her hand on Pearl's arm and fixed her gaze on her as she said: 'I want you to know that I love my daughter very much and I'll do anything I possibly can to protect her. In fact, I'm selling my house in London and moving here to be with Christina and my grandson. I've told you the truth today – and that's what I did with Steven.'

Though her eyes were the same topaz blue as Christina's, in that moment they seemed to burn with a quiet rage. Pearl looked down at the hand on her arm and felt Sally's grip finally loosen.

'We'll talk again,' Pearl said.

Stepping out of the car, Pearl walked to her front door and looked back to note that Sally was still observing her. Slipping her key into the lock, she entered her home and closed the door behind her, leaning back against it until she finally heard the sound of Sally's car starting up – and driving off. That was soon replaced by the welcome racket of children playing on the beach beyond Pearl's window, and she took a deep breath as she reflected on the exchange with Sally Ferguson. Before she could make sense of it, however, her mobile phone rang, shattering a brief moment of peace. Reaching quickly for the phone, Pearl heard Christina Scott's voice sounding strained on the end of the line.

'Thank you for coming today,' she began. 'I'm sorry if I seemed a bit stressed. The way I reacted about the coffee?'

'I understand,' Pearl said gently. A pause followed on the line before Christina spoke again. 'Yes,' she agreed. 'I think you do.' Then she continued, this time more confidently. 'I just talked to Linda and Alan. Steven's parents. They said they'd be happy to meet you tomorrow. Late afternoon, if that's OK?'

Pearl's first instinct was to resist this suggestion – she had plans of her own – but the keen sense of expectation in her client's voice was difficult to challenge. 'Look, Christina . . .' she began carefully.

'I'll text you the address,' said Christina quickly. 'Thanks for everything, Pearl.'

The phone in Pearl's hand went dead and she found herself staring at it for a moment before she sat down on the sofa and took the recorder from her bag. Setting it on her coffee table, she was about to press Play when an incoming text sounded on her mobile. As good as her word, Christina Scott had just forwarded a contact address and phone number for Linda and Alan Scott. Pearl felt distinctly uneasy – she didn't like having plans made for her, particularly during an investigation. She always preferred to follow her instincts. Nevertheless, she made a quick decision and picked up her mobile again. This time she dialled a stored number and asked the person on the end of the line: 'How do you fancy a trip to Herne Bay tomorrow?'

Chapter Four

Pearl could have taken a fast route to Herne Bay using a dual carriageway, but instead she chose a more scenic journey through town which took her, and Dolly, past the harbour and towards the gatehouse entrance to Whitstable Castle, where she turned her open-topped Fiat seaward to enjoy a coastal view shared by the swanky homes on Marine Parade. The sea in Whitstable could take on various shades of colour according to tide, wind and general weather conditions, and though today the waves appeared an emerald green, rough seas churning the estuary bed could create hues ranging from pewter grey to a muddy brown – something to perplex visitors from sunnier climes. A dinghy race was taking place, making good use of a fresh breeze that was turning the sails of the wind farm on the horizon, and the lowering tide had just begun to expose what was known to local people as the Street – an abbreviation of the Street of Stones, the name for the narrow spit of shingle that stretched at least half a mile out from the shore. This had been the location given by Christina Scott as the place where Steven's young twin brother, Mark, had met a tragic death, and today the shingle bed appeared above the water like a sharp arrowhead pointing towards the horizon. Wavelets rippled around it, shimmering in the early sun, while offering a dangerous indication of currents lying in wait for inexperienced swimmers – or those unfamiliar with the area.

No one could say for sure how the Street had come into existence. Some believed it to be the remains of a Roman road, built on land that had subsequently been surrendered to the sea, while others said it had originated as an ancient landing stage for vessels. Ultimately it was as much a mystery as Steven Scott's disappearance. Dolly checked a text on her mobile phone, then slipped it back into the pocket of her 'coat of many colours' before she looked sidelong at her daughter and commented: 'You know, I swear all this is down to the afternoon I left you with Polly Parrot.'

Pearl glanced back at her mother as she drove. 'Polly …?'

'Don't pretend you've forgotten,' Dolly said quickly. 'Florrie Parrot,' she continued, 'though as soon as she joined the police force she became "Polly". I bumped into her yesterday. She's eighty-two years old and bright as a button. And she happened to remind me about the day I left her looking after you.' She eyed Pearl knowingly.

'I can't say I remember,' said Pearl.

'Well, you were only seven years old at the time,' Dolly

explained. 'But she swears she remembers letting you wear her helmet – and I'm sure it must have affected you.'

'I'm sure it didn't,' Pearl countered, driving on for a while before adding: 'In any case, it wasn't a helmet – it was more of a peaked cap.'

'Ah, so you *do* remember!' said Dolly triumphantly. 'Seven is a very impressionable age,' she insisted. 'Obviously so,' she went on. 'Because now you can't resist snooping around in other people's business ...'

'I'm offering a service,' Pearl argued.

'Yes. Trying to run two businesses when you could be relaxing a little, taking your foot off the pedal ...' She paused before adding her *coup de grâce*, 'And finding yourself a nice man.'

Pearl said nothing to this, knowing all too well her mother's opinion of McGuire – or the 'Flat Foot', as she preferred to call him, demonstrating her natural antipathy towards authority figures like the police.

'You're a beautiful woman,' Dolly continued. 'And it's quite right what they say: Life begins at forty – *if* you allow it to.'

Her mother's smug look was more than Pearl could bear. 'That's precisely why I started up the agency. I am doing something different ...'

'Yes,' Dolly conceded. 'Hankering after old police dreams instead of moving forward with new ones.' She took a breath before adding, gently this time: 'You can't live in the past, Pearl.'

'And neither can Christina Scott,' said Pearl knowingly.

'Her husband's been missing for almost seven years and she needs the truth.' She gave her mother a telling glance but it failed to silence her.

'And what if she can't handle the truth?' Dolly asked. 'What if her husband *did* commit suicide – or he's hiding out somewhere not wanting to be found?'

'Then at least she'll have an answer,' said Pearl. 'But at the moment, she has nothing.' Pearl glanced challengingly at her mother, then gave her full attention once more to the road, recognising that it wasn't only Christina Scott who needed answers because, although Sally Ferguson's warning to Pearl had been a firm one, it had merely served to spur Pearl on …

A short while later, Pearl's Fiat was driving along Hampton Pier Road, which offered a clear view out to the west of the dark silhouette of Sheppey across a choppy sea. Cyclists and dog walkers were enjoying the western esplanade belonging to Whitstable's seaside neighbour, Herne Bay, and the last remaining section of the town's old pier, a landing stage, soon appeared like an island stranded out at sea. Dolly wasn't looking at it. Instead her attention had been caught by something on the land side of the road. 'Would you believe it,' she said, 'that old crazy golf course is still there.'

Pearl glanced across towards an elegant white terrace that had once been home to the largest covered swimming baths in the county, but which now housed a garish amusement arcade and a mini golf course. The sight of the little putting green immediately took Pearl back to a summer during which six-year-old Charlie had aimed to complete the course for a much-coveted prize of a stick of candy floss. Pearl now wondered whether Christina brought her own son here too – Martin Scott, a boy being brought up by his mother and grandmother, just as Charlie had been.

Pearl managed to find a parking space close to a white, single-storey Art Deco building at the foot of the newly renovated pier. There, in the window of the Petit Poisson restaurant, a dark-haired woman in her early fifties looked up as she turned a page of a broadsheet newspaper and caught sight of Dolly, who was now waving excitedly through the windscreen of Pearl's car. Dee Poulton's face broke into a warm smile. Quickly folding her newspaper, she waved back.

Dolly turned to Pearl. 'Come in for a second. Let me introduce you.' Then she went on ahead, leaving Pearl to lock her car. On entering the restaurant it looked to Pearl as though Dolly was about to embrace her old friend, but instead she realised that the two women were striking the same flamenco pose – one arm raised above the head – before they collapsed into laughter.

Dee Poulton was dressed for the sunny weather in a white cotton shift dress and Roman sandals. Her shiny hair was cut into a stylish bob and her dark, almond-shaped eyes fixed directly on Pearl as she held out her hand. 'I've heard a lot about you,' she said, smiling warmly before adding: 'And all good.'

Pearl returned her smile. 'Same here.'

Dee's perfectly arched eyebrows gave her a look of childlike curiosity. 'Take a seat,' she said, but Dolly quickly explained: 'No. I'm afraid Pearl has to be somewhere, so we mustn't keep her.'

'What a shame,' said Dee. 'But it's good to meet you, finally. Here ...' She picked up her handbag and began rooting inside it, finally producing a small card. 'That has my new address on it,' she said. 'You never know ... one day you might be passing through again, and if you are, do drop by.'

She handed the card to Pearl and offered another smile.

'I'll do that,' said Pearl, slipping the card into her pocket. She was about to ask Dee how she was finding life in her new home when she noted that Dolly had already taken her place at the table and was now staring back at her. 'I'll call you later about a lift home,' she said, making it clear there was no present need of Pearl's services. Offering a slight wave, Dolly then turned to her old friend and began chatting animatedly as Pearl recognised she was now redundant.

Ten minutes later, she had managed to locate the home of Steven Scott's parents, Alan and Linda. A modest pebble-dashed bungalow with a tidy front garden populated by a few gnomes, it was tucked away on a side road off the pedestrian precinct, and might have remained forever unknown to Pearl if Christina Scott had not been so intent on setting up this meeting. Pressing the doorbell, Pearl heard the first few notes of a familiar tune, 'London

Bridge is Falling Down' before Alan Scott quickly opened the door. 'Pearl, is it?' he asked keenly.

Pearl nodded and introduced herself and he welcomed her inside. In his mid-fifties, Alan Scott was of a medium height with kind open features beneath short-cropped grey hair. Dressed casually in baggy jeans and a bright blue T-shirt, he led the way through a short passageway and into a tiny kitchen, the walls of which were painted canary yellow. Here, Pearl found Steven's mother, Linda, stirring a pot of tea which she set on the kitchen table, while Alan moved near the kitchen door where some sheets of tabloid newspaper were spread out on the floor together with a wooden frame and some sandpaper.

'You don't mind if he carries on with that, do you?' asked Linda. 'Only it's the new chapel hymn board and we promised the minister it would be ready for service tonight.' She smiled weakly, leaving Alan to explain: 'The other one had woodworm.'

Pearl gave a nod, noticing that Linda's hair was the same chestnut colour as Steven's – but there the resemblance ended. Linda's own hair was gathered back into a ponytail pulled high up on to the back of her head, and her general style made her look like a middle-aged teenager, with her thin body encased in black leggings and a pale pink top with a thread of silver running through its neckline. Seeming suddenly unsure of herself, she glanced at Alan for support. 'Or . . . we *could* go in the front room?'

Pearl replied quickly. 'Here is fine,' she smiled. 'I'm only grateful for your time.'

Linda looked relieved at this and offered a seat to Pearl at the kitchen table before sitting down herself to pour three mugs of tea. She passed milk and sugar to Pearl, then sipped her own tea before tapping the mug in her hands with nervous fingers as she asked: 'So ... this was all Christina's idea, was it? For you to come here today?'

Pearl began carefully: 'I ... do appreciate how difficult things have been.'

Linda blinked quickly a few times, then agreed, 'You're right there.' She looked away to the kitchen window, where sparrows brawled noisily on a branch of clematis. When she looked back again at Pearl, she asked: 'Have you ever lost someone dear to you?'

Taken aback by such a candid question, Pearl's thoughts instantly turned to her father, Tommy, who had died when she was only a teenager. But the word 'lost' also prompted thoughts of Charlie's father, Carl, and of a school friend 'lost' to Pearl when she moved to America with her family.

'Yes,' she replied.

'Then you'll understand,' said Linda gently. She offered a sad smile and a soft look that showed she viewed Pearl differently now – not with fear or scrutiny, but with compassion and empathy. She went on: 'For a long time I asked myself: "Why *me*?"' Then she closed her eyes as she murmured softly: '*How long will you hide your face from me?*'

At this, Alan stopped sanding the wooden surface of his hymn board and stared across to note Pearl's reaction. He explained: 'The Lord has been a great comfort to us.'

'Yes,' said Linda. 'So I no longer ask "why me?" but instead, "why *not* me?"' She cocked her head to one side like one of the small sparrows outside her window. Alan Scott blew wood dust from the top of the hymn board before offering a supportive smile, but he said nothing more and allowed Linda to continue.

'I'm sorry,' she said. 'You wanted to know more, didn't you? About my boy?'

'That's right,' Pearl nodded. 'I know it must be difficult but whatever you can tell me will be helpful.'

Linda drew a deep breath, as though preparing herself, then said: 'He was very special.' Her smile was less sad than serene. 'I knew that, even when he was a baby. We had a bond. Mother and son. Very strong.' She broke off for a moment before asking: 'Do you have any children?'

Pearl nodded. 'Just one. A boy.'

'Then you'll know what I mean,' said Linda.

Alan Scott continued to work in the background, and Pearl's list of prepared questions began to fall from her mind as the rhythmic sound of sandpaper on wood filled the silence. 'You . . . mentioned a church service?' she said finally, trying to restart the conversation.

'Chapel,' said Linda. 'Minister Cameron has been a wonderful support to us. He's shown us the way . . . helped us to bear our loss.' She smiled sadly. '. . . *every branch in me that does not bear fruit, he takes away; and every branch that bears fruit, he prunes so that it may bear more fruit.*'

Linda gave a beatific smile and another silence followed,

which her husband now filled: 'John. Chapter 15. Verse 2,' he said, before returning to his work.

Pearl spoke gently: 'Steven's wife, Christina, she—'

'Doesn't understand,' said Linda, curtly. 'She has yet to come to the fold. But one day she will. She'll come to know, as we do, how important it is to *trust in the Lord with all your heart and lean not on your understanding. In all your ways, submit to him and he will make your paths straight.*'

'Amen,' said Alan softly, almost to himself.

Linda Scott gave Pearl an assured smile but in the awkward silence that followed, a sudden beep sounded with the arrival of a text on Pearl's mobile.

'I'm so sorry,' she said quickly. 'I thought I'd turned this off.' Confused and annoyed with herself, Pearl quickly switched off her phone and gave the couple her undivided attention, determined to steer the interview back to the questions she had wanted to ask.

'Could you possibly tell me about the last time you saw your son? When that was? How he seemed?'

At this, Linda Scott closed her eyes, her face taking on a peaceful expression; she finally appeared to relax, as though allowing herself to be drawn back to the past.

'It was a warm summer's day,' she said softly. 'Just like today. He was in a good mood, talkative, happy. He always loved to make me laugh.' She gave a small giggle which seemed to surprise her, then she opened her eyes and nodded at Pearl. 'He was sitting where you are right now, promising me he'd be back in time for dinner . . . then he gave me a hug.' Her smile began to fade and her face clouded. 'I didn't want him to go. I had a feeling that something was going to happen ... Later, when I was making dinner, scraping some carrots at the sink, I suddenly fell to my knees ... I'd lost all strength – couldn't even stand to switch off the tap.' She put a hand to her throat. 'I couldn't breathe and then the water came running ... over the sink ... all over the floor. Cold water everywhere.' She began to tremble and Alan, concerned, quickly got up and moved to her. She took his hand and continued. 'It was our cross to bear,' she said starkly. Confused, Pearl said nothing, but Linda Scott was staring at her as though she should have understood.

Pearl's gaze shifted to Alan but he shook his head quickly, unnoticed by his wife who continued, this time in a steely tone. 'Stevie could have saved our Mark because he was always the better swimmer. But, for some reason, he couldn't do that.' She frowned. 'Instead he had to let him drown.' She looked in quiet desperation at Pearl, as though waiting for some explanation, but Pearl exchanged a knowing look with Alan and quickly got to her feet.

'I'm so sorry,' she said. 'I ... didn't mean to upset you. Perhaps I should come back another time.' She quickly picked up her bag but Linda Scott spoke again, in an urgent whisper: 'They see us,' she said.

Pearl saw now that Linda's look of distress had been replaced with one of hope. 'Minister Cameron explained that ... this life of ours it's ... just like a merry-go-round. Our loved ones may have stepped off it, but they still see us ... spinning ...' She broke off for a moment, then:

'Spinning so fast *we* can't see them, but if we look hard, sometimes we can catch a glimpse. They're always there, you see. Watching us?'

She glanced up at her husband, who slipped a comforting arm around her before he offered Pearl a helpless look. Pearl read its meaning. 'It's OK,' she said gently. 'I'll see myself out.'

Pearl made her way quickly through the gloomy hallway and out into the warm street – and a far brighter world. Gathering her thoughts, she grabbed her mobile from her pocket and checked the text that had come through during her meeting. It was from Dolly. Sent in her usual perfect prose, which she never abbreviated for a text message, it read: 'Don't worry about me. I'm going to spend the evening with Dee and she'll give me a lift home later. Hope your meeting comes up trumps. Mum x'

Pearl stared back towards the Scotts' bungalow then down to the foot of the road where the sea was visible as a thick stripe of blue in the bright sunlight. Drawn towards it, she slipped her phone into her pocket and had just set off when she stopped in her tracks on noticing an old chapel building set back from the road. It looked insignificant, a simple oak cross in its front yard, and a board offering the service times of the Chapel of the Wooden Cross, but Pearl's gaze was drawn to a single name on the board: Minister Russell Cameron. Reaching into her bag for her phone, she used it to take a photograph and, after checking it, she paused for a moment to reflect on what she had heard from Steven Scott's parents about their abiding confidence in the ministry. Wanting to know more, she approached the chapel doors only to find them locked, but a wooden gate at the side of the chapel was secured with only a simple steel latch. It opened beneath her hand.

Throwing a quick glance down the empty street, Pearl moved on to find herself on a narrow pathway which led to a garden overgrown with gorse and brambles. Another gate was visible at the foot of the garden, locked with a slide bolt. Unlocking it, she found it opened into an alley, which led in one direction towards the shopping precinct and in the other straight down to the sea. Looking back towards the rear of the chapel building she saw it was studded with a few windows. Some old crates lay scattered across the overgrown garden, which was clearly disused, and Pearl wondered how the fervour of Linda Scott's religious zeal could have been fuelled in such a mundane environment before she remembered what Christina's own mother had told her only yesterday: 'You've yet to meet Linda Scott but when you do, you'll understand.' In fact, Pearl knew she understood little at that moment, except how the loss of a child could send a parent to the limits of despair. Exiting the yard into the alley, she closed the gate behind her and reached up over it to re-lock the slide bolt.

The alley, too, was overgrown with unpruned branches and vegetation from neighbouring gardens, but Pearl soon found herself down on the seafront. She hadn't visited Herne Bay for some time and hadn't yet been on the newly renovated pier, but the unsettling interview with Linda Scott, short though it had been, now led her to seek some distraction there. The old Pier Pavilion, disliked by so many and dubbed 'the cowshed' due to its corrugated metal appearance, was no longer in existence, though many a child, including Pearl herself, had enjoyed the roller-skating rink it had once housed. Now, years later, the new structure restored a more familiar purpose to a pier promenade with various entertainments: a children's fun fair and at least a dozen retail outlets.

As Pearl approached the pier entrance, she couldn't help but think how Herne Bay's pier so suited the kiss-me-quick character of the town itself, for the new shopkeepers were housed in a 'village' of mock beach huts, the shutters of which were painted in the style of old saucy seaside postcards featuring heaving bosoms and henpecked husbands. Candy floss was on offer, and good old English fish and chips, while at the very end of the pier, hurdy-gurdy music was carried on the air from the children's fun fair. A few parents were climbing on to a carousel with their young kids and, as Pearl watched them, both the scene and the music took her back to the many times across the years when she and a young Charlie had taken rides on a beautiful old carousel that formed part of the annual local regatta celebrations. It also caused her to reflect again on the strange meeting with Steven Scott's mother, a woman who seemed trapped back in time by the loss of her beloved child – so much so that she had failed even to discuss the disappearance of his twin.

The operator was just heading back to his controls when Pearl decided to take her own place on the carousel. The music, and the gold horse on which she sat, prompted her to think about the upcoming carnival in Whitstable, reminding her that she was still without a suitable marine creature as the main focus for her restaurant float. A warm breeze blew in from the sea, and the carousel began to spin, offering Pearl a 360-degree view of the town.

The sunken Waltrop Gardens lay near the seafront, close to plenty of guesthouses and an old bandstand which now served as an ice-cream parlour and coffee lounge. The old pier's landing stage continued to stare back from its stranded position at sea towards a helter-skelter that had replaced it – though whether from envy or disdain, no one would ever know for sure. All Pearl felt in that moment was a sense of growing relief at having escaped the cloying atmosphere of the pebble-dashed bungalow in which Linda Scott had mouthed her Bible phrases with a look of muted desperation, while trying to include Pearl in a fellowship of suffering. The description she had offered of the dead looking on at the living like the spectators of a merry-go-round made for a compelling image at that moment, and one that filled Pearl's mind even when she closed her eyes in an effort to clear it. Abandoning herself to the music, she began to lose herself in the steady rhythm of the carousel creatures rising and falling, but it wasn't long before that rhythm began to slow. Pearl opened her eyes, jolted suddenly to glimpse a familiar face amongst the onlookers. The carousel gave a final turn – but the face had disappeared . . .

Pearl looked around again, searching in vain among the crowd of parents and children who had begun queueing for the next ride, but the operator now climbed the carousel, moving straight in front of Pearl to block her view as he held out his hand to take her money. She paid him and quickly dismounted, searching the pier for the face she had seen. But it had vanished as quickly as it had appeared. As the deafening hurdy-gurdy music started up again, Pearl now began to doubt what she had seen until, sensing a presence behind her, she spun round quickly to face the man who was now standing before her. Alan Scott.

Chapter Five

'I'm sorry. About what happened earlier. With Linda, I mean.' Alan Scott looked genuinely troubled as he turned to Pearl on the pier. 'I thought Christina might have prepared you but . . . I realise that must have been very confusing.' He looked both ashamed and apologetic in equal measure. 'You have to understand . . . how hard it's been. For both of us,' he said quickly. 'But especially for Linda.' He wiped his face with his hand then wandered slowly across to the pier rail where he stared out to sea. 'She's lost both her boys and she thought the world of them. I did too. But she was their mum.'

Pearl filled the silence that followed. 'And you were their stepfather.'

Alan nodded. 'Yes,' he said. 'Their real dad was a gambler, a waster. He didn't last long after they split up. Drank his way through some compensation he got from a work accident, so . . . since they were three years old, I was the only dad the boys ever really knew.'

Pearl moved closer. 'And they took your name.'

He nodded again before turning his body towards her. 'Look, I came to find you because there's something you should know. It might be important. I don't know. That's for you to decide but . . . I think you'd do the same if it was your boy?' He paused before admitting: 'And Stevie was always my boy. From a tot, he'd follow me around so much I used to call him my "shadow".' He offered up a sad smile. 'You did say anything we could tell you would be helpful?'

Pearl nodded. 'It will be,' she said. 'Please tell me about him.'

'OK.' Alan nodded and continued. 'Our Stevie was never too practical. A bit of a dreamer. A boy who never grew up? But he was an artist,' he said proudly. 'You'll know that if you've seen any of his pictures . . .' He broke off to correct himself: 'Paintings, I mean – though he'd always drawn little pencil cartoons for me and his mum as well.' He paused, collecting his thoughts. 'He liked to take himself off and study places. Just look at them. For days. Places you might see every day. Nothing special to you or me. But he made them special.'

'Like Faversham Creek?'

Alan nodded. 'Yeah. He knew it well. We all did. We'd go fishing out there. I've got a workshop down the way near Hollowshore? I used to help him with his frames.'

'Because Steven wasn't too practical,' Pearl remembered.

Alan smiled. 'That's right. I'm a carpenter by trade. And basic woodwork's a knack, a skill at best. But what Stevie had was talent. A real gift.' He paused again and frowned this time. 'But he felt things deep. Always did. And when Mark went, it hit him bad.' He pressed a hand against his chest.

'And . . . is this what you wanted to tell me?' Pearl prompted, sensing there was more.

Alan looked away, conflicted, and when he spoke again, it was with an admission.

'He ran away – when he was a boy.'

Pearl took this in. 'When?'

'After Mark drowned. They say you never get over grief, you just find a way of getting on with it. And that was true all right. It was a terrible time.' He shook his head slowly. 'I'd been the one who'd identified Mark – to save his mum having to do it. I . . . couldn't get that last image of him out of my mind – seeing him lying there so pale, like a waxwork – it haunted me. And sometimes I'd have to get up at night and go for a drive just to try and make sense of things. Whereas Linda's way was the chapel.' He frowned. 'We both needed something. Something . . . bigger than our grief? I didn't seem to be able to comfort Linda but the minister could.' He added quickly: 'And Minister Cameron's a good man. He does a lot for the community. And us. Runs a special group – grief counselling.' He frowned and went on. 'After a while, I started going to it too. And Linda's way became my way.' He looked back at Pearl. 'Linda and me, we had each other – and the chapel – but Stevie was alone. Adrift?' He broke off and looked away, as though ashamed. 'I didn't see it at the time and I should have done,' he said firmly. 'One day, he just took off.'

'How old was he?'

Alan took his time to reply, in an effort to be precise. 'It was about a year after the accident so he would've been around thirteen. We reported him missing to the local bobby.' He looked at Pearl. 'They've all gone now, haven't they? Anyway, he thought he'd seen Stevie down on the pier so we came down – together – and asked around, and sure enough a few people said they'd seen our Stevie over at the amusement arcade, with a young girl.' He broke off to collect his thoughts again, then: 'Linda was livid that he was putting us . . . everyone, to all this trouble? She said that he'd come back when he ran out of pocket money – but he didn't. He didn't come home at all that night and I got worried. Kids that age? You hear stories . . .' He broke off and composed himself. 'I couldn't sleep that night, so I got up, made myself a drink and lay on the sofa. His mum was angry . . .' he broke off. 'But not just about him running away.' He looked at Pearl knowingly.

'For his brother's death?' Pearl asked.

For some time, Alan said nothing, conflicted by the thought, then he finally nodded. 'But he was just a kid, it wasn't his fault, and like Linda said, Stevie was a strong swimmer . . .' He broke off again then continued with his story. 'Even so, that night I heard her praying, upstairs in our room? She was praying for our Stevie to be found. And the next day, he was. The owner of some holiday park in Reculver had rung the police to say he'd found two kids in one of his caravans. They'd broken in and spent the night there.'

'Two kids?'

'Yeah, the bobby went up and found Stevie and the girl. He said she was a bit older than Stevie – or maybe she just looked it.' He frowned again. 'At that age, girls often do?'

'And who was she?'

At Pearl's question, Alan shook his head. 'I dunno. No one special. Just someone he'd got talking to on the pier. But the police said she was trouble – so maybe it was her who'd persuaded our Stevie not to come home?' He broke off, looking fearful now, as though he had betrayed a trust.

Pearl took this in. 'Did you . . . tell the police about this when Steven went missing seven years ago?'

Alan nodded his head and admitted: 'Yes – or rather Linda did. We were just being honest but . . . we wanted them to do their job, not go thinking he'd done a runner, that he'd gone missing on purpose or . . .' He trailed off, leaving Pearl to articulate what he had been unable to. 'Taken his own life?' she asked.

'Of course not,' said Alan fiercely. 'Why would he? He wasn't a kid any more; he had a wife, and a kid of his own on the way – and a future.'

'But he left a note. Christina said it had definitely been written by Steven.'

'I know,' said Alan, frowning. 'But all the same, it's difficult to believe he would do something like that. He had everything to live for.' He took a moment to collect his thoughts. 'They talk about starving artists but Stevie's paintings were selling. I couldn't make his frames fast enough ... and he had an exhibition all lined up. It could have been the making of him—'

Pearl broke in. 'But he went off that morning . . . without a word to Christina?'

Alan shook his head dismissively. 'That wasn't so strange for Stevie. Like I say, he'd sometimes *need* to take himself off and . . .' He broke off for a moment before offering two words: 'Just be.'

Pearl considered this. 'Why do you think he would drive to Oare and leave his car on the slipway there?'

Alan raised his hand to his forehead and rubbed his brow. 'I don't know, but he'd done some drawings . . . sketches there, and I . . . think he was planning on painting something on the other side of the water. At Shellness. On Sheppey? He always said the light was special there – and at Oare – but he never worked from photos and liked to get out before the twitchers and birders arrived.' He paused for a moment. 'Christina was expecting,' he added. 'Maybe he just wanted to let her sleep that morning?'

Pearl reflected on Alan's question and looked away to some children mounting the helter-skelter at the end of the pier. 'What happened when he ran away as a child?' She looked back at Alan and clarified. 'After he was found at the caravan park?'

Alan shrugged. 'He got a ticking-off from the police – and from me. But his mum found it hard to forgive him for causing us so much worry.' He looked up quickly. 'It wasn't his fault. It was a cry for help. He had some counselling after that, through the school. They mentioned something called . . . survivor guilt. He'd been the one who'd survived that day off the Street. But his brother had died.'

'And he hadn't been able to save him,' said Pearl, thoughtfully.

'That's right,' Alan agreed. 'No matter what his mum might say . . . Stevie couldn't help what happened.'

Pearl considered this. 'Were they identical twins?'

Alan shook his head. 'They couldn't have been more different – in every way. Mark was a clown. He loved people, playing jokes, having fun. But Stevie was always the quiet one. He could spend hours in his own company, teaching himself guitar, painting his pictures? You'd hardly know he was there.' He paused again, clearly holding back emotion. 'I loved 'em both.'

'But you talk about Steven in the past tense,' said Pearl gently.

Alan looked at her. 'It's been a long time,' he said. 'Too long. But I've never given up hope that one day he'd come home.' In the next instant, he moved closer. 'So, if you're really serious – about finding my boy? I promise I'll help all I can.'

It took just twenty minutes for Pearl to drive home, but now she appreciated the truth of Dolly's comment that Herne Bay was separated from Whitstable by more than mere distance. The 'other side' now seemed an apt description to Pearl. Back at Seaspray Cottage she fed her two cats, Pilchard and Sprat, then opened the kitchen door, from where she had a clear view across her garden to the beach. A warm breeze continued to blow in from the sea and she longed to take a walk to clear her mind, but instead she took to her laptop to do some research. She was aware that various police forces had set up special teams to investigate what were known as 'cold cases', crimes that remained unsolved, some stretching back for decades, but no crime had actually been committed in this instance and an online search on the website of the local Swale Police force showed no appeal for information about Steven Scott, nor for any other missing person going back as far as 2011. Pearl was just reflecting on this when her landline phone rang. She responded quickly, but found it was only Dolly.

'We need a proper concept.'

'Concept?' asked Pearl, confused.

'For our carnival float,' Dolly huffed, as though Pearl should have realised.

'Well, I'm sure you'll come up with one,' she said confidently.

'But it has to be the *right* one,' argued Dolly in frustration. 'I happened to mention this to Dee today and confided to her that I'd been thinking about a mermaid ...'

Pearl tried to respond but Dolly continued over her. 'Don't say a word!' she ordered. 'Because Dee already said it.'

'Said what?'

'That my mermaid should be consigned to the depths – as an idea, of course. And she's quite right. It's a terrible cliché. So we need to come up with something else – and soon. Another sea creature.'

'All right,' Pearl said, 'I'll get thinking.' She smiled to herself, knowing how happy Dolly would be once she was fully engaged with constructing the float, as she was when involved in any creative endeavour. In the meantime, Pearl tried to distract her. 'So you had a good day with Dee?' She sat down on the sofa and took out her smartphone.

'Wonderful,' Dolly said. 'But I feel very sorry for the woman. She's isolated over there and a brain like hers needs to be occupied – and not with a bingo club. There's no flamenco group and she's met hardly a soul since she moved.'

Pearl was silent for a moment as she reflected on what Dolly had just told her, then said tentatively: 'So . . . she has a low profile in town?'

Dolly reacted to Pearl's question with more than a hint of suspicion: 'What are you thinking?'

'Me?' said Pearl in all innocence.

'Come on. I know that tone of yours and it always creeps into your voice when you're up to something.'

'Now what could I possibly be up to?' Pearl asked, knowing full well that her mother was unable to see her studying an image on her smartphone – the photograph she had taken earlier that day of the Chapel of the Wooden Cross.

PART TWO

Chapter Six

Detective Chief Inspector Mike McGuire tore the ring pull from the can in his hand and took a sip of lemonade, wishing it was something stronger. It was almost midday on Saturday and he had checked out of his hotel and stuffed his meagre luggage into the boot of his car before leaving it in a car park and taking a trip across town on the stuffy Underground. The journey had taken far too long due to delays and, as he walked along the Old Kent Road, jostled by shoppers, his path blocked by young mums pushing buggies, he felt as though he might be invisible. The trial had brought him to London for several weeks, but it seemed more like a lifetime, because he had spent some considerable time before that liaising closely with a London force, preparing evidence involving a group of criminals with Kent connections – a bunch of thieves who had used a disused farm on the outskirts of Canterbury as their hideout. They had finally been brought to justice but the trial had dragged on, and throughout that time, though a Londoner himself, McGuire had begun to feel oddly like an outsider in the capital.

Crossing Tower Bridge each morning to reach Southwark Crown Court, he had felt dwarfed by the sheer scale of the city, and though he had been stationed in Kent for only two years he now realised he had allowed the definition of Canterbury as a city to fool him into thinking that he was still working in a metropolis. Canterbury was anything but. Its heart consisted of a shopping thoroughfare dominated by the central attractions of an historic cathedral and a newly renovated theatre; even with a large floating population of tourists and students, it was a mere parish compared to London.

McGuire had once confidently negotiated London without being fully conscious of its teeming crowds and towering architecture, because he had felt part of the same landscape. But now he realised how his perspective had shrunk to fit his new environment, in the same way that it was said goldfish might grow or reduce in size to fit a small bowl or large aquarium. After a session in court each day he had walked the city streets, aware that he must have appeared much like the tourists who surrounded him – viewing London as if for the first time. His stay would have been so much different if Pearl had been with him. She would have insisted on trying out the menus of vibrant new restaurants, while he, not wanting to be thought by fellow diners as a 'Billy No Mates' for eating alone, had existed for the most part on pub grub and hotel room service. In the evenings, while catching up with Pearl over a hastily snatched call or text, he had often pictured her in his mind, gazing out at the estuary coastline at the foot of her beach garden while he, himself, had made do with taking walks along the Thames embankment, watching the great river finding its way to the sea. Certainly there had been many occasions when he had wanted to make further contact, then reconsidered, knowing that just at the time he was finishing at court, Pearl would be busy dealing with customers at her restaurant. Added to this, McGuire was a man who found it difficult to occupy two worlds at once, and preferred instead to give himself exclusively to one or the other. Work had been the one constant in his life so far – especially since his former fiancée's death. His police work had managed to fill the vacuum created by Donna's absence – an absence so great that for a time it had become a haunting presence. But inexorably, like a great river itself, Life had moved on, taking him along with the flow, convincing him that today he should make a final visit to the last place Donna had been seen alive.

Having taken the Tube to the Elephant and Castle, McGuire had stepped out of the Underground station to find not the shabby junction of his memory but slick new apartment blocks reaching up to the sky. An old family trattoria that had stood for generations on the Walworth Road had vanished, to be replaced with something far more modern, boasting 'fusion cuisine', something to satisfy the appetites of those who lived in the gentrified properties surrounding Burgess Park. But walking on beyond the Regency-style homes that lined the only expanse of greenery in the area, it wasn't long before he had found the old social housing estate, where balconies were still strung with washing lines, and smashed windows were barely covered with plywood panels. Here, one wet winter's evening, two young kids had hot-wired a stolen car and headed off into the night, high on drugs and adrenaline. Who wouldn't want to escape this place – as fast as possible – and allow a dream to grow like a bubble blown with soap and water . . . But the bubble had burst. The kids hadn't got far before an obstacle had appeared, blocking their escape. A woman had stepped out into their path. A target too great to miss.

McGuire now found himself standing on the same spot. Cars still thundered past on the busy road, but nothing was actually the same. Everything felt different. Everything had changed – including McGuire. He breathed deeply and put a hand in his pocket, his fingers tracing the outline of a small square box with embossed gold lettering. Then he took a lungful of traffic-soiled air and recognised it was time to go home – to Pearl.

At exactly the same time that Saturday afternoon, Pearl was seated at a wrought-iron table, watching Dee Poulton dead-heading geraniums in a collection of terracotta pots in her small courtyard garden in Herne Bay. She was dressed casually for the warm weather in jeans, a blue linen smock and a pair of trendy pink plastic flip-flops. A straw hat, with a long blue scarf tied around its brim, shielded her face from the bright sun, but once she had finished her work, she took off her floral gardening gloves and pulled off the hat, shaking out her bobbed hair before she gave her full attention to Pearl.

'I must admit,' she began. 'I don't take on many clients these days. As I mentioned yesterday, I'm retired from bookkeeping, though I was happy to give your mum some advice.'

'And I'm glad you did,' said Pearl, aware that Dolly's bookkeeping skills left a lot to be desired. Dee joined Pearl at the table and stirred a jug of homemade lemonade before pouring two glasses. She heaved a little sigh and then explained: 'You know, I was hoping to make a bit of a fresh start by moving here but, to be honest, I feel rather in limbo. Don't get me wrong,' she added quickly. 'The neighbours are perfectly friendly, and it's nice to have a little more financial security behind me, but the main reason I moved to Kent from London was Ted.' Leaving Pearl with something to ponder, Dee stepped through French doors into her kitchen and reappeared with a plate of fruit scones which she set on the table.

'Ted?' asked Pearl.

Dee reached into the pocket of her smock and pulled out a set of keys. Staring down at a picture on their plastic fob, she then passed it to Pearl who saw a photo of a wire-haired fox terrier, mouth open, eyes narrowed as though laughing on cue for the camera.

'Cute,' smiled Pearl.

'Yes,' Dee now eyed the photo herself. 'Ted was ten years old when we moved to Whitstable. I had visions of us enjoying some long beach walks together, but sadly it wasn't to be. What I thought was a little arthritis turned out to be something more serious.' She took on a pained expression and replaced the keys in her pocket. 'They were very good at the vet's, but there was no alternative but to say goodbye.' Her face clouded. 'After that, walking on the beach at Whitstable was never quite the same.'

'I'm so sorry,' said Pearl.

'Don't be,' Dee said bravely. 'He had a good life.' She picked up the plate of fruit scones and offered them to Pearl. 'Here, try one of these. I can see I've made you feel awkward.'

'A little,' Pearl admitted. 'But not for the reason you think. You see . . .' She broke off, then confessed: 'It wasn't actually bookkeeping I came to talk to you about.'

'Oh?'

'It's my case.'

'Ah,' said Dee, looking up from buttering her scone. 'Your detective agency, you mean. Dolly told me you're in search of some missing person?'

'That's right. And his parents happen to live here – in Herne Bay.'

Dee carefully spooned some jam on to her scone. 'I'm afraid I wouldn't know them,' she said, confidently. 'So I don't think I could help.' She took a bite of her scone, savouring it for a few moments before commenting, 'Your mother doesn't actually approve of this detective work, does she?'

Pearl shrugged. 'True.'

'Nevertheless, I can see why you've taken it on.'

'Can you?' asked Pearl, surprised.

'Why, of course. You've proved yourself with the restaurant, but now it's served its purpose – much as bookkeeping has done for me.' She smiled knowingly. 'You're not really like your mum, are you?'

'In some ways,' said Pearl defensively.

'In looks, I meant.' Dee reflected for a moment. 'They always say it's a difficult relationship – mother and daughter. Love, of course,' she mused. 'But an element of competition there too. And an expectation that a daughter might do everything a mother couldn't?' She licked a bit of jam from her finger and wiped her hand with a napkin before adding: 'My mother taught me how to make scones. But she also wanted me to have a career. I think your mother would like you to settle down.'

'I am settled.' Pearl smiled.

'I meant . . . with a good man.' Dee cocked her head to one side and asked. 'What about this . . . "Flat Foot"?'

'DCI Mike McGuire?'

'Sounds rather formal.'

Pearl smiled. 'Yes, but I've always called him McGuire. And he's tall, blond, attractive, intelligent and . . . married.' As Dee looked up at her, she clarified: 'To his work.'

'Ah yes,' sighed Dee. 'So are a lot of men. It gives them an excuse to escape.'

For a moment, Pearl considered this, remembering what she had learned of Steven Scott so far – a man who liked to take himself off for days at a time – and just 'be', as his stepfather had related, though his mother-in-law harboured another view: of a man who had failed to grow up and take his responsibilities seriously as a husband and father-to-be. Dee caught Pearl's look. 'What are you thinking?'

'About what you just said.' Pearl steered her next question away from her case. 'And you?' she asked. 'What would you like for yourself?'

'To be honest,' Dee began, 'at this point in my life, I simply yearn for something to happen: to become involved in something other than other people's balance sheets.' She paused for a moment before deciding: 'An adventure.'

'Good,' said Pearl. 'Then perhaps you can help, after all.'

As Dee looked up from her fruit scone she saw Pearl's enigmatic smile.

At 6 p.m. that evening, Pearl was back at home, packing a shoulder bag with a few important items including her smartphone and a camera, as she spoke to Charlie on the landline.

'You're sure you'll be all right to cope? It's Saturday night, after all, and—'

'Mum, we'll be fine.' Charlie had cut in, aware that in the kitchen of The Whitstable Pearl, Dean, Ruby and the kitchen assistant, Ahmed, were all exchanging smiles, knowing full well what Pearl would be saying. Charlie moved off with the phone, out of the kitchen and into the seafood bar area. The restaurant was not yet open but the tables were all set with crisp white linen and vases of sweet peas and Charlie now switched on the fairy lights that were draped across the walls on which some of his own artwork hung.

'I can manage this place fine,' he insisted. 'But to be honest, I'm more worried about you.'

'Now you're sounding like your gran . . .'

'Well, she says you're on a case.' He paused for a moment. 'It's nothing dangerous, is it? A murder?'

'No,' said Pearl, trying to put her son at ease. 'A missing person. And he's been missing for some time . . .'

'So how do you know he wasn't murdered?'

'I don't.'

'Well, there you go. You need to be careful.'

'I'm *always* careful, Charlie.'

At the end of the line, Pearl heard her son give an exhalation and recognised he still wasn't convinced.

'Look, if you must know, I'm only going to Herne Bay,' she explained. 'To church.'

'Church?' Charlie echoed.

'The Chapel of the Wooden Cross, to be precise. It's just off the precinct, in the middle of town. And I promise you, I'll be fine.'

With the phone receiver jammed beneath her jaw, Pearl zipped up her bag but her son's voice sounded again.

'Can't McGuire go with you?'

'He's still in London,' she explained. 'At a trial.'

'Shame.'

In that moment, Pearl could only agree with Charlie, whose view of McGuire was quite different from Dolly's. McGuire had always treated Charlie with respect, and as his own person, not just as Pearl's son, and though Charlie accorded with equal respect his mother's decision to start up her agency, he shared McGuire's concern for her safety, knowing that she was apt to play down the risks she often faced. 'Look, Mum, I'd better go,' he said hastily, as he noted a young couple at the door. 'First customers are here . . .'

'That'll be the Pritchards,' Pearl remembered, as she'd taken the booking only that morning. 'Don't forget, Charlie, they like a window table . . .' But in the next instant, she realised her son had already left the line in order to attend to his customers.

For a moment, Pearl wished she was going to spend her evening at the restaurant, working alongside Charlie, whom she saw little of due to his studies and his increasing independence. As she replaced the receiver on its cradle, her eyes lingered on the old family photograph she always kept beside the phone, which showed Charlie as little more than a toddler on the beach, holding a festive flag he had been given for taking part in a crabbing competition off the Street of Stones. Now, he was managing the family restaurant while Pearl went off in search of another boy's father. There was an irony involved, for over the last twenty years Pearl had never once looked for her own son's father, having been content to live with memories of a summer long ago – a magical summer that had produced the person she loved more than any other: Charlie himself. And Pearl's love for her son was so strong that it had supported Charlie without any apparent need on his part to search for more answers beyond those which Pearl had already provided – that he had been born of love and how that love would endure; two things of which he could be certain. Pearl glanced across at her two cats, Pilchard and Sprat, spread out on the stone floor of the kitchen in an effort to escape the evening heat. Then she slung her bag across her shoulder and left Seaspray Cottage.

The drive out to Herne Bay left Pearl enough time to find a suitable spot on the seafront to park her car, close to the entrance to the alley which led to the rear of the Chapel of the Wooden Cross. She was late for the evening service – but intentionally so – and headed up the alley to the wooden gate which led into the overgrown chapel garden. Sliding the bolt, she entered the garden to hear the strains of a harmonium playing as voices sang the words to a familiar hymn: 'Holy, Holy, Holy . . . Lord God Almighty . . .'

Pearl was instantly transported back to her old school assemblies and Sunday School classes at her own family church. St Alfred's in Whitstable High Street was a large parish church, capable of seating hundreds of people, but tonight its own vicar, Rev Pru, would surely have been grateful for what appeared to be a huge congregation singing in this little out-of-the-way place – a fact borne out as soon as Pearl reached the rear of the chapel, where she grabbed one of the empty crates strewn around the garden and stood on it to gain a furtive view through an open window. The organist was just on the other side of the wall from Pearl: a woman of indeterminate age with short grey hair and thick-lensed glasses, who failed to see Pearl as she was giving her complete attention to the sheet music on her stand. From Pearl's viewpoint, the chapel's interior looked less like an ecclesiastical building than a scout hut, its walls absent of any paintings or stained-glass windows. No flowers were on display, or candles to increase the stifling heat of the evening, which was clearly affecting some members of the congregation in the pews. Men were using handkerchiefs to dab foreheads and throats, while a few women were fanning themselves with the 'order of service'. Pearl was careful to switch off the phone in her pocket and leaned forward towards the window while concealing her presence from the congregation. The chapel was packed. A few self-conscious teenagers stood beside fresh-faced mothers and earnest fathers, while pockets of elderly citizens swayed on walking sticks or stood propped on Zimmer frames. But every member of the congregation was singing, joining in the hymn, proudly, in full voice. A familiar couple stood in the second row, an expression of religious fervour on Linda Scott's face as her husband, Alan, sang on beside her. Pearl assumed that Linda's clear enthusiasm might be for singing the hymn itself but, as it came to an end, the look on her face remained and Pearl recognised this was due to the presence of the man who now moved forward from the back of the chapel into her line of vision.

Tall and informally dressed in a white open-necked shirt, dark trousers and sandals, he raised his arms to greet his congregation. 'Greetings, brothers and sisters,' he began.

'Greetings, Minister Cameron!' came the enthusiastic response. Extraordinarily, this was followed not by a reverential silence but by informal applause. The minister turned quickly back to pick up his Bible, and almost came face to face with Pearl at the window, but she moved out of sight just in time while having managed to note that Minister Cameron was in his late fifties with dark good looks, thick black hair and regular features. He reacted to the applause with a nod of his head, then turned back to his congregation once more, striding down the central aisle of the chapel – a man sure of himself, or his faith, or both, thought Pearl. Acknowledging familiar faces, he thanked everyone for coming out on such a glorious summer night to 'praise the Lord', to which his congregation responded with a loud 'Amen'.

He then returned to the head of the chapel, where he took the hand of a young girl in the front pew and encouraged her to come forward. Introducing her as Jenny, he invited her to read a specific passage from his own Bible. The girl, a young teenager, with long fair hair drawn back in an Alice band, quickly cleared her throat, while Pearl noted that all eyes were now focused upon her as she read. '*Many people were travelling with Jesus,*' she began. '*He said to them, "If you come to me but will not leave your family, you cannot be my follower. You must love me more than your father, mother, wife, children, brothers, and sisters – even more than your own life."*' In the pause that followed, Pearl looked beyond Jenny to the back of the chapel, searching for another familiar face. Finally, it appeared . . .

Leaning out into the aisle, Dee Poulton made her presence known to Pearl with an almost imperceptible nod of her head, before leaning slowly back into the body of the congregation. Jenny continued her reading, her voice rising to fill every corner of the chapel, commanding Pearl's attention: "*Whoever will not carry the cross that is given to them when they follow me, cannot be my follower.*"

At that precise moment, another sound told Pearl that she was not alone in the overgrown chapel garden. The insistent buzz of mosquitos prompted her to search quickly for the cardigan she had brought with her in her shoulder bag. In spite of the evening heat, she put it on, but by the time she had done so, Minister Cameron was speaking again, his voice carrying on the night air beyond the window. Pearl leaned in once more to catch a glimpse of members of the congregation, now rapt in full attention as the minister's voice rang out.

'Thank you for that reading, Jenny, from the Gospel of St Luke, verses 25 to 27 – a message that is also brought to us in Matthew, Chapter 10, verses 34 to 39: "*Think not that I am come to send peace on earth: I came not to send peace, but a sword. For I am come to set a man at variance against his father, and the daughter against her mother, and the daughter-in-law against her mother-in-law. And a man's foes shall be they of his own household.*"' The minister paused for only a moment, as though ensuring he still carried the congregation's attention, before continuing: "*Whoever loves father or mother more than me is not worthy of me, and whoever loves son or daughter more than me is not worthy of me. And anyone who does not take up his cross and follow me is not worthy of me. Whoever finds his life will lose it, and whoever loses his life for my sake will find it.*' The minister hung his head for a moment then raised it, looking suddenly positive now, with a broad smile on his face. '*This* is the message that comes to us in the Gospels. The message to leave behind our own flesh and blood and become one with God. What sacrifice that must be – to turn our backs on our own family? But this is our destiny – to be with God – and so we must heed the message and unshackle ourselves from family ties and step forward as mature adults to do God's work.' He paused again and then began to recite: '"*When I was a child, I spoke as a child, I understood as a child, I thought as a child ...*"' Pearl leaned forward to note that in the front pew Linda Scott was reciting along with the minister: '"*But when I became a man, I put away childish things.*"' Minister Cameron's voice had almost lowered to a whisper, but now it suddenly rose to echo in the chapel as he called: '*Now* is the time to leave behind our childish ways and take up the Lord's work. Who is ready for that task?'

'We are ready!' came the thunderous response.

'Who will work to show the power of the Lord?'

'We will work!' the congregation called back.

As though primed, the harmonium started up again, and all eyes moved to a hymn board on the wall – the same board that Alan Scott had been working on in his kitchen just the day before. The minister made sure that no one needed to search their hymn books as he ordered a call to arms with: 'Onward Christian Soldiers!'

The singing began once more and Pearl now took out her camera, raising it to the window. She took a single photo of the view beyond it, and checked the image before she slipped the camera back into her bag. Looking through the window again, she saw that Dee was sharing a hymn book with the woman beside her. Once the singing had come to an end, the minister announced news: the success of various initiatives to raise chapel funds, an outing for local disadvantaged children and an upcoming charity sale which required further support and contributions for its organiser, Linda Scott. Once more, applause sounded, but now the minister became increasingly animated as he made his way along the aisle, thanking everyone for their efforts before he paused in his tracks, his attention drawn to one particular member of his congregation. 'Stand, sister,' he commanded. All eyes turned to view the woman rising to her feet from a pew at the back of the chapel. Pearl held her breath on seeing they had focused upon Dee.

'We have a new member of our family this evening,' noted the minister. 'What is your name, sister?' Under everyone's gaze Dee looked uncomfortable and vaguely unnerved at being unmasked as an infiltrator in their midst, until she summoned sufficient resolve and smiled before replying confidently. 'My name is Dee.'

The minister considered her for a moment, holding her under careful scrutiny before he turned to his congregation, his hand clamped firmly upon Dee's shoulder. 'Sister Dee has come to us tonight and what do we have for her?'

After a pause the congregation responded as one. 'A welcome!'

'Indeed,' said the minister. 'We say welcome, Sister Dee.' As he looked back at her, he held her gaze for a second while applause rang out, before the introductory chords of an upbeat hymn began to sound from the harmonium. The minister strode back to the front of the chapel and Pearl dared to breathe again as the music continued. A short time later, once final prayers were said, Pearl watched the congregation file from the chapel.

Slipping her camera into her bag, Pearl headed quickly to the foot of the garden where she opened the gate and peered left and right before stepping into the alleyway. It was impossible to see far in either direction due to the overgrown vegetation from neighbouring gardens, but she slipped away, heading for the seafront, confident that if she were discovered, she could simply pretend to be an innocent visitor to the area taking advantage of a short cut, as tourists did every day in Whitstable with the network of alleys that had once been used by smugglers as escape routes to and from the sea. Darkness had begun to fall as she reflected on the service she had just witnessed, confident in her decision not to have taken part in it herself. It was one thing for Dee to have been present, an innocent new resident to the area, but another altogether for Pearl – a private detective with connections to the local police.

Moving past the thorny branches of white roses and buddleia that encroached into the alley, Pearl suddenly paused as she heard a sound behind her. The soft crack of a twig had sounded underfoot but, listening intently, her keen senses aroused, she heard nothing else and so continued on for a few steps more. A dark form suddenly sprang out in front of her. Pearl gasped in fear, then saw it was a cat that had just leapt down from a garden wall. No more than a few months old, it was friendly and mewing, brushing its body up against Pearl's ankles in the same way her own cats were apt to do when hungry. She leaned down and took some time to stroke the creature, and it was only when she stood up again that she saw the black silhouette framed in the alley's opening just ahead of her. A tall figure stepped forward towards her, blocking out the light at the end of the alley.

Falling back on her instincts, Pearl looked quickly behind her, considering whether she could possibly make any kind of escape. But she realised it was futile. Instead, she quickly reached into her pocket and shone the beam of a high-powered LED torch straight into the man's face. His hand moved instantly to cover his eyes but it was too late – he was blinded. 'Turn that thing off!' he ordered.

Stunned, Pearl looked back down at the torch in her hand and did as she was told before asking: 'What are *you* doing here?'

'What do you think I'm doing?' McGuire replied with a smile. 'I'm looking for you.'

He held out his arms – and Pearl fell into them.

Chapter Seven

A few minutes later, McGuire sat down with Pearl on a bench in the sunken municipal gardens. 'You're the last person I expected to see in that alley,' she said. 'Couldn't you have given me a little warning you were back?'

'I tried. I left a message on your voicemail?'

Pearl reached quickly into her bag for her phone before she remembered: 'Oh . . . I'm so sorry, I switched off my mobile.' Taking it out, she switched it on again.

McGuire asked with an arch look, 'Because you were at church?'

Pearl looked at him sidelong. 'How did you know?'

'Charlie told me. I went to the restaurant to find you.'

She noted two missed calls on her phone, both from McGuire, who now added: 'He also said you're on a case.'

'I am,' she confessed, slipping her phone back into her bag. 'A Misper.' She saw McGuire's interest was piqued and explained further: 'Name's Steven Scott. He was twenty-eight when he walked out on his pregnant wife one morning in August 2011. Left his car at a disused ferry point, with his jacket and a suicide note on the passenger seat. Nothing heard since – so his wife came to me.'

Over his years as a police detective, McGuire had grown adept at taking in information given to him by anyone at any time, but at that particular moment, with Pearl's face tilted up towards his and the glow from an old street lamp falling softly upon her pretty features, he didn't much care about the case she was talking about, or the man who had gone missing; instead he was recognising how much he had missed her and how good it felt to be back, but the moment was broken by Pearl's phone ringing.

She quickly took it from her pocket and, when she saw the caller ID, she looked back at McGuire. 'Sorry, d'you mind if I take this?'

He smiled. 'Go ahead.'

Pearl took the call, immediately responding: 'Are you OK?'

'Absolutely fine,' said Dee Poulton on the other end of the line. 'Mission accomplished for "Sister Dee" – and not too challenging either. You'll have noticed they're a welcoming lot at that chapel – especially the Scotts,' she added.

'So you made contact?'

'Easily,' said Dee. 'We struck up a conversation at the end of the service and, once I explained about losing my best friend, Ted, Linda invited me to the next Lazarus meeting.'

'Which is?'

'Thursday evening at eight p.m.'

Pearl mused on this for a moment. 'Good work,' she said finally.

'Thanks,' Dee replied, puffed with pride, before she added, tentatively: 'I'm ... still not sure what you're after, though.'

'To be honest, neither am I. Yet,' she added. 'But I appreciate your help.'

'No problem,' said Dee. 'I'll report back after the meeting. And I promise I won't breathe a word to Dolly.'

'Thanks. Good night.'

Pearl reflected on the call for a moment before she looked back at McGuire, and found him eyeing her with more than a little curiosity.

'A new friend,' she confessed. McGuire nodded, unsure if the caller had been a man or a woman, and as he watched her slip her phone into her pocket, he recognised this wasn't quite the reunion he had envisaged when he had left London earlier that day. He had imagined turning up at The Whitstable Pearl and whisking Pearl off for a sunset supper near the beach in Whitstable, but now it was almost 10 p.m. and he was perched with her on a council bench in some empty gardens in Herne Bay. Glancing down at his watch, however, he refused to give up hope. 'Not too late to eat around here, is it?'

Pearl considered this, knowing for sure that Herne Bay restaurants would have stopped serving for the evening – except one. She gave a slow smile. 'Come on, I know just the place.'

*

A short while later, Pearl was sitting with McGuire at a table on the Central Parade near Herne Bay's famous clock tower, as a waitress ferried tartare sauce and quartered lemons for the meal Pearl and McGuire had just been served.

'Nothing like fish and chips on the seafront,' Pearl said.

As McGuire looked up and returned her smile, Pearl saw he was looking pale and tired – tired of spending the last few weeks in airless courtrooms, no doubt, though she liked to think he was also tired of spending time away from her.

'So your trial went well?' she asked.

He nodded. 'Guilty as charged, but the sentencing is still to take place.' He took a sip of coffee and considered something. 'This new case of yours,' he began. 'A lot of people go missing but most return of their own accord – sooner or later.'

'But some don't,' said Pearl. 'And from what my client says, it seems the Swale Police might have suspected pseudocide.'

McGuire failed to respond so Pearl went on: 'They seemed to think he might have faked his own—'

'I know what pseudocide is,' McGuire said. 'But why would they suspect it?'

Pearl shrugged. 'Perhaps because no body was ever found? There may be other reasons but, if there are, somehow I don't think they'll want to discuss them with a private detective like me. The SIO who was in charge has now retired and the case is so cold it's positively cryogenic

– which is why Steven's wife came to me.' She set down her fork and looked away to the old town clock. Over 24 metres high, it was an extraordinary structure, and some-thing of an architectural chimera, with a large bell tower, neoclassical columns and a lighting system programmed to change according to the tide levels. Pearl went on. 'Surely it's got to be difficult to fake your own death these days?'

McGuire gave a nod. 'But not impossible. You said his wife was pregnant when he left?'

'Yes. And she admitted they'd had some problems, and an argument just a few days before he went missing. But she doesn't believe that would have been the cause of him leaving.'

'Maybe she just doesn't want to,' said McGuire knowingly.

'Maybe,' Pearl agreed. 'But she's had no news in all that time. Their son was born in March the following year and she's brought him up alone since then with only the help of her mother. Can you imagine how difficult that has been?'

McGuire scanned her features and answered. 'Yes,' he said, softly. 'Though I imagine you'd understand better than I would.'

He reached across the table and took Pearl's hand, looking directly at her, so boldly that she felt exposed. Seeing this, he smiled and reached his other hand into his pocket and took out a small black box which he placed in her palm.

'For you.'

Taken aback by the sight of the stylish embossed gold lettering on the lid, Pearl looked at him.

'Go on,' he said. 'I've been waiting all evening for the right moment to give you that.' Seeing his smile, she quickly opened the box to find a pair of pale grey freshwater pearl earrings lying on a cloud of white satin.

'Pearls for a Pearl,' he smiled. 'Corny?'

She shook her head. 'No,' she said softly. 'Not corny at all. These are beautiful.' She took one from the box and held it up by its delicate silver clasp while McGuire explained: 'I tried to find something to match the colour of your eyes.'

Pearl quickly tried one on. 'Well?'

At that very moment, a loud bell began to toll. McGuire smiled. 'Even that old clock agrees.'

But Pearl said nothing as she found herself lost in his gaze. He leaned in slowly and kissed her. The bell ceased tolling and, as they broke away, he saw Pearl's eyes were still closed. When she opened them, she said: 'Look, I know you're going to be busy with work tomorrow but . . . do you think you can find time to help me with my case?'

McGuire was still looking at her as he admitted: 'I thought you'd never ask. Besides,' he added, 'how else am I going to get to see you?'

Pearl smiled. 'I'm glad you're back, McGuire.'

'So am I,' he said truthfully.

An hour later, Pearl entered Seaspray Cottage, switched on the lights, threw down her bag and glanced around the living room. The cats yawned a sleepy greeting and stretched their limbs before heading upstairs to take up a new position on Pearl's bed. She moved instantly to the mirror above the fireplace to inspect the earrings she was wearing – McGuire's gift. Caressing the delicate pale grey freshwater pearls that were catching the reflected light, she smiled to herself, exhilarated by the fact that McGuire had returned, but also relieved that she could look forward to counting on his help with her Misper case. Stepping into the kitchen, she opened the fridge and poured herself a large glass of chilled Pinot Grigio, then hesitated before taking a sip as she allowed her thoughts to stray to Christina, who would be spending the night alone with only her young son and her mother for company. For twenty years Pearl's own family members had been the pillars of her existence, supporting her but also providing sufficient motivation for her own ambitions for The Whitstable Pearl. It was a family business, initiated by family, run by family – but her thoughts now shifted to the chapel service earlier that evening and to the Bible passages she had heard. Minister Cameron had exhorted his congregation to put family ties to one side in order to pursue another path. Was this an arbitrary sermon, or a recurring theme for his own ministry?

Moving back into the living room, Pearl switched on her laptop, set down her glass of wine and waited until the screen came to life. She put in a search for the Chapel of the Wooden Cross in Herne Bay and found a simple website with the following information on its page:

We are a Non-Denominational Chapel with no set liturgy.

Non-Denominational means that we are not affiliated to any Church organisation because we aim to be fully acceptable to ALL denominations.

Non-Denominational also means that we are in charge of our own finances. Our collection goes either to our building and maintenance costs, or as donations to other charities and to local outreach.

We are not obliged to pay money to a central authority in order to fund our administration costs, expenses and overheads.

We are a fully Christian Chapel, and we listen to different opinions from people of different backgrounds and experiences.

As you will see on the 'Service Rota' page, members of our congregation can read selected Bible passages and lead the prayers.

Pearl also noted the service times and a group of regular meetings: a Sunday School, a Bible Study class and something called the Lazarus Group.

At the top of the website page was a photo of the modest Herne Bay chapel building, and another, of Minister Russell Cameron, dressed in clerical white collar, smiling confidently, and looking more like the charismatic Pentecostal ministers of American TV than a small-town English minister. Pearl noted the Bible quote centred beneath his photo: *'For where two or three are gathered in my name, there am I among them.'*

Reflecting on this for a moment, Pearl then moved back into her e-mail programme and had just begun writing a short note to Christina Scott, promising her new client she would have an update for her very soon, when a text came through from McGuire. It read: 'Dinner tomorrow night? Harbour Garden Restaurant at 8?'

Pearl smiled and tapped out her reply: 'Can't wait.'

Chapter Eight

The man who was walking back and forth, pushing the mower that was cutting neat stripes into the emerald-green lawn at the Reculver Holiday Park, looked to Pearl to be somewhere in his early fifties. He had begun to lose his hair, along with anything resembling a zest for life. A thin roll-up hung from his lower lip and he moved slowly, with no sense of urgency or enthusiasm for his task. Pearl observed him for a few moments before calling out above the noisy engine: 'I'm sorry to bother you ...'

He looked across.

'Reg, is it?' Pearl asked.

The man switched off the mower, abandoning it as he slowly ambled across. Pearl explained: 'Someone said you might be able to help me.' She gestured back towards an old pub, outside which some summer tourists, toting backpacks, were being served with Sunday lunch as they photographed the ruins of a medieval church that stood on a cliff facing out to sea.

'What with?'The cigarette still hung from his lower lip.

'The barman said you used to own the old caravan park here?'

The man now peeled the cigarette from his lip. 'Before it went upmarket, you mean?' He glanced, unimpressed, at the spacious static holiday homes behind him, surrounded by the perfect lawn and a Grecian statue overlooking a white fibreglass fountain. Then he looked back at Pearl. 'I sold up about ten years ago,' he said. 'Thought it was a good deal at the time. Turned out to be the worst move I ever made.' He paused as he put a cigarette lighter flame to his roll-up.

'I wonder if you might remember about two teenagers who once broke into your caravan park. A boy and a girl? The police were called . . .'

'The police were always being called.' He looked up. 'Vandalism.'

Pearl shook her head. 'No, I don't believe they did any damage apart from breaking into a caravan and spending the night in it. It was around twenty years ago.'

The man took a deep draw on his cigarette then shook his head. 'I don't remember,' he said finally. He had begun to move back to his lawnmower but Pearl persisted: 'Please try?'

Reg looked back and saw she had taken a wallet from her bag. 'It's important,' she added pointedly. She offered him five crisp £5 notes. The man looked down at the money then back at Pearl. 'Who to?'

She handed him her card. He checked it. 'A detective?'

'A private investigation,' she explained. 'Someone has gone missing.'

'And what's that got to do with this place?' he asked with some suspicion.

'It's the same boy who once ran away here.'

The man shook his head. 'It was a long time ago . . .'

'But you do remember?'

He paused and looked down at the money she offered before taking it. 'I remember calling the cops after finding some kids here,' he said. 'It was out of season. Most of the caravans were empty and they could have chosen one of the luxury models, but they aimed too low and went for one of the cheaper caravans. Maybe they thought they stood less chance of being found. But they were wrong. It was in bad shape and I was due to do some repairs on it. That's how I came to see the window was broken. There was music playing inside. A radio. They didn't hear me coming.' He broke off, pocketing the money.

Pearl prompted him. 'What else do you remember?'

He shrugged. 'Not much. I let myself in and just found them there. They'd helped themselves to some tinned food and . . . biscuits. Crumbs everywhere. Made a right mess. The boy looked scared but the girl was cocky, sitting there, just chewing gum? She had long blonde hair and black eye make-up. Gave me some lip. Maybe if she hadn't, I might not have called the police.' He considered this for a moment then shrugged: 'But they were too young to be out here on their own.'

'And what happened?' asked Pearl.

He shrugged again. 'Nothing. A copper came. They were only kids so they got a warning. End of story. They never came back again.'

Pearl viewed the holiday homes behind him. 'Would it be difficult to break into one of these? To squat here during the winter?'

'And some,' he said. 'The place is full of CCTV now. You wouldn't even get past the gates.'

The sound of water from the fibreglass fountain filled the silence that followed. Reg finished his cigarette and dropped the stub to the ground before stepping on it. Then he looked back towards the mower again, this time seeming torn.

'Is there . . . anything else you remember?' Pearl asked quickly.

He shook his head. 'Like I say, it was a long time ago.' He went to hand back her business card but she pressed him to keep it. 'If you remember something else, anything at all, please call me?'

He looked at her, then nodded slowly. 'OK,' he said, slipping her card into the same pocket he had put the money.

As he returned to his mower and started up the engine, Pearl turned away, noting that the tourists were now seated at a decked area outside the pub, chatting over their food, ignoring the old ruined church whose twin towers still dominated the skyline of Herne Bay. The towers also served as a navigation marker for ships at sea, on a stretch of coastline so secluded it had been used to test prototypes of the 'bouncing bomb' during the last war, and the same piece of coast had also provided the spot where two young kids had once come to hide – but from what? Had it been Steven Scott's idea to come up here that day? Or had he allowed himself to be led astray by another runaway? Out of season, the caravan park would have been a desolate place, much like the slipway at Oare where, years later, Steven had abandoned his car and disappeared into thin air. Pearl took out her mobile phone and dialled a number, deciding she needed to find out more.

It took only half an hour for Pearl to drive to her next destination, on an unmade winding road across the desolate marshes, until she reached a place called Hollowshore – a seemingly forgotten area of flatlands where the tidal water from the River Swale splits into Faversham Creek to the east and Oare Creek to the west. At that very point, an old weather-boarded pub had stood for over three hundred years, having served smugglers, pirates, and the Thames estuary fishermen and sailors, who had been grateful for an inn while waiting to travel back up the creek to unload their cargoes at Faversham.

Alan Scott had answered Pearl's call and agreed to meet her in one of the three interlinked bars – filled with nautical paraphernalia – of the old Shipwright's Arms. As she waited for Alan to arrive, she thumbed through a tourist brochure explaining how the old pub was reputed to be haunted by the ghost of a captain whose ship had sunk in the Swale one stormy night. His crew having drowned, the captain managed to drag himself across the muddy flats, finally reaching the pub's door, only for a fearful landlord not to let him in. The captain's frozen body was found the next morning on the steps, and his spirit was now said to haunt the inn, his presence announced by a sharp drop in temperature and an overwhelming smell of 'rum, tar and tobacco' …

'Sorry to keep you waiting.' The voice startled Pearl until she looked up to see Alan Scott standing there. He quickly took a seat opposite her at the table and glanced out of the window, to where an old boatyard still carried out work on the Thames barges that had once so heavily populated the creeks.

'Thanks for meeting me here,' smiled Pearl. A waitress came across and took an order from Alan of a small sweet cider. As she moved off, Pearl explained: 'I just wanted to ask a few questions about the exhibition Steven was about to have before he disappeared. You and Christina both mentioned this to me – a businessman had offered him gallery space?'

Alan nodded. 'That's right,' he began. 'I never met the fella but he owns the Oyster House.' The name meant nothing to Pearl and she shook her head. Alan explained: 'It's a huge old building down at the quay on Faversham Creek.'

The waitress returned with a glass of honey-coloured cider. Alan sipped it and then continued, 'It used to be a warehouse, but this fella took it over and did a big restoration and conversion job on it and offered our Stevie an exhibition there. Stevie was thrilled about it.'

'And apprehensive?' Pearl guessed.

Alan looked up at this and shrugged. 'He wasn't feeling under any real pressure, if that's what you mean. He had plenty of finished paintings, but I was helping with his frames, working on them from morning to night, so that he'd have nothing to worry about.'

'All the same,' said Pearl. 'He must have been wondering how his work would be received? Or whether people would even come to the exhibition?'

Alan Scott raised his eyebrows to concede this. 'Maybe. But the guy seemed to have got it all covered. He'd told our Stevie he didn't need to do a thing – just produce the pictures . . . the paintings,' he corrected. 'He didn't even want a share of the take. 'Said it was a . . . "community" thing and he wanted to make use of the space, that's all.'

Pearl considered this. 'And when was this due to take place?'

Alan rubbed his brow thoughtfully. 'Just a little over a week after Stevie went missing. The paintings were going to hang for a fortnight with an opening night on the Saturday. Early evening. There was wine being put on – the lot.' He paused and gave another slight shrug. 'I know it sounds odd, someone going to all that trouble for nothing but . . . well, maybe this fella wanted to use Stevie's show as a dry run for something else. Something he could make money from next time?' He shook his head. 'I don't know. I never got to meet the man but I know our Stevie trusted him.'

'And the exhibition never took place,' mused Pearl.

'That's right. But only because Stevie went missing. Christina had to explain to the bloke. I never had any contact with him.'

'But you knew his name?'

'I did.' Alan frowned as he tried to summon it up. 'Jonathan,' he said. His expression was still one of concentration until he finally remembered the surname. 'Elliott. Jonathan Elliott.' He looked pleased and rewarded himself with another sip of cider.

'And the paintings?' asked Pearl. 'Christina has a few on her walls and said there are some stored in the garage, but there must be more elsewhere?'

Alan nodded. 'Quite a few,' he said. 'At my workshop.'

Pearl looked at him expectantly. 'Could I see them?'

After finishing their drinks, Alan Scott led the way, on foot, along a muddy path separating the marshland from what appeared to be a series of makeshift huts, boathouses, caravans and trailers lying on some open land that faced a few boat moorings on the creek. Pearl wasn't familiar with the area and noted that it was an out-of-the-way place, the kind of location where a person might go off radar. All that would be needed was to lie low and remain quiet – something she expected someone of Steven Scott's disposition would be able to do.

'How long have you had your workshop?' she asked.

Alan took a set of keys from his pocket and explained. 'Must be almost thirty years now. I had a boat moored here at one time. Just a little thing we'd go fishing in. Me and the boys. But then I sold it on and kept the workshop. The rent's peanuts but there's not much provided apart from the space. I call it a workshop, but you'll see that's a bit of a loose description.' He smiled and pointed the way to a strip of lawn on which a white painted bench faced an old railway carriage. Opening the door, Alan allowed Pearl to enter what appeared to her to be a tidy, functional workshop space. 'It's an old goods wagon,' he said. 'Not much, but it is to me. You know what they say about men and sheds? Nice to have somewhere to escape to. Linda says it's a "cave" thing.' He pointed out of the window. 'But it's peaceful here – now, anyway. A while back we had youngsters coming down here for raves in the fields, but that all stopped and there's only ever a few "boaties" around. Even then, most of them only come down at the weekends so I can get on with my projects in peace.' His smile began to fade. 'I . . . must admit, I did lose interest when I no longer had Stevie's frames to do.' His expression clouded.

'I can understand that,' said Pearl. She offered him a sympathetic smile and turned her attention to a large piece of oak on a bench saw. Alan pointed to it. 'That's going to be a table for the chapel garden,' he explained. 'It's a bit of a mess out there at the moment but I've offered to tidy it up. Linda has her charity work. I have the workshop. You could call it occupational therapy. Something to do?' He walked over towards something bulky propped against the wall and covered in a tarpaulin. Hesitating for a moment, he pulled the tarpaulin off to reveal a number of canvases. He began to turn each of them around.

'These are all unframed,' Pearl noted.

Alan nodded. 'That's right. All the framed paintings went to the house, ready to hang,' he explained. 'These were yet to do but . . . like I say, when Stevie went missing, I . . .' He broke off, a pained expression on his face before he finally admitted: 'If truth be known, I suppose I didn't want to finish them. There's an old saying, "If a man finishes building his house, he dies". I felt like that with these paintings . . . that if I finished framing them, there'd be nothing left to do. So I promised myself I'd finish them when I saw him again.' He summoned a brave smile and allowed Pearl to inspect the canvases. As she did so, she noted that Alan stood twiddling a set of keys in his hand, waiting apprehensively for her reaction, as though they might have been his own work.

Spreading out the canvases on the plywood-panelled floor, Pearl viewed large oil paintings showing the ochre-red sails of Thames barges gathered on the Swale for an annual race; atmospheric studies of birds taking flight on the marshes in the early morning light; a view from Oare across the water to the Ferry House Inn. Somehow each of the paintings had managed to capture the magical, ever-changing light of their locations, and Pearl began to lose herself in the images, trying to conjure up in her mind's eye Steven Scott working in each of these settings, quietly and at his own pace. Then she looked up, as if from another world, remembering where she was, as she saw some tools hanging neatly on a rack on the wall of the former railway carriage: chisels, awls and small framing hammers. Beside them, she also noted a small framed drawing, a cartoon showing Steven Scott with his arm around his stepfather in front of a collection of his own paintings, each with a red spot and the word 'Sold' beside it. Looking back at Alan Scott she saw his sadness as he explained: 'Stevie did that just a few days before he went missing – to say thanks for helping with the frames. It was the last time I saw him.'

Pearl tried to distract him from his sorrow. 'Thank you,' she said softly.

'For?'

'Allowing me to see these. You're right,' she added, 'Steven had a real gift.'

Alan corrected her: '*Has* a gift,' he insisted. 'I understand how it must have looked to the police, him leaving his car on the slipway like that but ... if he'd drowned out there, his body would have been found. I know that must have influenced the police's thinking because they were taking things seriously right up until the coastguard's report and ... then they seemed to let go of all this.' He looked suddenly bereft then began to busy himself, as if for distraction, stacking the canvases carefully together once more. Once he had done so, Pearl asked: 'Does your grandson ever get to come out here?'

Alan shrugged. 'Not as much as I'd like,' he said sparingly. He paused, his hand still on the blue tarpaulin as he admitted: 'If you ask me, it's a damn shame, because I think he'd enjoy being here – with me? Same as Stevie did when he was a boy.'

Pearl saw that Alan was trying hard to rein in some emotion, but she couldn't be sure if it was anger, sadness, or a mixture of both.

'Is that by Christina's choice?' she asked gently.

Alan considered this. 'Maybe her mother's,' he said. 'Sally's never really spent any time with us. And I'm not sure she ever liked Stevie.'

'Why wouldn't she?'

Alan shrugged. 'Maybe she's too grand for us. Her husband was an architect, in London, but now she spends all her time down here with Christina and ... well, it doesn't take much to see she rules the roost. So, Linda and me, we ... don't get to see much of Martin – and the boy misses out as much as we do.' He looked plaintively at Pearl. 'He wouldn't come to any harm here with me,' he said, as though Pearl might possibly have some influence on things, though it was all too clear to her that she had none. As though reading her thoughts, Alan Scott looked down at the blue tarpaulin in his hand and wrapped it quickly but carefully around the paintings that faced the wall.

Once back in her car, Pearl checked her phone for any messages from McGuire but, finding none, she drove off through an area known as Ham Marshes and on to Faversham, arriving beyond a stretch of beautiful creek-side homes interrupted only by the odd fancy restaurant overlooking the water. The creek itself was a tidal inlet with convenient access to the River Swale and the Thames estuary, so it provided a safe and spacious haven that was reasonably shallow but perfectly adequate for coasting boats and barges. The quay was part of the local conservation area, and an important piece of the jigsaw of Faversham's maritime heritage, but Pearl saw that in the last couple of years since she had visited the area, a number of shops and cafés had been integrated into many of the old buildings on the creek's southern side, as well as a large restaurant called the Quayside. The area was still home to several classic ships and boats as well as the Thames sailing barge, *Greta*, which offered day trips from Whitstable, ferrying passengers out to the various locations in the bay. A number of other large vessels were also moored here: a restored Danish fishing trawler that had taken part in the Icelandic fish wars some forty years ago, and a coastal Thames sailing barge, the *Tollesbury*, which had been requisitioned by the Royal Navy to help in the Dunkirk evacuation and had later opened as a bar and restaurant, only to sink at her moorings during the Provisional IRA's bombing of the Docklands in 1996. But it wasn't a boat Pearl was looking for. Taking out her smartphone she put in a search, not for a vessel, but for the Oyster House, mentioned by Alan Scott. An image appeared on her phone's screen, perfectly corresponding with a building further along the creek on a section known as Chambers Wharf.

As Alan Scott had described to her, the Oyster House was an enormous quayside warehouse. It had once been used for the storage of hops before their transportation to London by barge. But the building gave no clues away about its current owner or purpose, because the original signage had been left on the exterior – the faded name of the old fertiliser company that had once used it. As Pearl approached, she noted that it was actually located on the cusp of a section of creek known as Iron Wharf, which was as utilitarian as the quayside itself was picturesque. She also noted that a vast dry-dock facility lay nearby alongside the quay – a sealed unit measuring around twenty-five metres by six, into which a boat could be floated before the creek water was drained out, leaving a dry platform from which work could be undertaken. With a walkway along three sides, the unit left all parts of a boat accessible for construction or maintenance – but for now it was empty, looking much like an enormous rusting iron bath. Beyond it, at Iron Wharf, Pearl could also see that owners of other long vessels had eschewed the dry-dock facility and craned their boats out of the water to lie propped up on great beams, ready for work to take place.

Pearl stopped short of entering the wharf, and turned instead towards the Oyster House, opening one of two wrought-iron gates to enter a large L-shaped area that surrounded the property on two sides. Serving as a front garden to the property, it was topped with pea gravel and contained a number of raised beds planted with culinary herbs, including mint, rosemary and sage. Half a dozen old bistro chairs, painted a deep cerulean blue, matched the metal table they surrounded, on which stood a terracotta pot containing some pretty marguerite daisies. An expensive bicycle was left unchained, and a low flight of steps led the way to a porch door, which had been left invitingly open. Pearl headed towards it, mounting the steps to ring an outer bell. It was part of an entry-phone system, and clearly in place to save the owner traipsing down from any of the upper floors to open the front door. Though she waited some time for a response, it failed to come, so she rang the bell again. Still no reply. Tempted by the open door, Pearl now glanced back across her shoulder but saw only a few boat owners working industriously on their vessels at Iron Wharf. She took a step forward and entered the house.

Pearl immediately found herself in a large entrance hall with a black tiled floor and stylish wall lights. To her left, a plush carpeted staircase led straight up to the next floor. To the right, a door had been left ajar. Pearl moved towards it, and called out: 'Is anyone home?' With no response, she pushed the door further open and called out again. 'Hello?'

Under her hand, the door now fell wide open, offering her an unexpected view. The entire length of the lower floor of the building formed a single room. Eight cast-iron columns ran through its centre; along one side glazed doors opened out on to a Juliet balcony, which looked over the creek itself and farmland that lay on the opposite bank. A square archway led through to a further section, leading Pearl to calculate that the entire area comprised at least twenty by ten metres – more than enough space in which to stage an exhibition of Steven Scott's paintings. Stunned by the sheer scale of the room, Pearl moved through to where a black grand piano stood at its rear, striking an appropriate note of theatricality in the enormous space. A collection of artwork was displayed on a single wall above the piano – a variety of styles: a lithograph in an aluminium frame, a large, colourful study of a coastal scene with a sandy beach, and, sitting between two further abstract works, a small watercolour which looked instantly familiar. In Steven Scott's own style, it showed the nearby creekside area: moored barges and the ancient warehouse buildings.

Pearl was just moving closer to see if the work was signed when the sound of a ringing telephone broke into the silence. She stopped in her tracks, glancing around until she noted a white phone on a stylish coffee table. Her gaze automatically shifted to the ceiling above her as she waited for someone on the upper floors to respond to the call, but instead an answerphone clicked on and a man's well-spoken voice suddenly sounded in the room. 'This is Jonathan Elliott. I'm not here right now to take your call, but if you leave a message after the tone, I'll get back to you as soon as possible.' A beep followed – then a woman's voice, high-pitched, almost like a child's, though her tone was flirtatious: 'Jonathan, darling, it's me, Sukie. Will you please stop playing hard to get and call me to let me know if you're coming to stay this week or not? Bye darling.' Another beep. As the line went dead, Pearl became aware she had been holding her breath. She finally exhaled, allowing all the tension to drain from her body . . . but in the very next moment, the click of a door sounded some-where behind her.

Turning quickly, Pearl saw a man had just entered the

room. He was in his late thirties, tall, with sun-bleached fair hair and wearing a loose white shirt, faded jeans and a deep tan. He said nothing, but simply stared at Pearl as she stood at the opposite end of the room, then he stepped forward, walking confidently towards her until his face was very close to hers. He was unnervingly good-looking and his tone was more intrigued than angry as he asked: 'Do you mind telling me what you're doing here?'

Chapter Nine

A few minutes later and at Jonathan Elliott's invitation, Pearl found herself mounting the plush carpeted staircase of the Oyster House to enter the kitchen area on the first floor. Elliott moved off to get himself a glass of water, but nodded to Pearl to move into the lounge. 'Take a seat,' he said. 'I'll be right with you.'

As she rounded the corner into the room, Pearl recognised she had never before been in a home approaching anything of this size. The kitchen, dining room and sitting room formed practically the entire first floor, apart from a study and utility room. There were more exposed cast-iron columns and walls of fashionably painted brickwork. Sash windows to the front and rear offered more breathtaking views of the creek and the surrounding countryside, and a slate blackboard, which lined a wall above a huge wood-burning stove, bore various notes and telephone numbers scribbled in chalk. It was loft-style living but on a colossal scale and with a great deal of comfort and style. Two large abstract canvases hung on opposite walls above a pair of enormous sofas which faced one another, the gulf between them bridged by a long, glass coffee table; all of which told Pearl this was the home of a man with both flair and money.

Jonathan finally appeared from the kitchen area, casually wiping his hands down his faded jeans before he explained: 'I've been dealing with the garden. Newly planted apple trees need plenty of watering.' He pointed towards a balcony which overlooked generous grounds lying fenced off from the footpath leading to the house. Viewed from this angle, Pearl realised that the path was actually a continuation of the Saxon Shore Way public footpath which ran across the front of the property, creating a divide between it and the main garden – which appeared to be at least a quarter of an acre in size, laid to lawn and planted with silver birch, bay and a variety of young fruit trees.

'So,' he said, finally, 'you were about to tell me what you were doing here.'

He looked at her quizzically with deep blue eyes and Pearl found herself momentarily lost in his gaze. 'I'm sorry,' she said. 'I came to the front door, saw that it was open and . . .' She trailed off, partly because she had no real mitigation and partly because his smile was putting her on the back foot.

'Do you always enter open doors?' he asked. 'If you do, you could find yourself in trouble.'

Pearl returned his smile and reached into her bag to hand him a business card.

'An occupational hazard,' she said.

Jonathan Elliott glanced down at her card and frowned, confused. 'The Whitstable Pearl Seafood Restaurant?'

Pearl cursed herself, grabbed the card back and quickly exchanged it for another, this time making sure it bore Charlie's distinctive graphic design for Nolan's Detective Agency. Elliott considered it then looked back at her, unsure if she was playing some sort of practical joke.

'And this is you?' he asked. 'Pearl Nolan?'

'Yes,' she said proudly. 'It's my agency. And I'm here making some enquiries – about a man called Steven Scott.'

Elliott took a moment to make sense of this, then he gestured casually to the sofa behind her. Pearl sat down on it and he took a seat himself on the one that faced her. 'And?' he asked.

Pearl hesitated before replying carefully: 'I understand you were going to stage an exhibition of his paintings – here?'

Jonathan Elliott looked momentarily unsettled before he finally gave a quick nod. 'That's right.' Then he leaned back against the comfortable sofa and slipped his arms behind his head, crossing one leg over the other so that he rested an ankle on his knee. Pearl imagined he might have done so in an effort to use body language to show he had nothing to hide. In spite of his casual clothes, she noted he was wearing an expensive Rolex diver's watch.

'I'd just bought this place,' he explained, 'and I wanted to do something useful with it. I've got around six hundred square metres here over four floors. Grade II Listed. An old warehouse.' He added, 'It's more than a hundred and fifty years old, but I've restored it sympathetically.' He nodded cursorily towards the balcony. 'Let's just say I don't much like what I see out there.'

'Which is?' asked Pearl.

'What brings people here every weekend throughout the summer – garden centres, tea rooms . . . commercialisation.'

He looked back at her, his eyes narrowing slightly with suspicion. 'Are you working for an insurance company?'

'Why do you ask?'

'Because the exhibition was to have taken place seven years ago. It didn't happen because the artist disappeared.' He paused and leaned forward towards her. 'Seven years is the time it takes for a missing person to be presumed legally dead, so it might just be worthwhile for a company to hire someone like you for a second opinion – before they pay out on a life insurance policy.'

'Someone like me?'

'A private detective. Just to check that there are no . . . irregularities?'

Pearl considered him for a moment, noting that he was not only good-looking and rich, but smart too.

'Have you had any contact with Steven Scott's family in that time?'

'No,' he said starkly.

'Then how do you know he's still missing?'

Elliott gave an amused smile and glanced away momentarily before looking back at Pearl. 'Very good,' he said. 'But I'm assuming if Steven Scott had reappeared he might

just have got back in touch with me. About the exhibition?'
He got to his feet now as he continued: 'But he bailed out
on us all,' he said stoically.

'Why d'you think he would do that?'

He shrugged. 'I'm not in a position to say. I know it
would have been the first time he'd shown his paintings.
Though I doubt it would have been the last – *if* he'd gone
through with it. Some people are afraid of success.'

'Don't you mean failure?'

He held her gaze. 'Steven Scott wouldn't have failed. I'd
have made sure of that. He knew it too. He trusted me.
He certainly had no reason to doubt me.'

Sensing Pearl was unconvinced he went on. 'Look, for
years I worked as a corporate lawyer. I've done well.
Financially,' he added. 'Now I'd like to put something
back.' He moved to the window and looked out. 'The first
time I saw Steven, he was right over there, on the quay. I
went down to check out what it was he was working on.
It was just a study, a sketch of some barges moored near to
the dry dock, but I could see he had something special –
real talent. I wanted to commission him to do an oil
painting of my boat. He agreed. I offered him the
exhibition.' He paused before deciding to explain further.
'You could say my life has been crowded out by commercial
interests – contracts, deals – but there are still people, here
in this place, who lead uncomplicated lives. They do what
they enjoy – and not for profit.' He turned to face her.
'To be perfectly honest, I'm envious of that. I'd like to be
a part of it.'

Pearl considered this and asked: 'Do you think he could have committed suicide?'

'Why would he? Just before his first exhibition?'

'Nerves?'

'No one's that nervous,' he said confidently. 'I told you – I would have made it a success.'

'So . . . you must have wondered what happened to Steven? Where he could possibly have disappeared to? And why? Just like that? If he'd done so on the spur of the moment, he wouldn't have had time to plan an escape . . .'

'If you mean, do I think he came to some harm?' He paused as though considering this question. 'I'm sure the police would still be investigating if that was the case – if they suspected any foul play. So . . . maybe he had good reason to disappear.'

'And maybe his wife has good reason to find him,' said Pearl.

Jonathan looked back and read Pearl's challenging look. 'I get it,' he said. 'So you're working for his family.' For a brief moment he looked conflicted then shook his head. 'I never met them,' he explained. 'Steven's wife called me after he disappeared but I didn't know what to say to her then – and I still don't. I just wanted to help, that's all – to offer the guy a break. It was no big deal for me to mount an exhibition here. I have plenty of contacts; people who would have taken great pleasure in owning a few of Steven Scott's paintings. I'm only sorry that didn't happen.'

Pearl took this in as Jonathan moved away from the window.

'When did you last have any contact with him?'

Elliott took some time to think about this, then offered a slow shake of his head. 'He came down here about ten days before the exhibition – gave me a small painting of the quay.'

'The one downstairs in the gallery space?'

He looked back at her. 'It was just a gift – to say thanks. Then he called a day or so later sounding upbeat about the exhibition.' He broke off and stroked his brow. 'Look, I'm very sorry . . . for his wife and his family, but, to tell you the truth, one of the reasons I bought this place – in fact the most important reason – is because . . .' He broke off and pushed open the doors to the creekside balcony, stepping back to allow Pearl a bird's-eye view of what lay directly below. On a private mooring, the deck of a beautifully restored ninety-foot sailing barge was visible, mast towering beside the building itself. Pearl looked back at Jonathan, who said only: 'Sometimes, some of us just need to get away.'

After leaving the Oyster House, Pearl decided against investigating Iron Wharf and began heading back along the quay. Following her conversation with Jonathan Elliott, she took a more careful look at the amount of development the area had undergone, and the historic old warehouse that was now home to the Quayside restaurant. Its black timber frontage looked much the same as ever, but its cavernous interior was now a vast white architectural space with a clever use of etched glass to define certain areas. It certainly matched any fine London restaurant in style, and its tables were fully occupied in spite of the high price of its menu which was shown on a panel of the door: smoked eel, lovage and gazpacho; crab in a delicate pistou with herbs; oysters with nori, soy and lime ... Pearl had hardly got beyond reading the appetisers when she realised how little she had thought of her own restaurant that day. Instead she began to wonder if Jonathan Elliott's rejection of his former lifestyle extended to the fine dining he must have enjoyed in the course of his previous career.

The quay had indeed been commercialised: apart from the restaurant and garden centre, there was a wine bar, a few antiques shops and a collectables market, as well as a record shop, a beauty salon, and even a wedding dress store – everything on tap for visitors. Elliott may have taken a disparaging view of all that, but there was also the provision of essential services for boat owners, including quayside water, electricity, and access to maritime profes- sionals and tradespeople for boatyard repairs, as well as the dry-dock facility. It occurred to Pearl that, having profited from his former corporate career, Elliott might now want a quieter life in order to enjoy his beautiful sailing barge, but there was no way progress was going to stop for him. The world had grown smaller, with fewer places to hide – though it was becoming increasingly apparent that Steven Scott might have successfully managed to do so.

Heading on towards the car park, Pearl noticed a figure on the quayside before her – a woman, leaning in towards a pretty houseboat, concentrating intently on her work as she carefully touched up the paintwork on the boat's transom. She looked to be in her thirties and was dressed casually in faded black jeans and a pale denim shirt over a white singlet. Her long red hair was fiery in the sunlight. As Pearl grew nearer, she saw that the woman was, in fact, cutting in the name of the boat in gold lettering, *The Seahorse*, beside which was a wood carving, also in gold, of the sea creature itself.

'Beautiful,' Pearl commented softly, almost to herself. At this, the woman glanced back, but only momentarily, and barely acknowledging Pearl, before she continued with her work. Pearl remained, nonetheless, admiring the charming features of the boat: a wooden table on the deck with a sunshade above it, some planters filled with geraniums, and brightly coloured curtains in the saloon windows.

'Is she yours?' Pearl asked.

'Yep,' said the woman. Pearl understood that living on a moored boat could mean having as little privacy as Pearl herself enjoyed in her cottage by the sea. Tourists and visitors were apt to treat Seaspray Cottage as a goldfish bowl, spying through Pearl's windows as they ambled along the prom and even taking the odd trespassing stroll around her beach-facing garden. Pearl now recognised she was in danger of invading the privacy of the woman on the quayside and decided to take a different tack.

'Is she a . . . 1930s trawler?'

At this question, the woman now turned, paintbrush in hand, and Pearl offered a smile as she explained: 'I really don't want to disturb you, but my dad was an oyster fisherman, working out of Whitstable, and all I have is a small dinghy.' She looked back at *The Seahorse* and smiled. 'I'm very envious.' The woman's gaze followed Pearl's to the boat. Then she appeared to do a swift reassessment of Pearl before saying: 'No problem. Care to take a look?'

'If I'm not stopping you?'

The woman returned Pearl's smile. 'To tell the truth, I could do with a break.' She set down her paintbrush, wiped her hands down her faded jeans and held one out to Pearl. 'I'm Celia.'

'Pearl.'

'Come aboard.'

Mounting the gangplank, Celia explained: 'The conversion's taken me forever but I'm almost there. She's got a fully working engine for cruising but she also makes for a very comfortable home.'

'I can see that,' said Pearl, as she paused to enjoy the view of open farmland on the northern side of the creek. 'I've always loved the idea of a life afloat,' she added, turning to Celia. 'You're living my dream.'

'And mine – finally,' said Celia. 'It took quite a few years before I could even afford a boat like this, let alone make her habitable. Here . . .' She opened the door to the wheelhouse. 'I've tried to keep things original and just brought them up to date.' She led the way for Pearl, who saw that the wheelhouse still retained its use as a navigation point but part of it had been converted as a shower. 'All mod cons,' said Celia proudly. She smiled and headed down below deck, revealing a well-equipped galley in the forward cabin, a separate cabin used for storage, while the main saloon doubled as a sleeping and living area with a wood-burning stove as a central feature. 'That heats the whole boat,' she explained, 'but there's also an electric hot-water heater.'

'No cold showers then?' smiled Pearl.

'Not if I can help it,' said Celia. 'My first boat was a bit more rough and ready.' She indicated a framed photo of a modest fishing boat with herself at the helm, looking at least ten years younger. 'But she served me well. I worked hard to renovate her and with the profit I managed to pick up this beauty.' She climbed the steps back on to the deck and surveyed her new boat. 'She needed plenty of work . . .' she added. 'Together with a new name.'

Celia hopped back on to the quay and, as she picked up her paintbrush once more, she saw Pearl's look and followed her eyeline to the boat's transom. 'I know what you're thinking,' Celia said. 'It's meant to be unlucky to change the name of a boat? But a new name often makes for a new start, and I think *The Seahorse* will work out just fine for me.' She looked back at the carving on the boat's transom and explained: 'Seahorses are special creatures – beautiful but strong. D'you know that during rough seas and stormy weather, they use their tails like an anchor, locking them around something stable on the seabed? In ancient Greece and Rome, sailors always kept a seahorse charm to protect them.' She offered an unexpected smile, as though reassured by what she had just said. 'It's my totem . . .' She pulled a chain from inside the singlet she wore. On the end of it was a single piece of silver, curved into the shape of a seahorse. 'My spirit creature. It keeps me safe.' She gave a quick smile and slipped the charm under her vest before she looked back at the boat. 'I've only just got her out of dry dock. She was there for over a week while I got the hull painted.'

Pearl nodded and asked: 'And is this your first time in Faversham?'

Celia shook her head. 'Nope. I did most of the restoration work here back in 2011.' She stirred her paint then looked back at Pearl. 'Are you a . . . friend of Jonathan's?'

'Jonathan?' echoed Pearl.

'I just saw you coming out.' She nodded towards the Oyster House.

Pearl realised. 'No,' she said. 'We've never met before today. How about you?'

Celia shrugged. 'I don't know him well but he moved into that place when I was last here.' She remained thoughtful for a moment as though reaching a decision. 'He's a good guy,' she said finally. 'He's tried to oppose some of the developments that have been taking place around here. That place, for a start.' She nodded towards the Quayside restaurant. 'But he's really into sailing barges. Owns a beauty.'

'Yes, I just saw her,' said Pearl. 'How about you? How did you get into the boating life?'

Celia paused for a moment as though gathering her thoughts, then looked back at Pearl. 'My dad was a pilot on the creek. I was always out with him as a teenager, so I got the bug early.' She smiled and changed the subject. 'Are you here looking for a boat?' She looked at Pearl, curious.

'No,' Pearl admitted. 'As a matter of fact, I'm searching for someone.'

Reaching into her bag, she took out a folded piece of paper and handed it to Celia, watching as the young woman unfolded it to view the poster showing the photo of Steven Scott. Celia looked down at the image, then shook her head slowly. 'Don't think I can help you.'

'Are you sure?' asked Pearl, disappointed. 'He would have been here in the summer of 2011. An artist. He never used photographs for his work so he would have spent quite a bit of time here.' Celia looked at the poster again, then across to the quayside, and frowned. 'You're right,' she said. 'He was here . . .' She broke off as she tried to collect her thoughts. 'A . . . quiet guy.' She looked up at Pearl. 'You'd forget that he was even there because he . . . just seemed to blend in with the scenery. He used to sit right over there.' She pointed in the direction of the Quayside restaurant. 'The first time I saw him, he was writing in a big book – at least, I thought he was writing, but then I realised he was sketching. He always seemed to look more than he drew?' She frowned. 'I . . . didn't like to disturb him but I got curious one day and asked what he was doing. He showed me a sketch for a painting. It was of the quay here and the barges sitting on the mud at low tide.' She broke off for a moment and shrugged. 'Like I say, he was just doing his own thing.' She handed the poster back to Pearl then asked with a little suspicion: 'Are you . . . with the police?'

Pearl shook her head. 'A private investigation.'

Celia nodded. 'Well, I wish I could help, but it's a long time ago. I haven't been here since. Like I say, I only came back to use the dry dock. A few more days and I'll be off again. I want to start doing some charters with *The Seahorse*. This life is about never staying in one place too long.'

She turned to pick up her paintbrush but Pearl spoke again: 'This man, Steven Scott, he was married – his wife was expecting a baby when he went missing.'

Celia's hand faltered as she painted. She failed to look back but asked: 'No one's heard from him since?'

Pearl shook her head. 'No one.'

Celia considered this for a moment before looking back at Pearl: 'Then perhaps he doesn't want to be found.'

'Yes,' said Pearl. 'Perhaps you're right.' She reached into her pocket and took out one of her agency business cards. Handing it to Celia she said: 'Please feel free to contact me – any time.'

Celia hesitated for a moment. Her eyes locked with Pearl's as she took the card and slipped it into the pocket of her jeans, then she turned her attention back again to her boat and began painting the last of the letters on its transom, as though Pearl had never existed.

Twenty minutes later, Pearl drove slowly along a narrow country road beyond a gastropub called the Three Mariners near Oare Creek. An expanse of fields soon spread out to

her left, overlooked by a variety of properties on her right
– a small parade of workmen's cottages, the parish church
of St Peter's and its vicarage and some recently converted
barns. Finally, the landscape opened up before her, with
marshland on either side and the River Swale straight
ahead. Birdwatchers were drawn to monitor the variety of
wetland birds that used the tidal banks and fringes of the
Swale as home and a winter stopover but, at this time of
year, when many birds had completed their nesting cycle
and were already heading south, the 'birders' and 'twitchers'
were also fewer in number.

Pearl drove down an old dirt road to the slipway for
Harty Ferry, noting how the surrounding area was riddled
with mudflats and water channels. Parking up, she headed
on foot past an old wooden boathouse to the slipway itself,
now exposed by the low tide. This was the spot on which
Steven Scott's car had been found abandoned. But why
was the car ever here at all? And what had happened to
him after leaving it? Ahead of Pearl lay the thirteen-mile-
long channel of the Swale. A hundred years ago it would
have been filled with Thames barges and fishing vessels
carrying cargoes up to London on the Thames estuary but,
today, there was only a single red and white fishing boat
lying at anchor. Off to the right was the public footpath of
the Saxon Shore Way, though Pearl saw no walkers upon
it. The area seemed abandoned – wild and desolate – and
Alan Scott's words came back to her: 'Stevie liked the light
there. He said it was magical . . .' and Pearl had to agree.
Steven Scott might very well have been preparing to paint

here, and possibly also across the river, on the Isle of Sheppey, at the very point where another old slipway mirrored this one. In years gone by, it had been used to launch a small sailing boat to take the local priest back to the mainland at Oare after he had performed his daily service on the island, but Pearl now wondered whether Steven Scott might possibly have used a small boat himself to cross the Swale almost seven years ago. But if he had, why had he never returned? Could Christina have been right when she said she felt instinctively that her husband would never have left her of his own free will? Had some danger befallen him that day which had prevented him from returning to his wife? If so, what could it have been? And if he had not been contemplating taking his own life, why had he left a note behind: 'I never thought what I did was of value – so I really can't go on like this any more.'

The note would remain out of Pearl's reach with the local Swale Police, but she hoped McGuire would have some news for her when they met for dinner tomorrow night. She closed her eyes, remembering McGuire's kiss at the sound of an old clock tower bell and, as a sudden breeze blew in from the Swale, she turned her face towards it, feeling the warmth of the last rays of sun on her skin. Taking a deep breath, she tried to summon up a picture of Steven Scott standing on this very spot seven years ago – a young man who, despite a few marital and financial problems, still had much ahead of him: a new role as a young father and perhaps even a successful future as an artist with an upcoming exhibition at Jonathan Elliott's

Oyster House. She tried hard to conjure up an image but found it impossible to see anything but a shady figure, a silent presence – a ghost; nothing more substantial than the phantom of an old captain that haunted the Shipwright's Arms across the marshes ...

Chapter Ten

'What about a seahorse?' Pearl was busily preparing a *salade Niçoise* in the kitchen of The Whitstable Pearl when the idea suddenly came to her. Dolly, deep in concentration as she arranged fronds of samphire on a grilled sea bass fillet, echoed: 'A seahorse?'

'For our carnival float.'

'Oh, they're beautiful creatures,' said Pearl's young waitress, 'everyone loves them!' Over the last few years, Ruby had flourished in her job at The Whitstable Pearl, gaining confidence and evolving from the troubled teenager Pearl had once taken under her wing into the pretty young woman who now stood before her, with her fair hair gathered back off her face in a neat plait. She appeared delighted by Pearl's suggestion, smiling expectantly as she waited for Dolly's response – and for the plate of sea bass she was fussing over. Dolly finally straightened, paying attention now. 'Yes,' she said. 'You're right.' She seemed to ruminate on Pearl's idea for a moment before plucking Ruby's order pencil from her pocket and using it to scribble quickly on the back of a menu. 'Seahorses are also a good-luck symbol in China, did you know that?'

'No,' said Pearl honestly, though she wasn't surprised that her mother should be aware of such a thing because Dolly was an expert in crystals, astrology, and adept at some palmistry too. 'They have all sorts of significance,' she continued.

'A good-luck charm for sailors?' Pearl suggested, remembering what Celia had told her.

'True,' said Dolly, before deciding: 'What an excellent idea! How on earth did you come up with it?'

Pearl took Ruby's pencil from her mother and handed it back to her waitress, along with the order of sea bass that Dolly had been preparing. She waited until Ruby had returned to the restaurant floor before she turned to Dolly to remind her: 'I *am* capable of some good ideas,' but she admitted: 'actually, it was a piece of serendipity. I happened to be over at Faversham Creek yesterday and met a woman with a boat of the same name.'

'*The Seahorse?*' Dolly computed for a moment. 'And was this on your search for the missing man?'

Pearl nodded.

'No nearer to finding him, I suppose?'

'Not yet,' Pearl admitted. 'But I'm trying to build up a picture. A profile of him. It's the only way I'm going to make sense of what might have happened – by talking to those who knew him.'

'That could be misleading,' said Dolly. 'People have different relationships with their friends and family so their views could cloud the issue. Besides, not everyone might be telling the truth.'

'I realise that,' said Pearl. 'Someone may well be lying, and I recognise everyone has a different opinion of Steven Scott. I think his marriage had hit a few problems and his mother-in-law certainly had reservations about him, but his stepfather positively adores him. Nevertheless, if I assemble all the facts I learn in the right way, I should end up with a result.'

'Like that salad?' asked Dolly drily, looking down at the *Niçoise* that Pearl was still assembling. Ruby entered the swing doors again and Pearl handed the dish to her, the girl disappearing again with it as swiftly as she'd entered. Pearl licked the bitter salt traces of anchovy oil from her fingers, then washed her hands at the sink, wondering to herself now if she might have dismissed too lightly the technological advances that had been offered to her a couple of years ago by a sales rep on a cold call. Technology played an important role in the business of any private detective, with the use of new apps and online search tools providing important checks on criminal histories as well as divorce and driving records, but the sales rep had been trying to interest Pearl in some genealogy software with which she could research family histories, together with some 'face-reading technology', by which he claimed a 'personality evaluation' could be created merely from facial characteristics. At the time, Pearl hadn't been too impressed by his 'hard sell' approach, not least because he had tried to make her feel ill-equipped and unprofessional, but now she began to wish she had something in her armoury which could help throw some light on the shadowy figure of Steven Scott.

She dried her hands quickly as she thought aloud: 'It can't be easy to lose yourself these days. I mean, wherever you go, you're likely to need a credit card, passport, or at least a new driving licence?' She frowned. 'In order to work, you'd also have to obtain another National Insurance number ... unless, of course, you were employed in the black economy – cash in hand – and for low wages?'

She looked back towards Dolly, who had remained uncharacteristically quiet while she allowed Pearl to organise her thoughts. But Dolly now checked that the kitchen was quite empty before she admitted in a low voice: 'I *once* thought about it.'

'Thought about what?'

Dolly paused for a moment before whispering: 'Bolting.'

The word caused Pearl to turn in shock. 'Bolting?'

Dolly nodded quickly. 'Walking out. And not coming back.'

Pearl looked sidelong at her mother but saw she wasn't joking.

'It was a few days before Christmas,' Dolly said. 'A bitterly cold winter. Your father and I had been married less than a year and ... well, times were hard. He was doing his best with the oyster fishing but he was also spending far too much time down at the Neppy.' She broke off and frowned. 'It was our first Christmas together and I'd been so looking forward to it. I'd bought all the presents, decorated the cottage, put up the Christmas lights on the tree and he came home – a bit worse for wear – and knocked the whole thing over.'

Pearl smiled and Dolly joined her. 'Yes, Pearl. I should've seen the funny side. It was Christmas, after all. But I got upset – not that I showed it; I was far too proud for that. I told him I was going out to pick up some holly from a neighbour, took a bag with me, walked to the top of the road and then walked on a bit further . . . past the harbour. The masts of the fishing boats were strung with fairy lights, all the colours reflecting in the water . . . and before I knew it, I'd walked on and found I was sitting at the bus shelter, just beyond Reeves Beach, wondering whether I'd really done the right thing.'

'By leaving Dad on his own?'

Dolly shook her head before admitting: 'By getting married.' She gave a defensive look and carried on. 'I was twenty-two years old, and we had very little. I'd never had to compromise before but . . .' She paused. 'I was fast learning that compromise is what marriage is all about.'

Pearl took some time to absorb this then asked: 'What happened?'

Dolly shrugged. 'I just sat there on the bench and I watched the tide come in. It was a bitterly cold night but I stayed there, shivering, trying to imagine what I'd do if I didn't go back. But I didn't have any answers.' She looked lost for a moment then went on. 'I set off home and when I opened the door, I found your father had . . . put the tree back up, and the lights on.' She paused. 'He had a glass of sherry waiting for me. I kissed him and I wished him a Happy Christmas.'

She looked down, as though embarrassed at a sudden wave of emotion that had just come over her. Pearl moved closer and offered her a tissue. 'Here.'

Dolly took it, blew her nose noisily and stuffed the tissue up her sleeve.

'You didn't walk out for long,' Pearl reminded her knowingly.

'No,' Dolly agreed, washing her hands at the sink. 'And a good thing I didn't, or *you* wouldn't be standing here right now.' She returned to Pearl and picked up the menu on the back of which she had scribbled a rough design. 'A seahorse,' she said. 'I love it.' And with that, she headed towards the swing doors to the restaurant, then paused and looked back at her daughter. 'And I love you too,' she said softly.

An hour after the busy lunch service had finished, Pearl spent some time putting up new posters all over town, appealing for help in finding Steven Scott. She then met with her client at a car park on the seafront and walked with Christina Scott in the direction of the old gate-house entrance of Whitstable Castle. 'I'm sorry I couldn't meet you at your office,' said Christina as Pearl kept pace with her. 'Mum phoned to say she's finally found a nice cottage to buy in Whitstable. She's at the estate agent's right now, putting in an offer, so I have to pick up Martin from a birthday party. They had a treasure hunt in the castle grounds and we're heading to a friend's house for supper.' She smiled but Pearl saw tension written on her face.

'It'll be good for you to have your mother here,' she said.

'Yes,' said Christina automatically. 'She'll be downsizing, of course, because she no longer needs a big family home – but that's left her with a good profit,' she said. 'You know what London house prices are like these days?'

'Yes,' smiled Pearl. 'And I won't keep you. I just had a few more questions, that's all.'

'About?' asked Christina.

'I spoke to Jonathan Elliott yesterday – the man who offered Steven the exhibition space at Faversham. He mentioned you were the one who had broken the news to him about Steven's disappearance.'

'Yes,' Christina nodded. 'The exhibition was coming up imminently so I . . . had to call and let him know. To be honest, I also thought there might be a chance Steven might contact him. The police had told me to check with everyone Steven knew.'

She looked at Pearl, who asked: 'And did you ever meet him?'

'Mr Elliott?' Christina shook her head. 'Steven had told me about him, of course – how he had liked the paintings and wanted to help.'

'Did he ever mention anything else?'

'Well, he . . . said Mr Elliott was a successful business-man with a wonderful home and a beautiful space in which to show the paintings.'

'But he didn't offer a view of why a successful business-man wasn't acting as "agent" for the exhibition – and taking a cut of any profits from sales?'

Christina frowned at this before shaking her head. 'No, he didn't. Though Mum did. She was rather suspicious about the whole thing, but then I'm afraid that's her nature. She's very good at business and managed Dad's company before he died. But Steven and I simply accepted the offer at face value. The exhibition never happened, so we'll never know if that was a mistake.'

A sporty open-top roadster went past, bass thumping from its car radio. Pearl waited until it had receded into the distance before she asked: 'The chapel that Steven's parents go to,' she began. 'Have you ever been there?'

'To a service, you mean?' Christina shook her head firmly. 'But that's not for want of trying on Linda's part. Ever since Steven went missing, she's been on at me to join them, but frankly I'm not impressed by what I've seen.'

Pearl frowned. 'What do you mean?'

Christina looked at Pearl and a dam of frustration seemed to burst. 'Linda uses that chapel as an emotional crutch,' she said. 'I don't think she's ever properly dealt with Mark's death – never moved on. It's like . . . she's trapped in time?' She bit her lip. 'And I know you might think the same of me with Steven's disappearance, but it's really not the same. Mark has been dead for over twenty years, but for Linda it might just as well be yesterday. The clock stopped for her that day. No wonder Steven had problems.'

'As a child, you mean?'

Christina nodded. 'I told you, the counselling helped him to move on and Linda could have learned from that . . . tried it herself? But instead she relies far too much on that bogus vicar.'

'Bogus?'

'Well, it's hardly a proper church, is it? Steven looked into it all. It was just a village hall till the minister took it over and began some kind of charm offensive in the local community.' She glanced at Pearl. 'He's involved in all sorts of local initiatives and activities, but it's always members of his congregation who seem to put in all the work – and a lot of that is about raising money . . .' She paused and offered a knowing look. 'And the dead?'

They had just passed through the gatehouse entrance to the castle. Pearl turned to Christina. 'What do you mean?'

'There's something called the Lazarus Group,' said Christina. 'The clue's in the name. Lazarus is the man in the Bible who rose from the dead, and the group's supposed to offer comfort to those who've experienced grief, but I wouldn't be surprised if there isn't some kind of . . . spiritualism involved. That's what Steven suspected. And why would I possibly go to something like that when I have no firm evidence that Steven is dead?' She shook her head in frustration. 'I don't know how Alan manages to go along with it all – but he does so for Linda, of course. He'll do just about anything to keep her happy. He deserves a medal, because she's like a child in many ways. I don't think she could ever manage without him. He's always been her rock – and Steven's.'

'The father he never knew?' asked Pearl gently.

'The only father he ever had,' said Christina with conviction. 'Alan never tired of helping him. He framed the paintings for the exhibition and, if he hadn't, I'm not sure we could ever have afforded to have done them. Steven wasn't ungrateful but ... I'd have to remind him to thank his dad for what he did. I didn't want him to go taking that for granted.'

'I was at the workshop yesterday,' Pearl said. 'I could tell how proud Alan was of Steven.' Christina's face clouded and she took on a pained expression. 'I so wish Martin could have spent these last years with his dad.'

Pearl recognised that those words had an added reson-ance because, at that very moment, having just reached the castle grounds, a group of young children came into view, playing on the central lawn. 'Does Martin see much of Steven's parents?' she asked.

Christina's eyes remained fixed on the children as she replied, 'Not as much they would like. I don't keep him from Linda and Alan, but I don't like the control the minister seems to have over them, so I like to be around when he's there. There's a chapel charity event coming up that I said we would go to – tomorrow in Herne Bay. It's at the Waltrop Gardens – the sunken ones near the seafront? We'll go along for a while but Martin really wants to try out the crazy golf.' She brightened at the thought, and Pearl returned her smile, ready to confide about Charlie's previous mini-golf efforts when she saw that Christina's attention had been suddenly taken by the sight of a familiar face among the children – a little boy with russet-coloured hair and a party bag in his hand, waving to Christina before hurrying across. Martin Scott stood breathlessly, looking up between his mother and Pearl. 'Hello,' he smiled brightly. Christina hugged him as she said: 'This is Pearl.'

'Good party?' Pearl asked.

'Brilliant.' Martin smiled again. 'I found this in the treasure hunt.' He fished inside his party bag and pulled out a plastic crab.

'I serve those in my restaurant.'

Martin's eyes widened. 'You eat them?'

Pearl nodded. 'Real ones,' she said. 'Not plastic.' She looked at Christina now. 'I'll be in touch,' she said softly.

'Bye,' said Martin Scott. He waved to her, the plastic crab still in his hand. Pearl moved off, then looked back to see Christina fastidiously straightening her son's collar and running a hand through his hair before they walked off together, her arm around him, clutching his shoulder protectively. Pearl watched them until they disappeared out of sight and then moved on herself.

It was almost eight o'clock that evening before Pearl finally managed to start getting herself ready for her dinner date with McGuire. After putting up yet more posters around town, she had become tied up with unexpected problems concerning a delivery from a supplier, which had resulted in her having to drive to the seaside town of Deal in search of fresh herring for Dean's Special Menu that evening. Returning to Seaspray Cottage, she had quickly showered to lose all trace of fish, and tried on a number of outfits before settling on a simple white cotton dress, gathered at the waist, and smothered in tiny red hearts. Pinning up her hair in a variety of ways, in order to show off her new pearl earrings, she had finally decided to let it fall loose around her shoulders before picking up her red vintage clutch bag and keys and heading for the front door. Opening it, she was taken aback to find somebody already standing there.

'Dee . . .'

'I hope you don't mind me dropping by, but I wanted to let you know about the Lazarus meeting.'

Pearl frowned. 'It's on Thursday evening, right?'

Dee shook her head. 'No. That's just it. It was rearranged. I've just come from it but I couldn't warn you . . .' She took her mobile phone from her coat pocket and held it aloft. 'Battery's dead.'

Pearl realised her mouth was gaping open like a fish. 'Sorry,' she said quickly. 'Come in.' She held the front door wide open for Dee to enter, who noted: 'You're looking very nice, Pearl. I do hope I haven't descended at an awkward time?'

Torn, Pearl admitted: 'Well, I . . . was actually on my way out, but . . .' She made a quick decision. 'It can wait. Can I get you a drink?'

'Glass of juice, if you have one? I'm driving.' Dee smiled. Pearl gave a quick nod. 'I'll be right back.' She headed off into the kitchen and, once there, took out her phone and tapped out a quick text to McGuire's number. It read: 'Something's come up. I'll be a bit delayed.' Then she opened her fridge, poured a glass of apple juice and dropped some ice into it. An incoming text duly sounded on her phone. 'How delayed?'

Pearl tapped back a response. 'Not sure. Half an hour?' She waited, but when no further text came through, she picked up the drink and took it through to Dee.

'Here you are,' she said brightly.

'Thanks.' Dee took a sip of the juice just as Pearl's phone sounded another text. 'Sorry,' she said to her guest, before she checked her phone quickly to see the new text was from McGuire. It read: 'No problem. I'm running late too. Have let the restaurant know.'

Pearl studied the text, unsure if she was relieved or disappointed that her date with McGuire was now delayed. Dee read her look. 'Are you . . . sure I'm not keeping you?'

'No,' said Pearl with a smile. 'It's absolutely fine. You were saying?'

'The meeting,' Dee replied. 'It was rescheduled because several people couldn't make it on Thursday evening.'

'I see,' said Pearl, thoughtfully. 'And?'

Dee noted Pearl's expectant look, but raised her shoulders somewhat helplessly. 'I'm not sure what I'm about to tell you is what you actually want to hear.'

Pearl frowned. 'What do you mean?'

'Well,' Dee paused for a moment then explained: 'I have to admit . . . I actually found it quite helpful.' She looked as surprised as Pearl, then took another sip of her drink before adding: 'There were eight of us in all.'

'Including Alan and Linda Scott?'

Dee nodded. 'That's right. Minister Cameron . . .' She broke off, searching for the right word before she found it: '. . . officiated. And he did so very well. He allowed us all to talk about our loss and how we felt. I can't say I've ever been tempted by the idea of counselling before, but I did find myself offloading, so to speak, and I feel better for it.' She looked at Pearl. 'That's the thing with sadness, isn't it? You spend so much energy trying to hold it in because you think it will just keep coming once you let go, but . . . actually sharing my experience tonight was quite cathartic.'

'I'm pleased to hear it,' said Pearl with mixed feelings, wishing she had learned something to reinforce Christina Scott's suspicions.

Dee went on. 'Of course I was talking about Ted and, though I did love him, he was only a dog, not a husband. A woman in her eighties called Mabel had just lost hers – husband, I mean – and they'd been together for almost sixty years.' She sighed. 'A young girl called Sandra spoke about losing her grandmother, Betty, who had passed on very recently – and quite unexpectedly. Sad.'

'Was . . . everyone in the group part of the chapel's congregation?' Pearl asked.

Dee nodded. 'All members of the flock,' she said. 'Sandra's thirteen and goes to Sunday school.'

'At the chapel?'

'That's right.' She gathered her thoughts and explained: 'You know, I was half expecting to experience something creepy . . . But the name, Lazarus, with all its connotations of rising from the dead, seemed only to be used in a symbolic way. Minister Cameron explained how we can all rise from this state of grief and loss if we understand we're all part of a greater truth – and in a way that brings a sense of rebirth itself.' She paused. 'It made a lot of sense, at least in the way he described it: letting out the sadness and remembering the good times? Simple, really. To be honest, I hadn't believed I could possibly entertain the idea of another companion but, after tonight, I . . . might just consider it. After all, companionship works both ways and there might very well be another little fellow out there I could give a good home to.'

'I'm sure that's very true,' smiled Pearl. 'And how did you find the minister?'

Dee shrugged. 'He was his same charismatic self – not as loud or sermonising as he was at the service the other night but . . . There's certainly something about him. He's persuasive . . . Inspirational . . .'

'Married?'

'Single,' said Dee. 'I asked.'

Pearl mused. 'And . . . being unattached, he's no doubt a favourite with the women of the "flock"? From what you've said, the only other man there tonight was Alan Scott?'

Dee nodded. 'Yes. And I got the impression he was really there to support his wife, but that's not to say he isn't carrying a great deal of sadness himself. Difficult to judge, because men tend to hold a lot back, don't they? But I'd say he also responds to the spiritual comfort the group gives.' She pointed a finger at Pearl and added: 'That's not to say I'm one for organised religion. Like most people, I attend hatchings, matchings and dispatchings – the usual church services for births, weddings and funerals – and I do like the odd Christmas carol service too, but I haven't read the Bible for years. Oddly, after only a couple of hours in the minister's company, I actually feel like revisiting a few chapters: the Psalms that gave me comfort as a child, and perhaps even some encouragement when required: 'Yea, though I walk through the valley of the shadow of death, I will fear no evil: for thou art with me; thy rod and thy staff . . . they comfort me.' She looked across at Pearl and offered an unexpectedly serene smile.

Chapter Eleven

The Harbour Garden Restaurant was one of the few establishments in town at which customers could eat al fresco; a good choice on McGuire's part for his date with Pearl, as the tide was high and the air was still warm and filled with the smell of summer – barbecued fish on the beach and the aroma of sautéed garlic from the restaurant itself. It wasn't quite the South of France, though it was Pearl's Riviera and, on the waiter's suggestion of a cocktail, she had duly opted for a French Negroni consisting of gin, sweet vermouth and the aperitif wine, Lillet, all balanced with a twist of orange. McGuire had chosen a Whiskey Sour. A young saxophone player was perched on a high stool playing some cool jazz as a waiter brought their order – a paella of monkfish and *vongole*, to share. Pearl took some time to admire the presentation of sweet red peppers strewn across saffron-gold rice dotted with baby clams, but McGuire saw only how stunning Pearl looked in the simple white cotton dress smothered in little red hearts. As night began to fall, the waiter brought a tea light to their table, the flame of which danced behind its glass container, as he poured some wine and left the bottle in a chiller on the table. The saxophonist began to play a laid-back number and Pearl raised her glass, touching McGuire's with it before taking a sip and saying: 'Thank you.'

'For?' He looked at her, noting that while the new earrings Pearl wore certainly complemented her moonstone-grey eyes, they couldn't match them in beauty.

'This,' said Pearl, indicating the table. 'It's such a pleasure dining out rather than playing host – not that I'm tiring of The Whitstable Pearl,' she added quickly. She took another sip of wine.

McGuire smiled. 'But you have got a new chef?'

As she looked up at him, he explained, 'I met him last night when I dropped in to look for you.'

'Dean,' she said. 'And he's doing fine. Plenty of enthusiasm – and some delicious new dishes on the menu.' She took a mouthful of paella and savoured the taste for a moment, and the sight of McGuire in a crisp white open-necked shirt, his ice-blue eyes looking playful in the candlelight. 'This paella is good.' She smiled and McGuire considered her, taking pleasure from just being in her company.

'I managed to get a few pieces of information for you.'

Pearl looked up. 'You mean, you talked to Swale Police?'

McGuire framed his response carefully. 'Let's just say I managed to pull in a few favours.' He took out his smart-phone and scrolled through it before finally setting it down on the table beside her. Pearl looked down at the image displayed, then back at McGuire. 'Steven's suicide note.'

She picked up the phone and took a closer look. McGuire replied, 'It doesn't exactly say "Goodbye cruel world" but . . .' He left the thought hanging as Pearl studied the words before her, noting they were written as two lines of almost equal length.

I never thought what I did was of value –
so I really can't go on like this any more.

McGuire added: 'And it's unsigned.'

'Yes,' Pearl agreed. 'But Christina confirmed this was definitely her husband's handwriting.' Still studying the image, she now chose to enlarge it.

'But . . . it's not actually a "note", is it?' She looked at McGuire, who shrugged.

'He's been economical with words,' he said. 'But there's enough there to suggest someone either wanting to end it all – or to make it look that way?'

'Was the pen left in the car?' Pearl asked. 'The one he'd used to write this?'

'Found in the pocket of his jacket.' McGuire nodded to her meal. 'Your food's getting cold.'

She savoured a few more mouthfuls of paella, but McGuire saw she was still looking thoughtful. 'What is it?' he asked, feeling she was leaving him in suspense.

She took another sip of wine before asking: 'Why do you think Steven took this note with him that day? I mean, he left the house very early that morning and, if he was really planning to fake his suicide, why did he not just leave the note behind on the kitchen table? Christina would have seen it as soon as she got up – instead of having to wait until the car was found?'

McGuire shrugged. 'Maybe he hadn't made his decision by then.'

Pearl looked at him. 'Right. But he *had* made it by the time he'd driven all the way to Oare? And why did he go there of all places?'

McGuire considered her question. 'It was high tide, and he wanted to give the impression he'd drowned?'

Pearl looked unconvinced. 'He lived forty paces from the shoreline at Seasalter.' She looked down again at the image of the note on McGuire's phone. 'And this seems to have been written on a long strip of paper.'

McGuire nodded. 'Part of a plain A4 page. Why?'

'The writing's quite large and bold and . . . these two lines are fairly long and written across the page in a land-scape orientation? Why did he not write on it the usual way, portrait style, using more lines?'

McGuire shrugged. 'Perhaps this was the only scrap of paper he had to hand?'

Pearl frowned. 'Well, in that case it would seem to rule out any premeditation?' As she took another mouthful of food, McGuire considered her question and tried again. 'Maybe he'd made a few attempts at writing what he felt, but hadn't been satisfied with them and used up most of the paper.' He paused. 'What're you thinking?'

He ate some more paella as Pearl asked, 'Were there

any forensic tests done on the car? Christina said the police had found it by ten past six that evening.'

McGuire shook his head. 'That's true, but it had actually been sighted much earlier.' He took a notebook from his pocket and flipped it open, searching for a specific page. 'Witness statements show it was first spotted about seven-thirty that morning. There were walkers and visitors around from that time, but shortly after four-thirty that afternoon someone had tried to move a boat from the slipway and found the car was in his way, so he enlisted the help of a few birdwatchers. The car was unlocked and they drove it off the slipway and back into a nearby parking area. They also checked it for signs of owner ID – and found the note on the floor well.'

'And the birdwatchers then called the police?'

McGuire nodded. 'But by that point they'd contaminated both the car and the scene as far as forensics went. It had also been raining from midday, so there wouldn't have been a great deal of evidence to log on the slipway.' He considered this. 'There was no sign of foul play and it's not actually a crime to go missing. He wouldn't be the first person to try to fake his own death,' he added. 'One guy on record pretended to his family that he'd died in a rail crash and managed to keep up the pretence for years before he was found out.'

'But from what I've read,' Pearl said, 'in cases where death wasn't faked for monetary gain, those involved were all suffering some kind of emotional turmoil – or they'd made mistakes that were sufficiently serious for them to need to escape. None of that seems to be the case with Steven.'

'That you know of,' McGuire qualified.

Pearl finished her food and pressed a table napkin to her lips before she said: 'I told you, Christina's convinced he would never have left like that of his own accord.'

'And I've said she's maybe in denial – especially if the argument she had with her husband was more serious than she's letting on.'

'So why would she mention that to me at all?'

McGuire gave this some thought, then said: 'Because he could have told someone else about it, and if you happened to find out, you'd then know she was lying.'

'True,' Pearl conceded.

'A word of advice,' McGuire added. 'Everything initially presented to you has come from Christina, so be sure to keep an open mind and don't let her control your thinking on this case.'

'I won't,' said Pearl, remembering how Christina had set up the meeting with Steven's parents. 'She's been trying to direct things but . . . that might just be down to her OCD. That's why I went off alone yesterday to interview Steven's dad and Jonathan Elliott.'

McGuire finished his paella. 'Jonathan who?'

'The man who was setting up Steven's exhibition,' Pearl explained. 'Former corporate lawyer. Seems to have retired early.'

McGuire looked at her as she went on. 'He lives in a huge converted warehouse on the creek in Faversham, with a ninety-foot sailing barge, and a need to put something back.'

'What's that supposed to mean?'

'He's what I think is called an ethical businessman?'

'Rich old guys sometimes go that way . . .'

'Oh, no, he's not old. I don't think he's even forty. And rather good-looking.' She was just about to pour some wine when she saw McGuire was looking at her.

'But not as good-looking as you,' she added pointedly. She smiled, but at that moment her phone sounded and she rummaged quickly through her bag for it. McGuire noted her reaction as she frowned at the caller ID.

'Who is it?' he asked, curious.

'I'm . . . not actually sure,' she admitted. 'Do you mind?'

McGuire nodded for her to take the call.

Pearl found it difficult to hear the voice on the end of the line as it was competing with background music which, in turn, vied with that of the saxophonist at the Harbour Garden Restaurant. Pearl looked back apologetically at McGuire. A gruff voice finally sounded in her ear: 'She was in care.'

'I'm sorry. Who is this?'

'Reg Taylor. From Reculver. You said to call if I remembered anything else about those kids at the caravan park? The girl was from a care home. I remember the copper saying so because he had to take her back there.'

'Back where?' Pearl was still straining to hear.

'I can't remember the name of the place, but it wasn't far from an old transport café on the A299 into Whitstable.'

Pearl listened, paying good attention as he continued. 'The copper said the place, the care home, was trouble. The girls – kids – would bunk off there at night and get lifts from the lorry drivers.' He paused for a moment. 'That's all I remember.'

'Thanks,' said Pearl. She was just considering what she'd been told when Reg spoke again. 'Look, if there's a reward for this bloke you're looking for, you will remember me, right?'

'I will,' said Pearl.

The line went dead. Pearl took a deep breath and a moment to absorb what she had just heard. McGuire registered the spark in her eyes.

'What is it?'

'A possible lead ... about an old café by the service station into town.' She looked at him playfully. 'It's always open late.'

McGuire smiled. 'Are you ... suggesting what I think you're suggesting?'

'Dessert?' she asked, mischievously.

Ten minutes later, McGuire had paid the bill at the restaurant and was driving Pearl up Borstal Hill, passing a picturesque windmill on the eastern side of the road. Pearl watched his strong hands on the wheel as he said: 'Your missing man was an artist, wasn't he?'

'That's right.'

'Aren't they all in search of meaning?' He turned to look at her.

'Meaning to what?'

'Life? Maybe he was asking some questions he just couldn't answer. Or maybe a settled life in a quiet seaside town wasn't what he wanted after all and he just didn't have the guts to own up to that.'

Pearl considered this, then shook her head. 'Doesn't feel right to me.'

'Why not?' McGuire asked. 'You just told me he ran away once before.'

'Yes, but he was a child then – not a grown man. He had problems in his childhood, making sense of survivor guilt – not easy to do at twelve years old and with a mother consumed with grief – but he'd moved on. He was about to become a parent himself. He had his work . . .'

'All the same,' said McGuire. 'There must be challenges involved in living with someone with OCD. Maybe he used his painting as an escape, and realised he couldn't go on doing that once his child arrived. You also said his mother-in-law had been on his case?'

Pearl reflected on this. 'That's true, but Sally Ferguson doesn't exactly fit the profile of a battle-axe mother-in-law. She's capable, confident, canny . . . and she seems to have run the business side of her late husband's company very successfully. She's also as fiercely protective of her daughter as a lioness with a cub.' She frowned. 'But she didn't have to admit to me about having warned Steven about his responsibilities . . .'

'It's possible she might have put more pressure on him, though.'

'Possible, yes.' Pearl admitted. 'But *if* she had, she would surely only have created more problems for her own daughter.'

McGuire spun the wheel of his car to turn on to the A299 dual carriageway and, as he did so, Pearl thought about her drive out to the slipway yesterday, to the spot where Steven's car had been left abandoned. That route now seemed to be a bit like this case: a winding road through the marshes that led only to Oare, and Harty Ferry, where a boat journey might just as well begin as end. She frowned as she suddenly remembered. 'Oh, and I nearly forgot to tell you, apparently Steven had been investigating the chapel that Linda and Alan Scott go to. It's non-denominational and has charity status. Seems there's quite a lot of fundraising going on so it might be worthwhile looking into. The minister, Russell Cameron, has quite a hold over his congregation.' She gave McGuire a knowing look, but before he could respond she indicated the old transport café which was just coming into view. Set back off the road by a service station, it had once been known as the Black Spider but had been renamed the Whistle Stop. McGuire pulled up in the car park and looked back at her. 'You're the only woman I know who would leave a quayside restaurant for a greasy spoon café.'

'And you're the only man I know who would understand why.' She smiled and kissed him. 'Come on.'

They left the car and entered the café to find its interior sported plenty of plastic and formica. McGuire looked around and sighed. 'Why are these fast-food places always so orange?' His question was rhetorical but Pearl provided an answer: 'Because it's the colour that's said to give customers the impression that time's passing faster than it is.'

McGuire looked at her. 'Really?'

Pearl nodded. 'Really.'

McGuire thought about this. 'Then we should use it in police interview rooms, and I might get home a little earlier.'

He took her arm and they moved to a table. A large menu on the wall was extensive but unappealing, offering a variety of breakfasts, burgers and various 'snacks', all of which seemed to Pearl to be a tribute to cholesterol. A smell of bacon fat hung in the clammy air. Still looking at the menu, McGuire asked: 'Do we really have to eat something?'

'How about jam roly-poly?'

'I can't wait,' he said with irony.

Pearl smiled and took a poster from her bag and pointed to the far wall near some fruit machines. 'Looks like there's a noticeboard over there. Would you mind putting this up for me – and I'll order?' She handed him a copy of the new poster. McGuire checked it out carefully and looked at her as he noted the contact details. 'You should have used a number other than your own. You're likely to get some crank calls.'

'Bit late now,' she said. 'They're up all over town.'

He gave her a rueful look and got to his feet to head across to the noticeboard. At the same time, a middle-aged waitress wearing a badge showing the name 'Valerie' headed quickly over to the table and scribbled Pearl's order of two desserts into her pad. As she did so, Pearl glanced around the place and said: 'It's been a while since I was last here. You've had a name change?'

Valerie sniffed and replied: 'Used to be the Black Spider.' She slapped a copy of Pearl's order in a saucer on the table before turning to move off, but Pearl quickly asked: 'Didn't there used to be a care home somewhere nearby?'

Valerie looked back at her. 'It's a motel now,' she said. 'New development.'

Pearl smiled. 'And . . . you've been here a while?'

Valerie heaved a sigh and looked around. 'Too long.'

Pearl noted that the woman was somewhere in her early fifties, with short hair dyed an unnatural blue-black shade and a figure that looked as though she had enjoyed too many items from the café menu.

'But you do remember the care home?'

Valerie glanced back at the counter to see the manager was giving McGuire a drawing pin for the poster. She looked back at Pearl, somewhat suspicious. 'Why d'you ask?'

Pearl admitted: 'To be honest, I'm trying to find out about a girl who used to be there.'

Valerie saw Pearl's urgency but shrugged and folded her arms across her ample bosom. 'The place was closed down fifteen years ago or more – and I can't say I'm surprised.'

'Why's that?'

Valerie glanced back again towards the counter and continued in a hushed tone. 'The girls. They'd come in here – all times of the night.'

'Girls?'

'From the care home. Barely more than kids, they were.'

'And you were here then?'

Valerie shook her head. 'No. But a friend was.'

'When it was the Black Spider?'

Valerie gave a nod. 'More like the Black Spider's web.' Valerie saw the manager looking across and indicating two plates of food to be served. 'I've got to go . . .'

Pearl spoke quickly. 'Your friend . . .' She quickly slipped a ten-pound note down on the saucer on which Valerie had left a copy of the order.

The waitress looked back at it, then at Pearl, before she said quickly: 'Irene. Lives above the chemist on the shopping parade in Swalecliffe.' The manager rang a hand bell, summoning Valerie back to the counter. As she moved off, McGuire returned to the table, and asked Pearl: 'Any luck?'

Pearl was just about to explain but McGuire's phone sounded and he answered it quickly, using only three words: 'Where?' Pause. 'Now?' Pause. 'OK.' He ended the call and looked back apologetically at Pearl. 'I'm really sorry. My DS needs assistance with a domestic violence call-out. Looks like I'm going to have to take a rain-check on the pudding.'

Pearl glanced ruefully up at the café menu. 'Lucky you,' she smiled.

Half an hour after McGuire had headed off back to Canterbury CID, Pearl crept into bed with only Pilchard and Sprat for company. She drifted off into a deep sleep, in which she dreamed that she was standing on the slipway at Oare. Behind her, the old boathouse appeared like a black silhouette, its wooden doors closed and windows shuttered. The Swale tide was ebbing away before her, reminding her of a biblical image of the Red Sea parting, leaving a pathway in front of her leading straight to Harty Ferry on the Isle of Sheppey. Drawn to it, Pearl began heading on foot towards the island but soon found her feet stuck in the tidal mud. A feeling of panic overtook her as she struggled in vain to free herself, issuing a silent scream that was drowned out by the sound of a bell buoy tolling across the estuary as she sank ever deeper . . . With a gasp she found herself suddenly awake and saw her two cats looking back at her in surprise, as if wondering why she wasn't answering the telephone that was ringing on her bedside table. She took a deep breath and noted her alarm clock flashing the time, 2.29, in red-hot digits, then she reached across and picked up the phone, certain who the caller was. 'McGuire?'

She smiled as she anticipated hearing the detective's voice but instead there was only silence on the line.

'Hello?'

Again only silence.

'Who is this?'

She listened hard, becoming sure she could now hear breathing on the line. Sitting up sharply she switched on the bedside light, trying hard to organise her thoughts as she remembered what she had been told by Christina about the hoax calls she'd received after Steven had first gone missing. She paused then said: 'Look, if you've seen the posters, you can talk to me . . . in confidence.' Silence. 'Hello?' She paused again then gently broached: 'Steven? Is that you?'

Pearl waited expectantly but the line suddenly went dead in her hand. She quickly dialled back – only to discover what she already suspected – the caller had withheld their number. A shiver ran straight through her and she reached up to pull her leaded bedroom window shut before she finally nestled down again beneath her duvet – recognising it might be some time before she finally fell back asleep.

Chapter Twelve

'It was a long time ago,' said the woman sitting across a kitchen table from Pearl in the flat above the chemist's shop in the nearby town of Swalecliffe. She was in her late fifties, short in stature with a trim figure and fair, pixie-cropped hair that made her look far younger. The clothes she wore were as neat and tidy as her home – a crisp pink cotton top, and jeans that had a crease ironed into them. The kitchen dresser was filled with crockery that was mostly concealed by a selection of family photos featuring a boy and girl throughout the years from babyhood to school and finally into adulthood. Irene continued: 'Nevertheless, all that stays with you – seeing girls of that age, in a place like that, at night.'

'At the Black Spider, you mean?' said Pearl.

Irene took a sip of tea and nodded. 'Yeah. Not a very inviting name, is it? But the owner, Leon Marris, was just out of the army. Mr Macho.' She sniffed, unimpressed. 'He didn't know a thing about running a transport café. He'd been used to taking orders from officers but now it was from truck drivers – for burgers. He was drinking too much as well.' She took a sip of tea while Pearl steered the conversation back to what she needed to discuss. 'And the girls used to escape the care home and come to the café?'

Irene nodded again. 'They'd get lifts with the lorry drivers, or sometimes just hang around the place. It was loud in those days. There was a jukebox, fruit machines and a pool table, but the girls weren't there for games – they were looking for attention they weren't getting elsewhere.' She gave a dark look to Pearl and bit her lip before adding: 'Then Leon started giving tattoos. It was a sideline of his. Next thing, he was offering them to the girls – nothing like the ones you see today. These were just little things – love hearts, flowers . . . But all the same, those girls were far too young, and I know myself it's against the law to give a tattoo to a kid without a parent's permission. If my kids had ever come home with one, there'd have been all hell to pay.' She glanced across at the display of photographs on the dresser, then added: 'I tried to warn Leon but he didn't take a blind bit of notice. "It's just a bit of fun," he'd say. "They don't have much, do they?" And that was true enough, but it still didn't give anyone the right to take advantage.'

'And you think that's what was happening to them?' asked Pearl.

Irene gave a nod. 'They'd come across all sharp and streetwise, but I'll never forget . . . one girl in particular, little blonde thing, covered in black eye make-up like a panda. She used to talk to me like I was her friend and not a waitress, and I knew she was easy prey.' She shook her head slowly. 'One night she showed me a tattoo Leon had done – a little butterfly . . . right here?' She laid a hand on her inner thigh and shook her head. 'It wasn't right. So when she told me she'd "fallen in love", I decided enough was enough. Young girls'll do a lot of things for love, so I handed in my notice and I didn't just walk away, I reported everything to the authorities. It wasn't long after that the Bay Care Home was closed down. I'm not ashamed of it, either, which is why I'm telling you.' She gave a satisfied nod and picked up her mug of tea.

Pearl asked: 'Was it Leon Marris that she was in love with?'

Irene gave a shrug. 'Who knows? But if you ask me, someone had got under her skin, giving her a load of guff about looking after her like she was a "princess"?' She shook her head at the thought.

'Do you remember the name of that girl?'

Irene took another sip of her tea and nodded. 'Alice,' she said. 'Alice Weston. I'll never forget because I used to think that without all that black eye make-up that girl might look like Alice in Wonderland.' She frowned, deep in thought.

'And how old was she?' asked Pearl gently.

'Just fourteen,' said Irene. 'The same age as my Nicola was at the time.'

She looked across at the dresser again, and Pearl followed her gaze to a photo of a young girl in school uniform with neatly braided fair hair and braces on her teeth, smiling innocently for the camera.

Ten minutes after her meeting with Irene, Pearl stood on a sunny street in Swalecliffe, watching the flow of traffic circle a roundabout which took motorists to Herne Bay in one direction and back to Whitstable in the other. She thought carefully about what she had just learned, trying to decide if it might be at all significant to her search for Steven Scott. Then she headed back to her car, where she sat for a while at the wheel, thinking about a young blonde teenager – a girl who might have looked like Alice in Wonderland if it hadn't been for the black eye make-up she wore and the tattoo on her thigh ... Pearl didn't like disturbing McGuire at work, but she took out her phone and texted him, asking if he could possibly find out anything about a girl called Alice Weston, who had been at the Bay Care Home twenty years ago, and a former soldier called Leon Marris who had owned the Black Spider Café around the same time. At the end, she wrote: 'I know it's a long time ago – but it's the only lead I have.' After sending the message, she reflected for a few moments on how true this was, before starting up her car and heading back to Whitstable.

A few hours later, in the kitchen of The Whitstable Pearl, Dolly took advantage of the end of the lunchtime restaurant service to convince Pearl that her carnival preparations were all in hand. 'Charlie and I have it covered,' she said confidently, as she washed her hands at the sink. 'He's already got the panels cut for the float and I'll be working on the seahorse tomorrow.'

'Tomorrow?' said Pearl, unable to hide her shock. 'Is that going to give us enough time? What about Ruby's costume?'

Pearl's young waitress was just putting away some baking trays but turned quickly to explain: 'It'll be fine, Pearl. I've been making some of the costume myself – to Dolly's design, of course,' she added. 'I found some lovely gold taffeta from the charity shop in Harbour Street . . .'

'And *I* decided to sacrifice my old Fish Slappers' outfit,' Dolly said, with a rueful look, as she summoned up memories of her time in the infamous women's dance troupe that had featured in so many previous Oyster Festival parades. 'If I'm honest, I'd never have got into it again,' she admitted with a sigh, 'so it's been recycled for our lovely new Seahorse Queen.' Dolly looked at Ruby, who smiled and took some fresh napkins back into the restaurant, while Pearl's new part-time chef, Dean, piped up: 'I'll be off then, Pearl.'

Dean was at the door, just getting into his jacket before taking his break. Tall, lean, and with cropped light brown hair and an unassuming manner, he was only a few years older than Charlie, but his passion for cooking matched Pearl's at the same age, and his dishes were being so well received by customers, Pearl wondered how long she would be able to keep him before he was snapped up by another restaurant, or maybe even started up his own.

'Thanks, Dean,' she smiled. 'See you later.' In the hiatus between lunch and supper, when holidaymakers usually took to the beach or the shops, Pearl's seafood bar satisfied any remaining customers by offering an extensive selection of cold buffet items, which included oysters served in numerous ways; herrings marinated in Madeira; fresh prawns; crab and potted shrimp. Pearl had checked that the bar was well stocked and everything under control when Ruby suddenly entered the kitchen again, pointing back towards the restaurant area. 'Someone's asking for you, Pearl.'

Pearl followed her young waitress back into the restaurant to see Jonathan Elliott standing near the door. She smiled and moved forward to explain: 'I'm really sorry but we've finished for lunch. I could offer you something from the seafood bar?'

'It's fine,' he said quickly. 'It's you I came to see.'

Pearl nodded for Ruby to return to the kitchen and then indicated a table and sat down at it with Jonathan. He was dressed rather more formally than at their previous meeting, in a white shirt and black jeans, with his sun-bleached hair slicked back off his tanned brow. His hand idly stroked a small glass vase of gerbera on the table as he said: 'You mentioned you're working for Steven's family?'

'His wife,' Pearl confirmed.

He gave a nod. 'Must be tough for her,' he said. 'With a child, and not having her husband around.'

'Yes,' Pearl agreed. 'But I think what's equally tough is ... not knowing what happened.'

Jonathan looked at her but said nothing more, so Pearl decided to broach something: 'There's a boat currently moored at the quay in Faversham, owned by a woman called Celia.'

'*The Seahorse*,' said Jonathan. 'She's been in dry dock getting some work done. I think Celia's planning on doing some chartering. What about her?'

'Celia and I talked the other day. She told me she remembers seeing Steven on the quay at the time he was painting there?'

A vague frown crossed Jonathan's brow. 'What else did she say?'

'Nothing more than you could tell me,' said Pearl. 'Just that he made for a quiet presence . . . barely noticeable.'

'Some people are like that,' he said. 'They prefer to observe rather than participate.'

'True,' Pearl agreed. 'But Steven still had something to contribute, to express, in his paintings?'

Jonathan shrugged. 'Yes, he did. And I don't know what his family might think of what I'm going to suggest but . . . it occurred to me that we could still go ahead, with an exhibition of his paintings. If his wife agrees.'

Pearl considered this. 'At the Oyster House?'

Jonathan nodded. 'It might help her. If not now, then when things are finalised. Death in absentia.'

Pearl reflected on this for a moment. 'Yes,' she said. 'It might.'

'So maybe you'd like to ask her?'

'Why not ask her yourself?'

'I'm going away for a few days so I'd rather you did.' His tone was confident, but Pearl saw that he seemed conflicted for a moment. As he got up, she spoke quickly: 'You ... haven't remembered anything more, I suppose?'

Jonathan shook his head. ''Fraid not,' he said sparely. He picked up his car keys and moved to the door, giving one last look back to Pearl as he did so. For a moment, Pearl thought he might be about to add something further, but he said nothing more and left. After he had gone, it seemed to Pearl that it might not have been solely tension she had seen written on his face, but a trace of guilt – though for what, Pearl couldn't be sure.

Straight after Jonathan Elliott's visit to the restaurant, Pearl headed out to the sunken Waltrop Gardens in Herne Bay. The sun was still shining but the sky had become hazy, with rain having been promised for the afternoon. Since her visit the other evening, Pearl noted that the council railings had been brightened by the addition of colourful sleeves, specially knitted by a local group of Yarn Bombers, whose mission was to reclaim sterile public places with fun pieces of unexpected knitting. Looking beyond the railings, Pearl saw that the gardens were populated by a number of stallholders who were setting out their wares. Among them was Linda Scott. At that moment, Pearl didn't hold out much hope that a further conversation with Linda would prove productive, but she steeled herself and headed over to at least try. As she approached, Linda had turned away, rummaging through a box on the ground for more items to join the old CDs, DVDs, pottery ornaments and unwanted books that were already on display. Finally Pearl asked: 'Can I help?'

Turning around, Linda saw Pearl and then looked down at the items in her hands before passing them to Pearl: bath salts and talcum powder – unwanted Christmas gifts, thought Pearl.

'Thank you,' Linda said briskly. 'What brings you here?'

Pearl began to set the items on the stall and explained: 'I . . . just happened to be passing and saw this little market.'

Linda corrected her. 'Charity sale.'

'Charity?'

'Yes. We fundraise for lots of local causes through our chapel.'

'Causes for local children?'

Linda didn't miss a beat as she set out more cheap junk on her stall. 'Among other things,' she said. 'Minister Cameron does a lot of outreach work.'

'That's good to hear.' Pearl offered a smile and hesitated before she said tentatively: 'I've been thinking . . . about the time Steven ran away as a boy.' Linda looked up and Pearl explained: 'Alan happened to mention that to me.'

Linda continued busying herself, adding more items to her stall. 'Did he now?' she said coldly.

'I was wondering,' said Pearl, 'if that incident might have influenced the police's view of his disappearance?'

Linda merely shrugged. 'I doubt it would have made much difference.'

'Why not?'

'Stevie was only thirteen when he ran off. And it's not as if he went very far. It was just his way of getting attention, that's all. He'd do that as a child.'

Pearl frowned. 'What do you mean?'

Linda paused for a moment. 'Steven always found a way of getting what he wanted. One time we were all off to Canterbury for the day. Alan wanted to take the boys to the Beaney Museum and I had some shopping to do. We were all looking forward to it – all of us except for Steven. He wanted to stay at home and do his drawing. We'd just reached the bus stop when he started making a fuss . . . saying he'd got something in his eye. He got Alan so worried we all ended up waiting in Casualty for the afternoon. And when we did finally see a doctor, he said there was nothing in Stevie's eye at all.' She shook her head. 'I felt so bad for our Mark because he'd been looking forward to the museum.' She set a jigsaw puzzle down on her stall and moved to find some more toys.

'It must have been very difficult for Steven,' said Pearl, taking time before adding, 'living in Mark's shadow.'

Linda looked up sharply but Pearl continued. 'You . . . mentioned that Mark was the joker, the son who made you laugh? It's a great bond to share a sense of humour, to laugh together? I do that with my own son.'

Linda Scott frowned. 'If you're saying that Steven felt pushed out, that's not true. Alan and I always included the boys in everything we did.'

'But it was Steven who enjoyed spending time with Alan in the workshop?'

'Yes,' said Linda. 'He did. And he must have got in Alan's way something awful, but my husband's a very patient man.'

'And he loved Steven.'

'We both do,' said Linda sharply.

'Of course,' said Pearl. 'And you don't believe Steven could possibly have come to any harm? You . . . just referred to him in the present tense?'

'Why shouldn't I?' asked Linda. 'Look, we all know what happened. There's no mystery to it. Like I said, Steven always managed to get his own way. And he left us. Like he did before . . .'

'But he was a child then, and you just said yourself, he didn't go far. He had problems, dealing with Mark's death . . .'

'Yes, but—'

'And he had counselling and therapy, to help?'

'I'm not sure it did help,' said Linda petulantly. 'It just allowed him to stay in a world of his own. Steven never really made friends, and he certainly never needed to after he met Christina. They cut themselves off – out there in Seasalter – all in a world of their own. Steven did what he wanted and no more. He didn't even finish his college course. He made a habit of not finishing things.'

'But he finished his paintings,' Pearl pointed out.

'He never went through with that exhibition though, did he?' said Linda.

Pearl recognised she wasn't in a position to challenge this. Instead, she looked around for a moment to gather

her thoughts, then turned back to see Linda efficiently setting out soft toys on her stall. Pearl asked: 'When Steven ran away to Reculver, he was found in the caravan park with a young girl. Do you happen to know who she was?'

Linda shrugged. 'Someone he met on the pier. Up to no good. A truant.'

'Did he ever mention her name?'

Linda shook her head. 'And I don't see what any of that has to do with a grown man walking out on his family.'

'Then what do you think?' asked Pearl, masking her own frustration at Linda's closed mind. 'You're Steven's mother, and you probably know him better than anyone. So where do you think he could possibly have gone? You must have some idea.' Pearl looked earnestly at the woman before her and Linda finally looked down at the soft toy rabbit in her hand, before placing it on the stall and fixing her gaze on Pearl, as though she was about to divulge something of great importance. She braced herself and said slowly in a voice devoid of emotion: *'Cain went out from the presence of the Lord and dwelt in the land of Nod . . . on the east of Eden.'* Pearl was shocked to the core by the biblical reference to Cain, the man who murdered his brother, but Linda merely looked back at her stall and began rearranging her display of soft toys as she started softly humming the familiar hymn: 'Oh God, Our Help in Ages Past'.

As she did so, Pearl stepped away, trying to assimilate what she had just heard, when her mobile phone began to ring. She plucked it from her pocket and, on seeing who the caller was, moved further away to answer it.

'McGuire . . .'

'You wanted some information,' he said, trying to sound businesslike as he strode past a few officers in a corridor of Canterbury Police Station. Once they were out of earshot he continued more informally. 'OK, here goes . . .' He began reading from some notes he had made. 'Leon Marris was demobbed in 1996, took out a lease on the Hot Spot transport café that year and renamed it the Black Spider. He'd only had it for two years before he went off the rails: a fight in a pub, leading to a charge of ABH. He pleaded guilty but court medical reports turned up a diagnosis of PTSD – linked to a term of military service in Bosnia. He got probation, help with alcohol abuse, and now lives on Sheppey.'

'With a café?'

'Tattoo parlour.'

'And no further offences?'

'None. He's kept his nose clean. Married a couple of years ago. Wife's name, Melanie. No kids.'

Pearl considered this. 'And . . . anything on Alice Weston?'

McGuire paused at the end of the line. 'No happy ending there,' he said. 'She died in 1998. Sixteen years old.'

Pearl was instantly taken aback by this news. 'How?'

'Death certificate shows bronchial pneumonia, but a coroner's report cites self-neglect. After the care home was closed down, she entered a placement in a foster home in Ramsgate but it didn't work out. She ran away and took to the streets, moving around quite a bit. She was known to a soup kitchen in Canterbury, told them she was about to move in with a boyfriend, but it appears she wasn't telling the truth. She was still rough sleeping. It was winter.' He said nothing more – as though nothing more needed to be said.

'But how could she possibly have fallen through the net like that? Sixteen years old? The local authority had a duty of care . . .'

'Autopsy showed she was almost twelve weeks pregnant.'

Pearl tried to absorb this news, remembering all she had learned about a young girl with long blonde hair and black eye make-up – a vulnerable girl looking for love. 'Why didn't she seek medical help?' asked Pearl, helplessly.

'Maybe she didn't realise she was pregnant,' said McGuire. 'Or maybe she was in denial.'

Pearl knew what McGuire said made sense. She also knew he would come across young teenagers like Alice Weston on a regular basis – kids who had failed to survive a harsh life on the streets. At that moment, McGuire had just reached the door to an interview room when he said: 'Look, I'm going to have to go now. I've got a suspect to interview.'

'I understand.'

He paused, torn. 'And I'm really sorry I had to run out on you last night – though I'm not sorry I deserted the dessert.' He managed a tired smile. 'Looks like it'll be another late one for me tonight . . . but I'll call you tomorrow and let's try to rearrange something?' McGuire broke off, waiting as a group of uniformed officers passed him in the corridor before he added: 'Until then I want you to stay safe – and do nothing.'

'But I—'

'Look, Pearl,' he had cut in quickly and now spelt it out for her. 'Searching for a Misper is one thing, but this guy, Marris, is another. Promise me you'll stay away from him?'

Pearl hesitated for a moment before reluctantly giving in. 'OK. I promise.' Then: 'McGuire?'

'Yep.'

'Did you . . . try to call me last night?'

'Chance'd be a fine thing. I was caught up with the DV incident. Why?'

Pearl paused. 'No reason. Let's talk tomorrow.'

As she slipped her phone back into her pocket, she realised she was standing on the same part of the Herne Bay prom on which she had stood with McGuire only a few nights ago – though it seemed so much had happened since then. Looking back towards the charity stalls in the sunken gardens, she could see Linda Scott had finished setting out her own stall and was now smiling at the man standing beside her. Minister Russell Cameron had an arm around her, clearly charming her with compliments, while other women from surrounding stalls came up to greet him. Pearl noted how he smiled benevolently at them all – like a member of royalty holding court – then she looked away, her attention suddenly caught by a figure standing motionless on the prom. Moving closer, Pearl realised it was a statue of the famous aviator, Amy Johnson, who had died in a flying accident at sea off the same piece of coastline when she had been only thirty-seven years old – just four years younger than Pearl. Neither her body nor the wreckage of her plane had ever been found, but a life-size bronze statue had been placed on the prom – ostensibly, it was said, so that the brave lone girl flyer could 'merge with the crowds during the day'. Dressed in her 1930s flying gear, Johnson was smiling and staring out to sea, one hand raised to the aviator goggles perched on her head, on which Pearl saw the words: 'Believe nothing to be impossible.' Emboldened by this message, she headed off.

Arriving back at Seaspray Cottage, Pearl immediately took to her laptop to research a number of issues. Firstly, she looked more carefully into pseudocide and learned that acquiring a new identity required considerable preparation – either with obtaining essential new documents such as passports and driving licences, or in assuming someone else's identity. In consideration of all this, Pearl found it difficult to view Steven Scott's disappearance as premeditated, and the existence of the cursory suicide note served only to reinforce her instinct that whatever had caused him to go missing had to have been sudden – and unexpected.

After a few hours she stared up from her laptop screen to the window above it and saw that night was falling. The horizon was studded with the navigation lights of freighters and ferries that were so far away they looked stationary, and she reminded herself that although her own progress with this case had been slow, nevertheless she must still be moving forward. She took a deep breath and tried once more to concentrate, this time reflecting on all she had heard that afternoon from Linda Scott. She recognised Dee Poulton was right – the minister was a charming and charismatic man who had clearly attracted a large congregation to his chapel and was capable of exercising power over women like Linda, but was his ministry or its activities monitored in any way? Pearl punched a simple question into a search engine on her laptop: 'What is a church?'

A number of links immediately appeared and she sifted through them to skim-read several articles, learning that there were different examples of the usual quasi-corporate institutions that most people would recognise as churches, the Church of England, the Roman Catholic Church, the Russian Orthodox Church and others being all single entities. But she also learned that there were various other forms a church might adopt: one without any formal structure at all – just a group of friends meeting to share a faith – or a formal but unincorporated group, like a society or club. A church could be an incorporated association such as a company, or, there again, it could adopt the status of a charitable trust which, in turn, could take ownership of a particular building for community worship. The definition appeared to be a loose one, and Pearl began to consider all that she had been told by Christina Scott – how the Chapel of the Wooden Cross had once been a village hall before the building had acquired a new purpose with the new ministry. The chapel had charity status and was being run by Minister Cameron as a religious institution, but nevertheless it still remained outside the control or structure of any formal established church.

Pearl sat back in her chair to consider this, but her concentration was broken by her landline ringing. She picked up the cordless receiver and answered automatically. 'Hello?'

Silence.

She braced herself and spoke again, calmly but firmly. 'Look, whoever this is, if you have any information about Steven Scott's disappearance, please speak now.' She waited but all she heard was the sound of someone breathing softly on the line. 'Please. Speak up and tell me who you are.' Another pause as Pearl strained to hear any sound in the background that could possibly give a clue as to who the caller might be, but instead she heard a sound far closer. Quickly replacing the receiver, she moved towards the window, certain she had just heard a footstep on the garden path that was strewn with leaves dried by the recent spell of sunshine. Making sure she was hidden by a curtain, she listened keenly to someone brushing past the banks of lavender that lined her garden path. She headed straight into her dark kitchen and, once there, peered through the window, but could see nothing except the dark shape of the beach hut that doubled as her office. Another sound. This time a muffled voice. Pearl slipped a knife from its block. Tucking it into her sleeve she summoned up courage to open the kitchen door and slipped quietly into the garden. The air was still warm and filled with the salt tang of the sea, but the fragrance of her French lavender, and the sight of tiny seed heads on her path, confirmed to Pearl that she hadn't been imagining things. Taking a quick look around she saw no one, and heard nothing more than some voices on the beach. Moving to her garden gate she looked out to see a small group of people heading in the direction of the Old Neptune. She waited until they had entered the pub, from which she could hear the faint sound of live music as the door opened and closed. Then she turned back to the cottage and stepped into her kitchen. McGuire's words echoed for her: 'Searching for a Misper is one thing, but this guy, Marris, is another.'

She firmly bolted the door.

Chapter Thirteen

Dolly's garden was in stark contrast to Pearl's. It lay at the back of her home in Harbour Street, crowded out by the extension she had built after she had sacrificed the rooms above her shop to create her little holiday flat – Dolly's Attic. Since then, her back garden had remained a largely undefined area comprising a variety of plants in a number of pots: mainly bamboo, which acted as a screen concealing the more ordered back yards of her neighbours. A mirror on the rear wall cleverly enlarged the appearance of the garden, and the area was dotted with various sculptures Dolly had crafted over the years from the *objets trouvés* she had discovered on her beachcombing walks – stones, rocks, shells but also fish bones, driftwood and sea glass. A small square lawn lay in the central part of the garden, usually with a colourful hammock on display strung between two small fruit trees, but today it was concealed by a number of wooden panels which Charlie was busy painting.

'Lovely blue, don't you think?' Dolly said, smiling

appreciatively at her grandson's handiwork as she looked on, with Pearl, from the doors of her conservatory. 'Very aquatic, and it'll contrast nicely with Ruby's gold costume.' She looked to Pearl for an opinion. Finally it came: 'You . . . don't seem to have got very far,' said Pearl tentatively.

'What do you mean?' exclaimed Dolly, miffed. 'We've had a lot of measuring up to do and a few problems getting the wood delivered . . .'

'But are you sure everything's going to be ready in time? There's less than a week to go before the carnival and—'

'Of course we'll be ready,' said Dolly, butting in. 'Charlie and I know precisely what we're doing.'

'I'm pleased to hear it,' said Pearl.

Dolly looked sidelong at her daughter. 'I don't go telling you how to cook, do I?'

'No,' said Pearl, knowing full well that her mother's talents failed to stretch to culinary creations. Dolly was a dreadful cook and was therefore entrusted only with garnishing or sandwich-making duties at The Whitstable Pearl – and then only under strict supervision.

'I also don't tell you how to solve your cases,' Dolly went on. 'Though I'm rather pleased this case turned up the seahorse idea for our float. Charlie's working on that tomorrow.'

'Good,' smiled Pearl.

Dolly stepped back into her conservatory, which was in its usual state of ordered chaos, with her feline familiar, Mojo, curled up asleep on some paperwork. 'I've been looking through my books,' she said, 'to see if there's anything else we could use in connection with the sea-horse.' She bent down and selected a large tome from a number of them lying on the floor. 'I knew I had something on them somewhere. Remarkable creatures.' She raised the book in her hand and let it fall open at a marked page. 'There's a lovely story in here about the seahorse being a guide to the afterlife for drowned sailors.' She looked up. 'Probably why they were used as nautical good-luck charms through stormy seas.' She considered this, then frowned to herself. 'But a "stormy sea" could be met-aphorical – with the seahorse helping us through difficult periods?' She went on, reading this time: 'Sometimes when you've hit a wall and can't see your way past it, the seahorse symbol is said to fire imagination and help with inspiration – and that's probably because the creature has eyes that can look in opposite directions at the same time. They're also meant to have a heightened sense of aware-ness and observation.'

'Something I could do with right now,' Pearl admitted.

'The missing man's still missing?' Dolly asked.

Pearl nodded and pointed to the book in Dolly's hands. 'The woman who gave me the idea about the seahorse,' she began.

'The one with the boat, you mean?'

'That's right. She told me the seahorse was her . . . totem. Her spirit creature.'

Dolly gave a shrug and considered this. 'Well, if you believe in such things, a seahorse would be an excellent choice of totem for a sailor, or for anyone who prizes their freedom, although it's also said to be a good symbol for fatherhood too.'

'Why's that?' asked Pearl.

'Why?' Dolly echoed. 'Because seahorses are said to mate for life. They form very strong partnerships and the male seahorse carries the female's eggs in his tail pouch right up until the young seahorses are born fully developed.'

'Interesting,' said Pearl, her thoughts straying once more to Steven Scott, but also to poor Alice Weston who had died so young – with no one to protect her unborn child.

Dolly saw her daughter looking distracted. 'Are you all right?'

Pearl nodded, but at that very moment she was actually reconsidering her warning from McGuire – weighing it against the responsibility she felt towards her client and any possible connection between the missing father, Steven Scott, and the girls of the Bay Care Home.

'Mum?' Charlie had entered from the garden behind her, concerned after hearing Dolly's question. Pearl turned to see him – tall, blond and handsome, but covered in splatters of blue paint. She smiled. 'I'm absolutely fine,' she decided. She kissed Charlie's cheek, and then Dolly's, before picking up her bag and heading for the door.

'Where are you going?' asked Dolly, confused.

'In search of a ghost,' said Pearl decisively.

It took only twenty minutes to drive to the Sheppey Crossing, the arching viaduct for traffic which, for the last dozen years, had eased travel on to the island for motorists who had previously had to rely on the old Kingsferry lifting bridge – still used by the railway. Though the island was barely nine miles by six, it still formed part of the local landscape of Whitstable and Seasalter because it was always visible from the coastlines of those towns. In spite of the development which had been taking place for some time on the mainland, Sheppey was still a fairly isolated place, so there were some who joked that inmates of the island's cluster of three prisons probably outnumbered the general population.

Pearl hadn't been on Sheppey for at least a decade, but soon found her way to the main holiday location of Leysdown. It stood in stark contrast to the gentrification of so much of her own home town, with a 'strip' serving holidaymakers in the caravan parks with a steady supply of fast food and crinkle-cut chips. Pearl was acting on instinct, with no clearly defined plan other than to follow up McGuire's information regarding Leon Marris – even if it meant breaking her promise to him to stay away.

As she drove slowly along the main road on which bars advertised Happy Hours and Karaoke, it occurred to her that on a hot day like this, she could be driving through any tourist strip in southern Spain or Greece – but for the fact that she was looking for a particular establishment. It soon came into view. Leon's Tattoo Palace would have been difficult to miss as it occupied two shop spaces and bore a highly conspicuous neon sign, its front window studded with photos of satisfied customers sporting a multitude of different tattoo designs.

Having parked her car, Pearl approached to hear music playing loudly inside – Beyoncé rapping with Jay-Z. Entering the shop, she found a young couple at the counter. In spite of the summer heat they were dressed in black, with pale complexions and numerous piercings in their lips and ears, as they discussed an appointment with the receptionist, a blonde girl in her late teens who wore high-cut flamingo-pink shorts. She clearly served as a walking advertisement for the business as her plump limbs were covered in elaborate Celtic designs of tree branches that disappeared into her clothes, only to re-emerge at her throat. Chewing gum, she acknowledged Pearl with a quick nod of her head, but continued talking to her customers.

Pearl used this as an opportunity to study various posters on the walls, her attention drawn to a framed Certificate of Registration from the local borough council confirming that Leon Trevor Marris was licensed to perform tattooing, semi-permanent skin colouring, cosmetic piercing and electrolysis at the business address of Leon's Tattoo Palace in Leysdown on the Isle of Sheppey. The certificate occupied only a quarter of the frame, while the rest was taken up with a photograph of a muscular man in his late forties with a bullet-shaped bald head. He was wearing a black vest and a silver skull hung from a chain around his neck. His arms were tightly crossed in front of his chest, exposing biceps and forearms on which not a single inch of unpainted skin was visible. He faced the camera, clutching a tattoo needle in a surgically gloved hand. While the smile on his face was clearly intended to inspire trust and confidence, it looked to Pearl to be somewhat forced, because other posters, showing him posed with men dressed in camouflage trousers and heavy metal T-shirts, seemed to offer an image with which he looked far more comfortable: a painted hard man, keen to enlarge his club.

As Pearl took in the various photos of Leon and his satisfied clients, she tried to imagine him some twenty years ago, as the owner of a rundown transport café, mixing with a clientele of long-distance lorry drivers and young girls who had escaped the confines of a care home looking for attention, affection and a free tattoo at the Black Spider Café. In the background, the girl at reception was still chatting to her prospective customers, explaining that they couldn't see Leon today as he wasn't at the parlour, but she'd be happy to make an appointment for them for next week. Pearl continued to study the images before her: a woman's back emblazoned with the words, 'Love With Passion'; a man's chest showing a lion roaring; a girl's shoulder on which a black rose bloomed. The young receptionist finished dealing with her customers and they passed by Pearl as they headed for the door. 'See you next week,' said the receptionist. At the door, the young man turned back, and called: 'Say hi to Leon,' adding: 'He's not ill, is he?'

The young receptionist smiled. 'Nah, but he probably will be tomorrow. It's his birthday so he's having a barbie down the beach.'

A doorbell sounded as the couple exited and the young receptionist gave her attention to Pearl: 'Sorry about the wait. What can I do for you?'

Pearl thought quickly. 'Leon,' she said. 'I'm ... meant to be at the barbie, but I'm not actually from round here and I can't remember which end of the beach I'm meant to be?' She pulled her phone from her pocket. 'Battery's dead so I can't call.'

The receptionist looked askance for a moment then smiled broadly. 'This end,' she said, as if no alternative was possible. 'Just go straight down past the amusement arcade and you can't miss 'em.'

'Thanks.' Pearl had turned for the door and was just about to exit when the girl called out. 'Good thing you stopped to ask.'

Pearl turned to face her and the girl explained: 'If you'd gone down to Shellness you'd have found it's a nudey beach.' She popped a fresh stick of chewing gum into her mouth, gave a slow smile, and waited for Pearl to exit before she switched up the music.

After leaving the tattoo parlour, Pearl walked back to her car and thought again about McGuire's warning concerning Marris and her promise to him to stay away. Time after time, Pearl found herself returning to the one tangible clue she had: an incident twenty years ago concerning a young boy running away from home. Was this really of no significance to Steven's later disappearance? Or did it show that the need to escape, to run away, was part of Steven's true nature? In order to find out more, Pearl had hoped to track down Alice Weston, only to discover that the girl had died – aged only sixteen – lost to the system, failed by the system; living on the streets with the anonymity accorded to those who understand a common need to erase a painful past. Alice Weston was lost to Pearl, but nevertheless she had now managed to track down the man who had owned the Black Spider Café – the former soldier who had given tattoos as 'favours' to girls like Alice who had been minors at the time. Pearl headed back to her car where she sat for some time at the wheel before looking back at the neon sign above Leon's Tattoo Palace. She made her decision.

Seeking out an off-licence on the 'strip', she bought a chilled bottle of Cava then walked on past an enormous amusement arcade, illuminated even by day. She didn't have to search long for the barbecue party as the smell of burning charcoal lured her towards the prom, from which she spied a swarm of people on the sands.

A cheap marquee had been set up on the beach while smoke rose from a portable barbecue closer to the water's edge. Music wafted across to her – party hits from more than twenty years ago: 'Runaway' by Janet Jackson segueing seamlessly into 'Gangsta's Paradise' by Coolio. High in the clear sky, seagulls circled in the hope of scraps to come and Pearl braced herself and moved on.

As she approached the party, she could see that a number of beach chairs had been arranged in a small semicircle for the comfort of some elderly guests, including a man in his late seventies wearing a handkerchief knotted in four corners on his head, his trouser legs rolled up and his bare feet half buried in the sand. The woman beside him sat motionless but for the battery-operated fan which she held close to her face, while another elderly couple sipped from plastic beakers as they munched on a shared bowl of crisps. Children played together, using water pistols shaped like machine guns, loosely supervised by a group of women who seemed overdressed for the occasion, wearing glamorous beach shifts over swimsuits with diamanté features. Sarongs and glitter-strewn T-shirts seemed to be the order of the day, so Pearl soon recognised she was underdressed in jeans and a loose pink top, but she then noted a woman in her late thirties who stood posing for a photograph on the beach as a man's arm circled tightly around her shoulder. She was smiling for the camera, her long, sun-bleached hair blowing freely in the breeze. She wore a scarlet bikini top and low-slung tight white pedal-pusher trousers on a slim body that clearly served as a canvas for numerous tattoo designs. Once the photo was taken, the man beside her pulled her closer and kissed her hard on the lips before releasing her to return to the group of children on the beach.

As she moved off, Pearl's attention remained on the man. Leon Marris took a swig from the can of beer in his hand and gave a satisfied smile as he cast an approving eye around the beach scene. Dressed in a tropical shirt and cut-off Levis, he lowered a pair of vintage Ray-Ban sunglasses from his head. Pearl waited for him to begin mingling with his guests before she made her way down on to the beach.

The music was deafening as she reached the marquee, below which a long trestle table was serving as a bar.

Behind it, a young man in his early twenties looked as though he had failed to pace himself, and drew deeply on a cigarette, his eyes closed as he swayed unsteadily to the music. Pearl produced the bottle of Cava from her bag. 'I brought this,' she said.

Opening his eyes, the young barman looked confused for a moment, leaving the cigarette stuck between his lips as he took the bottle from her. 'You shouldn't have, love,' he slurred. 'Leon's put on plenty and there's more in that.' He peeled the cigarette from his lower lip and nodded towards a white van on the road, adding: 'Brought it back from Calais last week.' He offered a lazy smile and dumped Pearl's bottle in a large builder's bucket, filled with ice, beneath the table. 'Shampoo?' he asked.

'Sorry?'

Seeing Pearl's confusion, he picked up an open bottle of champagne, poured a plastic beaker for Pearl and handed it to her. 'Here you go, girl. Happy days.'

Pearl took the drink from him and moved off into a group of party guests who were milling around a cold buffet of sausage rolls, slices of sweating quiche, potato salad and triangles of sandwich curling in the heat. Pearl took a paper plate and loaded a few items on to it while trying not to look out of place. Staring out towards the beach she could see Leon kicking a football passed to him by some children. It sailed up into the air to land in the sea and the kids rushed into the waves to retrieve it. Leon left them to it, dumping his empty lager can into a bin before heading back to the bar for another. Pearl waited until he had torn off the ring pull from his next can, before she headed across. 'Happy Birthday, Leon.'

Marris looked taken aback for a moment but quickly noted that Pearl held a drink in one hand and a plate of food in the other. 'Thanks,' he replied in a voice that sounded as though he had been shouting for the last twenty years. He took a quick sip of beer and asked: 'Sorry. You a friend of Mel's?'

He glanced across the beach towards the attractive blonde he had been posing with for the photograph, but Pearl shook her head. 'I've come all the way from Whitstable,' she said. 'Just to ask you a few questions.' She paused then added: 'About the Black Spider.'

The ghost of a frown flashed across Marris's sunburnt face before he asked, with some suspicion: 'Who are you?' His eyes narrowed and Pearl set down her plate of food and knocked back her drink for courage.

'My name's Pearl Nolan,' she began. 'I'm a private detective.'

Leon Marris didn't look too bothered by this and glanced around before fixing his gaze on Pearl. 'Look, this might be a public beach but it's still a private party.' He gulped his beer and had begun to move off when Pearl asked quickly: 'Does Mel know?'

As Marris turned back slowly to face her, the look on his face caused Pearl's mouth to dry but she held her ground and managed to continue. 'About the girls from the care home. The ones you gave free tattoos to?'

Marris seemed stunned for a moment, confounded as

to how he could possibly have such a question asked of him, today of all days. In the background, party music played on as he took a step closer to Pearl. 'That was more than twenty years ago.' His voice was now little more than a growl. 'If people had been doing their jobs properly, those girls would never have been out at night in the first place.' He paused and appraised Pearl, looking her up and down. 'You've got nothing on me.'

Pearl held her nerve in spite of his menacing look. 'They were underage,' she countered.

'Yeah?' said Marris. 'Well, they didn't exactly bring their birth certificates with them.'

'And you didn't ask for them.'

'Neither did anyone else.' He looked at her challengingly but she met his gaze without flinching, then he took a sip of beer and suddenly smiled. 'I don't know what they got up to. That was down to them. All I know is, I had a business to hold together – and myself. I'd just got out of the army, and if you think a little tattoo is some kind of abuse, you should have seen what I got to see out in Bosnia.' He paused then raised his hands. 'So I gave a few tattoos. Favours. Nothing more. There was nothing in it. A bit of fun, that's all. Those girls knew what they were doing, and I didn't offer – they asked.' He turned to move away. Pearl spoke urgently: 'Did they ever mention a minister? A clergyman at a chapel in Herne Bay?'

Leon smiled at this and shook his head, as though he had suddenly tired of her. Leaning in closer, he said: 'Let's just say they weren't the kind of girls who make it to church on Sunday.'

He had just started to turn away when Pearl spoke once more. 'Even Alice Weston?'

Leon Marris looked back and Pearl glanced knowingly across at the woman on the beach who was now staring over at him. She continued quickly: 'She was blonde – just like Mel.'

A slow smile spread across Leon's face before he shook his head. 'You're wasting your time, darlin'.' His expression suddenly turned to stone. 'Now get lost.'

The confrontation with Leon Marris caused Pearl to brood; she decided against returning to her car and instead headed further along the coastline, on foot, in an effort to clear her mind. She recognised that gatecrashing Leon Marris's birthday party had served little purpose at all, and that whatever had occurred all those years ago in the Black Spider Café was now history. Marris had shown no remorse, perhaps because he still laboured with problems of his own – PTSD – just as Steven had suffered after he had been unable to save his twin brother. But Marris had also appeared unconcerned by her enquiries – unless, of course, he was bluffing. But what irked her most was the fact she had broken her promise to McGuire – for nothing.

Taking the direction of Shellness, it wasn't long before she had left Leysdown's strip, beach and barbecue way behind and encountered a number of motorhomes lining the roadside close to the sea. The vehicles were laden with bikes and kayaks, their owners having taken up positions on collapsible chairs, from which men were preparing to begin fishing at high tide while their partners entertained children or prepared mobile barbecues. The question that kept returning to Pearl as she walked along the coast was why Steven had driven thirteen miles to leave his car abandoned on the Harty Ferry slipway? Was it because he had been planning to paint the area – or perhaps across the water here on Sheppey? A little way up the coast at Harty Ferry itself lay a hundred and seventy acres of grazing marsh, dissected by freshwater dykes like those out at Seasalter – nothing more than a mirror image of what lay on the other side of the Swale …

After a short while, the road Pearl trod began to turn into a bumpy track. Fields used as summer campsites opened up to her right, while the sea wall on her left grew higher, masking her view of the beach. Straight ahead of her, Shellness beach lay at the far southeastern tip of the island but, as she began to encounter 'Keep Out' signs, Pearl recognised she must have reached the boundary of a private estate of brick-built cottages known as Shellness Hamlet. A turnstile gate led inland on to a nature reserve which, like that at Oare, was frequented by birdwatchers, but today Pearl saw no one on the open land before her. A narrow tributary ran out to the Swale estuary, its banks studded with sea lavender and golden samphire, and, as a flock of sand martins took sudden flight, scattering against the blue sky, Pearl watched them and felt suddenly at peace and able, finally, to breathe. She took her time as she ambled back towards the gate to the hamlet, then decided to move on towards the sandy beach. It was only at that moment that she realised the coastline she could see facing her across the water was, in fact, Seasalter beach – a thirty-mile journey by road but only three miles or so across the Swale estuary. It was an unfamiliar vista for Pearl since her usual view was from across the other side of the water, but it prompted her to wonder what Christina Scott might be doing at this very moment – tidying her home in a fruitless attempt to regain control? It struck Pearl that in a desperate effort to tie up the flailing loose ends of her life, Christina was relying on Pearl to solve a mystery on which the police had long given up, and which was becoming an onerous task and responsibility for Pearl – one which was now weighing increasingly heavily, not least because she had come up with so few clues as to the reasons for Steven Scott's disappearance. She began to suspect that she had totally lost her way because the signposts that had been recently thrown up had only led here – to another impasse.

Every other one of Pearl's previous cases had centred around a crime, and the facts and events surrounding those crimes had been substantial, allowing her to interpret them as potential clues and arrange them in the same way that she might assemble ingredients for her own dishes. That usually led to a satisfying result for both Pearl and her clients, but now she began to question what, if anything, she really knew of the missing man – Steven Scott. She took a crumpled poster from the depths of her bag and stared down at the face that looked back at her – the same face that had surely stared back at Christina throughout the years, not just from a poster, but in her memories and her dreams. Contacting Pearl had given Christina renewed hope that she would finally see Steven's face again for real, so that he could explain what had happened and why he had abandoned her. But it was clear that solving the mystery Christina Scott had lived with for all of seven years was wholly dependent on Pearl's efforts and, at this point in time, all those efforts appeared to have failed. McGuire was right – unless an unlawful act had been committed, any adult had a perfect legal right to go missing and even to assume a new identity. And if that was indeed what Steven Scott had done, he had done so effectively, and without leaving a suitable trail of clues for anyone – including Pearl – to follow.

With that thought, she turned her eyes away from the coastline of Seasalter, almost in shame at her own sense of failure, and instead looked down at the sand at her feet, a contrast to the pebbled beach at Whitstable. She bent down to take off her shoes, suddenly reminded of the day-trips she had enjoyed as a child to the sandy beaches of Ramsgate and Broadstairs, which lay further along the eastern coast on what was known as the Isle of Thanet. Thanet had once been separated from the mainland by a six-hundred-metre channel of water, but over time it had become reunited with it. In the same way, Sheppey had once been formed by more than one 'isle': the Isle of Elmley to the southwest on which part of the prison cluster stood, and the Isle of Harty, where another old slipway mirrored the one at Oare at the very spot where Steven Scott's car had been found abandoned. But over time, the water channels between those locations had become silted up, resulting in the single island on which Pearl now stood, the shoreline of the sandy beach beneath Pearl's feet littered with tiny shells – cockle, clam and oyster – as well as tiny pieces of rose-pink glass polished by the tide.

Pearl walked to the water's edge and picked up some of the shells as the waves of a rising tide rolled up on the sand to reach her ankles. The sea-blackened timbers of old breakwaters reached up out of the water liked charred fingers stretching up to the sky, and a gull screeched as it soared up into the clouds, only for the sound to be swiftly replaced by another. It was one that was familiar to Pearl, a sound she heard increasingly these days on the beach at Whitstable. Looking up, she saw a dark shape dropping out of the sky – a black drone.

No one appeared to be operating the unit – the whole area seemed deserted – but the sound of rotors grew louder and Pearl recognised they were heading straight for her. She reacted quickly and turned, dodging out of the drone's path, but only just in time. It overtook her, as though being piloted on towards the direction of town, and Pearl observed it, watching as it became a small speck in the sky. She took a moment to calm herself and began to head back to the sea, but she soon heard the sound of rotors returning . . .

Rooted to the spot, Pearl looked up to see the dark speck in the sky becoming larger. High above her, she could make out twin rotors and a landing frame heading back in her direction. The drone suddenly swooped in low, and fast, swerving only as it came within a few feet of her, before soaring up into the sky again. Then it turned in an arc and returned yet again. This time, Pearl didn't wait. She broke into a run, heading up the beach away from the deserted nature reserve and on to where she had seen the motor-homes parked. Before she got anywhere near them, the drone dropped out of the sky again, focused in its path as it began to pursue her. The noise of the rotors grew ever louder behind her and Pearl ducked and swerved as the drone continued to chase her along the empty beach. With the rising tide, she now saw that she would have to cross a high breakwater that reared up ahead of her, and she turned to try to track the drone's progress, only to see that it was still flying low on her trail.

Breathless and panicked, a thought finally came to her, crystal clear, as though every nerve in her body had keenly sensed the need for survival. She threw herself down, low on to the beach, stomach flat to the sand, in the hope that the drone would follow and collide with the breakwater that was now just a metre away from her head. Her heart pounded. A terrifying jolt. Time seemed to stop with a sudden blow to Pearl's right temple. The sound of the drone began to recede into the distance …

Pearl heard nothing more but waves on the shore. Managing to open her left eye, she saw tiny pendant-shaped droplets of blood were falling on to the pink sand close to her face. She watched them for a moment before closing an eyelid that was now too heavy to keep open. The sand beneath her body was still warm but it no longer felt solid. It was shifting, undulating like water beneath her. A haze of swirling shapes appeared; a mosaic of tiny shells – cockle, clam and oyster – began drifting before her eyes, though she knew they were still closed. Relying on another sense, Pearl strained to hear footsteps approaching, a man's heavy breaths as he stood over her. She felt the same breath close to her face as he crouched down beside her and she waited, tensed for another blow – perhaps a final one – before every sound, image and thought was suddenly washed away like shells upon the shoreline.

PART THREE

PART THREE

Chapter Fourteen

The first sounds were undefined, as though travelling on the air to Pearl from somewhere very far away: birdsong, underscored by the beating of wings – a steady rhythm as reassuring as a heartbeat. She felt a kiss upon her skin close to her right temple. Strangely cold, it caused her to react in confusion, then to flinch in pain. A single word came to her – a question posed to another.

'Tony?'

With this came clarity, translating everything into rational order: not birdsong but music, sounding softly from a radio, not a heartbeat but the steady whirr of fan blades turning close to Pearl's face and a woman's hand gently holding a cool damp cloth to her temple. A hazy silhouette became focused into a young woman's pretty face, smiling benevolently. Then another came into Pearl's eye line – a young man coming closer, peering at her as he asked with concern: 'How are you feeling?'

Pearl raised a hand to her head and images flooded back

to fill a dark void: shells, sea, waves upon the shore, a gull soaring up and then a black form falling from the sky …

'Where am I?' Pearl asked. She tried to get up but the young woman placed a hand on her shoulder in an effort to gently restrain her.

'Take it easy,' she said. 'You're safe.'

Looking around, Pearl saw that she was lying on an old iron daybed covered in a red and white patchwork throw. Tongue-and-groove panelled walls, painted a vivid blue, were lined with various pieces of artwork and artefacts: an old mirror, a canoe paddle, a framed antique map. Wooden shutters had been thrown open to allow sunlight to flood into what appeared to be an old beach shack, judging by the sound of waves beyond the window.

The young woman explained: 'I'm Penny and this is . . .'

'Tony,' he said quickly. He took up the story: 'We found you on the beach. Thought you'd fainted until we saw the bruise on your head, so we brought you back up here to our chalet. What happened?'

As Pearl struggled to remember, she saw concern written on the young couple's faces. They were an attractive pair, almost like twins, with long fair hair and loose batik print clothes. They exchanged a look before Penny said: 'Tony can fetch some help. There's no mobile reception or services here,' she explained. 'Just some solar panels for what little electricity we need.'

With the sudden cry of a seagull outside, Pearl began to remember. 'It was a drone. On the beach. Coming straight for me. Was it yours?'

The young woman shook her head. 'We didn't see any drone.' She looked at her partner who explained: 'It's pretty isolated here, but we do still get some idiots at this end of the beach. They disturb the birds.'

Pearl frowned as she continued to recall: 'I . . . couldn't get out of its way.' She suddenly realised: 'It must have turned to avoid the breakwater and the landing gear clipped me.' She put a hand to her temple and the young man made a decision. 'We'd better get you checked out at the community hospital. The walk-in centre's open right now . . .'

'No,' Pearl argued. 'No, I'm fine.'

She pushed herself up into a seated position and took in more of her surroundings. The style of the place was like many of the beach huts in Whitstable – strewn with colourful bunting, and wind chimes sounding in the breeze – but it also had a functioning kitchen, a wood-burning stove and gas lamps hanging from the ceiling. It was clear this chalet was more than a hut – it was a home.

The young woman spoke up. 'You could have concussion,' she ventured.

'I don't think so,' countered Pearl. 'What is this place?'

'An old fisherman's hut,' Tony explained. 'There are just a handful left here now. Some have been washed away by the sea or taken by the wind, but the few that are left are mainly unoccupied.'

Pearl rose slowly to her feet and moved to the open door that led on to a verandah that faced directly out to the coast. Another cabin stood just a few metres away. 'That one's used by our neighbour, Derrie,' said Tony.

'But only during the summer,' Penny added. 'And just for fishing during the day. It's been in his family since the last war.'

Pearl looked beyond it, towards the Hamlet of Shellness and the stretch of beach she had been walking on before the drone had appeared.

'You found me over there?' Pearl pointed to the last area of beach that she remembered.

'No,' said Tony. 'You were lying here, just outside our chalet.'

Pearl looked back at him. 'But . . . I'm sure I was further up the beach when I saw the drone.'

Penny continued: 'Then you must have found your way here before you lost consciousness.'

Pearl tried to make sense of this but Tony spoke again. 'I really think I should fetch the car and take you to a hospital . . .'

'No,' said Pearl decisively. 'I'm fine.' She stepped back into the shack and moved to the mirror, pushing back her hair to inspect a dark bruise on her right temple.

The young couple exchanged another look before Penny said: 'Well, at least take it easy while I make you some tea?'

'All right,' said Pearl, finally offering a smile.

A short while later, Pearl was seated on a beach chair on the chalet verandah sipping a cup of herbal tea. 'This is a very secluded spot,' she said. Of the few remaining chalets it also looked to be the one most cared for – each strip of clapboard painstakingly decorated in a series of pretty pastel-coloured stripes.

'Which is precisely why we like it here,' said Penny. 'We really needed somewhere to escape to.' Pearl saw her smile but it was Tony who explained. 'We were living in London but hated it. It's just a scramble for survival – unless you have money.'

Penny shrugged. 'Which we don't. And we're not too bothered about that either. Parts of this island are really wild and deserted, which is why travellers come from time to time. New Age,' she added. 'But Tony and I can live very simply here. In fact, it's a bit like . . . being a castaway? It may look rough and ready but we have everything we need. You can even swim naked a little further along the beach,' she confided. 'Some of the locals call us freaks or perverts but we're nothing of the kind. It's a great liberation to be free of clothes.'

'And it's not actually against the law,' said Tony. 'But we're sufficiently out of the way that no one need be offended.'

Pearl asked: 'Did you . . . happen to see anyone else here on the beach today?'

The couple exchanged a shrug. 'Only you,' said Tony.

'And you didn't hear the drone?'

Penny shook her head. 'No. But then I was playing guitar earlier and Tony was taking a nap.'

Pearl nodded and looked out to sea. For a moment she felt as though she was emerging from a dream, though the dark bruise on her temple was proof enough that she hadn't imagined what she had experienced that afternoon.

'Thank you,' said Pearl.

'For what?' asked Penny.

'For taking care of me.'

*

The light was fading when, a few hours later, Pearl returned home to Seaspray Cottage. Opening her front door she was looking forward to taking a shower and getting some rest, but she heard the telephone ringing inside and braced herself to answer it. 'Hello?'

She was prepared for another silent call but found, to her relief, that it was McGuire on the end of the line. 'Sorry,' he said. 'I couldn't speak yesterday.'

'I understand.'

'What are you up to?'

For a moment, she considered telling McGuire about her trip to Sheppey, then decided against it and hesitated before replying: 'I . . . just got back from chasing a few leads.'

'Oh?'

'Dead ends.'

'Sorry to hear it. You sound tired?'

'Very.'

McGuire paused. 'Me too. But can we meet up tomorrow night – or do you have to be at the restaurant?'

'My new chef'll be working so they can do without me,' she explained. 'Why don't you come here – about eight?'

'Great. See you then,' said McGuire. 'Oh, and . . . I was thinking about your missing man,' he added. 'That note?'

'What about it?'

'Well, as an artist he was probably more accustomed to using a regular A4 page in landscape rather than portrait style – maybe even when writing an important message?'

'The suicide note?' said Pearl, reflecting on this. 'Yes you may well be right.' She said nothing more, prompting McGuire to ask: 'Are you sure you're OK?'

'I'm fine,' she smiled. 'See you tomorrow.'

Pearl set down the receiver and caught sight of her reflection in the mirror. Her smile began to fade as she moved closer to the glass, lifted her hair, and realised she would need to keep her injury a secret, not only from her concerned family but also from McGuire. It was possible that the drone incident had been an accident and nothing more – a new toy in the hands of an inexperienced operator – but it seemed far more likely to have been the result of somebody trying to warn her off. Leon Marris could have left his birthday celebration and followed her to Shellness, or asked someone else to scare her off the island as a favour. He was, after all, noted for handing out favours himself – like the free tattoos he had given to young girls at the Black Spider Café.

At that moment, Pearl was only grateful that a young couple had come to her aid that afternoon – and that McGuire remained unaware that she had broken her promise to him to stay away.

Chapter Fifteen

Early the following morning, Pearl set up a meeting with a charity specialising in helping the homeless in Canterbury. Her plan was to try to assess how easy it might be to go missing in the city – something she recalled Christina Scott having mentioned in connection with Steven; but the thought of the teenager, Alice Weston, who had fallen through the cracks of the care system, wasn't far from Pearl's mind.

The main Canterbury thoroughfare for shoppers that included St Peter's Street and St George's Street was like an artery running through the city, and in the summer months in particular it coursed with tourists and visitors from all over the world, attracted to the famous setting of Chaucer's 'Tales', the birthplace of the playwright Christopher Marlowe, as well as to the cathedral itself, with its connection to a murdered archbishop. But, even here, in the very seat of the country's established Christian Church, rough sleepers were in evidence, begging or busking for charity from any passing 'Good Samaritans'.

Pearl's appointment took her to the back streets, and to a single-storey building, around which a group of men, of varying ages, were milling as she arrived. Chatting and smoking by the front door, they moved aside to allow Pearl to enter, and she found herself in a small central passageway, which enabled the staff to monitor all visitors before allowing them entry. A middle-aged man with long grey hair greeted her, his tired features brightened by kind blue eyes. Introducing himself as Tim, he led her past a series of tables at which a few clients were seated, although breakfast was over and lunch was as yet hours away from being served. Unlocking a door, he ushered her into a quiet office and invited Pearl to sit down. She thanked him for agreeing to the meeting.

'No problem,' Tim smiled. 'We welcome visitors here because it's important that people get to see the work we do, especially if they'd like to support us. We're an independent local charity and receive very little statutory finance. In fact, we're almost entirely funded by the local community.'

'And so I'd like to leave a donation,' said Pearl.

'No pressure,' Tim replied. 'But I promise you it will be gratefully received.' He smiled. 'So what is it I can help you with?'

'Some information, hopefully,' said Pearl. 'I'm in the process of searching for a missing person, exploring all possibilities, including whether he might have gone under-ground here in the city. In your experience, is there an overriding common reason for people to find themselves living on the streets?'

Tim considered her question carefully. 'There are prob-ably as many reasons as there are rough sleepers,' he said. 'Everyone who walks through that door has a different story and a different experience, which is why we have to try and tailor our work to meet our clients' needs. But it's true austerity plays a part, as does alcohol and drug depend-ency, family problems, partnership breakups, mental health issues, depression, bereavement and trauma following domestic violence, sexual abuse and rape.'

'And ... presumably you would refer women to the police and specialist services for rape?'

'And men,' said Tim. 'Because rape isn't something that only happens to women. We would do an assessment for each of our clients,' he explained, 'and try to make referrals to the services they most need, many of which are dwindling. But at the same time, here at the centre we can offer meals, showers, help with applying for benefits – and we also campaign for change in social policy to tackle the causes of homelessness and rough sleeping.'

Pearl reflected on this before asking: 'Presumably, you'd also observe client confidentiality – for example, if someone came to you for help but didn't want their family to be contacted, you'd respect that?'

Tim nodded. 'Our responsibility is to our clients. That's not to say we don't help the police in the case of missing persons, but sometimes there are good reasons why people disappear and that's something that's understood and respected by those on the streets. The word "jungle" is often applied, and certainly it's a fight for survival out there, but there's often a community spirit at work, particularly on the campsites.'

'Campsites?' asked Pearl.

'A loose term for areas on the banks of the River Stour, behind the industrial estates, where rough sleepers have camped in tents before now. Some of them teamed up and developed makeshift facilities for themselves, although the weather or the authorities swept them away pretty quickly.'

'Tell me,' said Pearl. 'If a young girl came to you, sixteen years old, pregnant, a runaway living on the streets, what would you be able to do for her?'

Tim paused before slowly shaking his head. 'We can only direct minors to the local authorities for suitable care. Hopefully, they would be able to find some accommodation for her, but that would probably be a hostel or B & B.'

'And if she had cause not to trust the authorities? If she'd had a bad experience in a care home, for example, and felt safer on the streets?'

Tim explained: 'What I can tell you is that children placed in residential care usually arrive as teenagers after multiple foster-care placements. They can often have complex needs, including mental health, emotional and behavioural problems as a result of childhood trauma. A third of those children might well have been placed as a result of abuse or neglect, and another third may have experienced instability during five or more different place-ments. Over a third will have special educational needs and are also more likely to be in contact with the criminal justice system.' He paused. 'But I'm afraid there's absolutely nothing we could do for them here.' He looked helplessly at Pearl who, in turn, looked away towards various cardboard boxes on the floor filled with canned food, unwanted clothing, toiletries – donations from members of the local community, but of no possible use to Alice Weston.

On the way back to the car park, Pearl walked through an avenue of tall lime trees at Dane John Gardens, pausing at the fountain where she and McGuire had once shared a first kiss. The sun was still shining brightly against the white terrace of elegant Georgian homes that overlooked a vast lawn on which families were enjoying picnics, but as she walked on, she saw the upper floor of the police station above the city wall and imagined McGuire at work there. She couldn't help but think that if things had been different, if she had not become pregnant with Charlie at the age of nineteen, she could be working at McGuire's rank in the same station right now, with all the resources available to him. But instead she was trying to solve another case alone, as most private detectives do and have always done, relying on legwork, imagination and gut feelings to obtain results. Dogged determination, an appetite for seemingly innocuous detail and a good instinct for people had been the attributes which had singled Pearl out during her police training for possible detective work, and though that training had been abandoned, those same attributes still served Pearl well. But whether they would serve her well enough with this particular case still remained to be seen.

*

Returning to Whitstable provided a stark contrast to the visit to the homelessness charity, as a colourful banner was strung across the High Street, advertising the summer carnival that was due to take place in just a few days' time. 'We're all ready for it,' confirmed Dolly brightly in the kitchen of The Whitstable Pearl, as she slipped into her 'coat of many colours'. 'Charlie's built the float on to our trailer,' she explained. 'And I'm off now to put the final touches to Ruby's costume.'

'A seahorse?' Pearl asked, finding it a challenge to picture her waitress as the sea creature.

'Wait and see,' said Dolly. But her mischievous look soon transformed into one of concern as she added: 'You look dead beat, Pearl.'

'Just a bit low, that's all,' she admitted. 'I was at a home-less charity today.'

'Oh?'

'Looking for clues. Anything to help me see things more clearly.'

Before Dolly could respond, another voice sounded behind Pearl. 'Can't McGuire help?' It was Charlie, who had just entered the kitchen from the restaurant. He looked at his mother, waiting for a reply.

'Yes,' Pearl said. 'I do believe he can.' She summoned a smile in an effort to prevent her son worrying. 'And I'm seeing him this evening.'

Dolly's face set at this news and she began to grumble: 'The sooner this case is over, the better.'

Pearl was about to argue but Charlie interrupted her as

he came forward. 'Gran's right,' he said. 'You're not a police officer, Mum. You can't rely on backup . . .' He paused as he considered something. 'And what if this man you're looking for was murdered?'

'It's a possibility, surely,' said Dolly darkly.

'So, can't you leave all this to McGuire?' Charlie asked.

'I wish I could,' said Pearl truthfully. 'But this isn't even his patch. Don't worry,' she said, looking between Dolly and her son. 'I promise I'll be careful. And I *will* solve this case.' With that she picked up her jacket and hurried off, leaving Dolly and Charlie still unconvinced.

Whenever Pearl felt the need to clear her mind, she took herself off to the beach. 'Angels talk to a man when he's walking,' her father used to say, and that thought had stayed with Pearl, not least because it so often appeared to be true. Inspiration descended when she least expected it: watching the bait diggers out on the mudflats at low tide, or seagulls skimming the waves at high water. That evening, Pearl walked as far as the Street, below the grassy slopes, and looked out through the heat haze to where it seemed a few figures were actually walking upon water – a trick of the evening light, and a reminder that Steven Scott's twin brother had failed to survive the current that took his young life at that very spot.

Pearl took a deep breath of sea air and thought of all she had learned that day of the many challenges confronting vulnerable people that could result in the loss of everything – including a home. But in spite of Linda

Scott's description of her beloved son, Mark, the joker and the apple of his mother's eye, it occurred to Pearl that it was, in fact, Steven who had proved to be the stronger twin, for he had survived the accident off the Street of Stones and the further undertow of bereavement and guilt for having done so, while rejecting the dysfunctional reliance of his mother on an unconventional chapel minister whom Christina Scott had described as 'bogus'. In fact, Pearl now recalled that it had been Christina who had revealed Steven's own suspicions about the chapel – something Pearl felt the need to investigate for herself, since she had yet to personally interview the mysterious but charismatic Minister Russell Cameron. But for now, that would have to wait, because she needed to go back to Seaspray Cottage to get ready to meet McGuire.

Chapter Sixteen

McGuire arrived on Pearl's doorstep, precisely on time, at 8 p.m., in spite of the burden of paperwork he should have been dealing with about his new case. Instead, he had abandoned it until the next day, hoping he still had sufficient time to satisfy his superintendent's insatiable need for reports. Superintendent Maurice Welch was a constant stone in McGuire's shoe – the greatest impediment to his police work in Canterbury, but also an obstacle in his working relationship with Pearl, which had caused McGuire to cross several lines of police protocol in the course of as many murder investigations. At that time, Pearl had seemed to underestimate the importance of this, which had only served to create further complications for McGuire, who was well aware of the strict rules governing the way in which police officers were allowed to operate with private investigators and informants. Because of that, McGuire was constantly walking a tightrope in trying to keep his work and Pearl separate – though he recognised her help in serving his own cases had been immeasurable. What concerned him more than anything were the risks she took in her own work and, if he could mitigate those, he would do so with all the assistance he could give her.

After ringing the bell to Seaspray Cottage, he waited only a few moments before the front door opened to reveal Pearl, wearing a scarlet dress cinched at her narrow waist by a vintage fifties belt. Her smile was like sunshine after rain as she beckoned him in. Closing the door quickly behind him she kissed him; he took in the floral perfume on her long dark hair which fell loose about her shoulders, hiding the bruise on her temple which she had also taken care to further conceal with some make-up. 'Come through to the kitchen, I was just opening some wine.'

McGuire followed her there to find two glasses set in readiness. Pearl opened the fridge and poured some white Bordeaux for them both, then touched his glass with her own before they took a sip. She noted McGuire was clean-shaven and casually dressed, wearing jeans, a loose pale blue shirt and some citrus aftershave.

'Let's go outside,' she smiled. 'We've been so lucky with the weather lately, but we should make the most of it because it looks as if we could be in for a storm later.'

She stepped out into the garden and McGuire followed. 'It wasn't forecast,' he said.

Pearl nodded towards the sea view before them. The sky was still blue but a stripe of black cloud lined the horizon.

'There's a change coming,' she said. 'Can't you feel it?'

In truth, McGuire couldn't, but he was prepared to take

Pearl's word for it since she seemed to have an instinct for such things.

'I just hope it stays fine for the carnival,' she went on. 'It's on Saturday.'

McGuire nodded. 'I saw the banner as I drove into town. Big event?'

'For Whitstable,' she said. 'And one of the last of the summer.' She indicated a bowl of plump green Sicilian olives set on her garden bistro table and smiled as she added: 'Mum and Charlie have been in charge of the restaurant float – a marine theme; I'll say no more. We'll close the restaurant for an hour while the parade is on but we'll be open straight after for a celebration. It's a traditional thing – a private party for some of our best customers and local suppliers before the evening service begins. A good excuse for a get-together,' she added. 'Though we may really have something to celebrate if we manage to win a prize for our float. Will you come?' she asked. 'If you have time – with work, I mean.'

'I'll make time,' McGuire said purposefully with a smile.

For a moment, Pearl was lost in his ice-blue eyes, until a loud popping noise caused her to react quickly. She turned to find a seed pod had landed on the bistro table behind her. 'Look at that!' she said. 'The sweet peas are exploding. I could have mistaken that for an intruder on a dark night.' She held out her hand and McGuire took the seed pod from her, not interested in the slightest about botany or the results of an overactive imagination. Instead, he pulled her to him and kissed her. Straight afterwards, she looked up at him, breathless, and for the first time ever, McGuire saw that she was at a loss, and so he took advantage of the moment. 'I've been wanting to tell you,' he began. 'This last time in London, I realised . . . I don't belong there any more. You know that my transfer here was meant to be temporary.'

She smiled. 'Yes. But then we solved that first case. And you stayed.'

'Not because of the case,' he said. 'Everything changed for me . . . being here.'

'Everyone falls in love with Whitstable,' she said.

He held her gaze. 'But I stayed because of you.'

She looked up at him. 'Me?'

He smiled. 'You're a good detective, so don't look so surprised. You know how I feel. We've danced around each other for a long time, Pearl, but we can be honest now, can't we?'

'Honest . . .' she echoed, reminded of her broken promise to him to stay away from Marris. But she saw him smile again. 'There are a lot of things I love about you but . . . you've always said it like it is, Pearl, even when I haven't wanted you to. And trust is important with a partner.'

Pearl focused on the word, recognising this was the first time in their relationship he had ever used it. He continued: 'Especially when you're working together . . . when your life's on the line . . .'

Pearl suddenly realised. 'Oh . . . you mean . . . your work?'

McGuire nodded. 'Yes,' then: 'Is something wrong?'

Pearl shook her head. For all her hopes for this evening, she realised she could no longer keep her secret and needed to be straight with him. Perhaps, she thought, if she owned up now about her trip to Sheppey, her confrontation with Marris and the incident with the drone, McGuire would still feel the same – he would still trust her. The word 'partner' had raised her expectations, but now she felt disappointed by the work context in which he had placed it.

McGuire saw her confusion and tried to explain: 'Look, Pearl,' he began. 'All I'm trying to say is . . .' He was about to suggest that perhaps Pearl's agency cases were as much of a distraction from what was really important as his own police work, but he broke off and decided to kiss her again. His hands moved to frame her face but Pearl flinched beneath his touch.

'What is it?' he asked, shocked by her reaction.

She was still looking up into his eyes as her hand moved to his, then she pushed back her hair and wiped the make-up from her right temple.

McGuire saw the bruise. 'Pearl . . .'

'I went to Sheppey,' she said quickly.

'You did what?'

'You were busy with the DV case and I . . . broke my promise to you.'

'You went to see Marris?'

She nodded and McGuire's expression turned to stone. 'And he did this to you?'

'No,' she explained quickly, 'it was an accident. A drone. On the beach.'

McGuire saw she was conflicted. 'What happened?' he asked.

'I'm not sure. I'd . . . gone to talk to Marris.' She tried to explain: 'You'd told me he now lived on Sheppey, and that's only half a mile across the Swale from Oare, and then there was the other connection with him having owned the Black Spider Café, and the girl who had run away with Steven? So I went to see him but got nowhere, and while I was walking on the beach, the drone . . . just seemed to fall out of the sky. I couldn't get out of the way in time.'

'Marris?'

'I honestly don't know.'

'But you did report this?'

She looked up at him. 'There was no reason to call the police. I'm sure it was probably just an accident. I was looked after by some kind people . . . I'm fine.'

McGuire looked at her, wholly unconvinced, but he curbed his frustration, still hoping that the evening would bring them closer. He took a step towards her, but at that moment the telephone rang. Pearl looked at the receiver, half expecting another silent call, and decided to let it go to voicemail. A beep sounded. A voice was heard on her answerphone – quick, urgent. 'Hello, Pearl? It's Celia . . .' Pearl recognised the voice of the owner of *The Seahorse* at Faversham and quickly picked up the receiver. 'I'm here,' she said. 'What is it?' She listened to Celia while looking at McGuire. 'I have to talk to you,' said Celia. 'As soon as possible.'

Pearl watched as McGuire walked to the window, but she responded to Celia after deciding: 'I'll be over tomorrow morning ...'

'No,' said Celia quickly. 'Tomorrow's too late! You have to come now.'

'Why?' asked Pearl, confused.

'I can't explain. I've ... just seen someone ...' She lowered her voice. 'I think they're still here.' A pause followed, during which Pearl could hear what sounded strangely like cowbells on the end of the line. 'Are you still there?' she asked. 'Celia!'

Celia's voice returned. 'I'll be on the boat.' The line went dead.

Pearl looked at the receiver in her hand then replaced it slowly on the phone's cradle. McGuire turned back and saw her troubled expression. 'What is it?'

Pearl shook her head slowly. 'I'm ... not sure. She said she needs to see me. Now.' She looked up at him and McGuire read her concern. He made a sudden decision. 'Come on. We'll take my car.'

Pearl said little during the drive to Faversham. The roads were empty and, as McGuire parked up in a quiet cul-de-sac, Pearl turned to him and said: 'D'you mind if I see her alone? If she really has something important to tell me, I don't want to put her off by arriving with a police detective. I also don't want to have to lie to her about who you are.'

A sudden gust of wind blew across the creek, sending loose rigging clanking on some sailing boats moored on the quay. Pearl frowned at the sound of it and McGuire took this as a sign of tension on her part – the weather was indeed beginning to change, and for the worse. 'All right,' he said softly.

She got out of the car and began walking on towards the quay, only to hear McGuire behind her. 'Pearl?'

She turned to see he was also now out of the car and standing, leaning against it. 'I'll be right here.'

Pearl nodded and moved on.

Rounding the corner to approach the creek, Pearl saw the quayside was deserted, though a few lights still shone from the windows of the black timbered apartment buildings on the opposite bank, reflecting in the water. The towering form of the Oyster House was silhouetted by a pale moon rising behind it, and for a moment Pearl thought she heard music from a radio in one of the sailing barges, but it soon faded as she moved on along the quay. The teahouse, shops and services were all long closed but, as she headed on in the direction of Chambers Wharf, she saw the saloon light of *The Seahorse* shining like a beacon in the darkness. Pearl's spirits rose at the thought of hearing what Celia might have to tell her. Surely she would not have insisted on bringing Pearl out so late had this not been something important – something she had failed to divulge before? But, if that was the case, why had she not confided it during their meeting? Pearl reasoned that it had to be new information, perhaps something connected to recent events.

Due to the late hour, Pearl decided against calling out and instead took the gangplank from the quay across to

The Seahorse's deck. Once aboard, she tapped on the wheelhouse door and found it unlocked. It was her first time on the vessel at night and, as with all beloved boat interiors, it felt like a safe haven, womb-like, a protection from stormy seas. But it was more than that – it was Celia's home – and, feeling to be an intruder, Pearl knocked again on the door: 'Celia, it's me. Are you here?'

Silence.

Opening the door, Pearl moved through the boat, but soon found the saloon space, galley and cabins were deserted. Heading back up on to the deck, Pearl looked out across the still creek before she took her mobile phone from her bag and quickly found the number logged for received calls. Once back on the quay, Pearl looked again towards *The Seahorse*, recognising Celia could not be far away to have left the boat unlocked and with her lights on. Perhaps she was with another boat owner, or even at the Oyster House with Jonathan, though the windows of the old warehouse showed no lights on at all.

Dialling Celia's number, Pearl waited for the call to connect, expecting her to pick up quickly, but the phone rang a few times before she heard something beyond it – the faint ringtone of another mobile sounding from somewhere close by, and in time with her own call. Curious, Pearl followed the sound, heading further along the quay towards the Oyster House, when she suddenly realised the ringtone was now behind her. She took a step or two back, confused by the fact that there were no other vessels moored to the quayside at this point – but the ringing was coming not from land but from the direction of the water. This made no sense, until Pearl saw she was now standing only a metre or two away from the dry dock. The wind whipped up once more, blowing through the tall trees of the grounds of the Oyster House, setting halyards and boat rigging clanking again, this time seemingly in alarm. A chill ran through Pearl as she stared down into the basin of the dry dock.

In the rusting gulley, a woman was lying on her back, eyes wide open, staring straight up at Pearl, her mouth gaping as if she was trying to speak. Pearl quickly climbed down into the dry dock and bent down to help, then recoiled as she saw a thick glistening pool of congealing blood lying beneath Celia's skull.

'Don't touch a thing.' McGuire's voice, urgent and authoritative, sounded behind her from the quay. He jumped down on to the platform beside her and leaned in to lay his fingers against the side of Celia's throat. As he did so, a charm on a silver chain fell to one side – a small sea-horse; Celia's totem. McGuire tried to find a carotid pulse then turned back to Pearl, his look giving confirmation of what she already knew. 'We're too late,' he said gently.

Chapter Seventeen

It was barely light before Pearl had been released home by Swale Police after having given a full witness account of what had occurred at Faversham Creek the previous night. She didn't hold out much hope of the senior investigating officer finding mitigating circumstances in the fact that McGuire had been with her, because he had not been on the quayside when she had found Celia's body. There was therefore no guarantee that Pearl might not be arrested again for further questioning once the results of an autopsy had established an exact cause and time of death.

The first thing Pearl did on returning to Seaspray Cottage was to run a hot shower and try to wash away the smell of death. She stood for some time beneath the water, eyes closed in an effort to blot out the image of Celia's corpse lying in a rusting dry dock on a moonlit night, but that picture was inscribed on her memory as clear as the word, *Seahorse*, which Celia had carefully painted on to the transom of her beloved boat. Her words echoed in

Pearl's mind. *It's meant to be unlucky to change the name of a boat but I think* The Seahorse *will work out just fine for me.* Celia had smiled confidently that day, her red hair shining vividly in the bright sunlight. But the seahorse totem, the spirit creature she had trusted to protect her, had failed to do so.

Pearl stepped out of the shower and wrapped a warm towel about herself, wiping steam from her bathroom mirror to see her reflection staring back – a bruise still in place on her right temple, but nothing as grave as the injury that had caused the death of a young woman last night, her skull smashed against rusting iron . . .

Pearl heard her mobile ringing and answered it quickly when she saw the caller was McGuire.

'How're you feeling?' he asked.

'I'll be OK.'

'I'm still with Swale Police,' he explained, 'so I can't talk for long. Leon Marris has been picked up.'

'Arrested?'

'Only for questioning,' he said. 'The SIO here has taken on what you told him about your case: Steven Scott, the link to the girls in the care home – and the drone,' he said pointedly.

'And the fact Celia had something to tell me?' asked Pearl anxiously.

McGuire hesitated before saying: 'We'll never know what that was.'

'But I know it was important,' Pearl insisted. 'She said it wouldn't wait.'

McGuire answered carefully. 'Procedure will follow. An autopsy . . .'

'She was murdered,' said Pearl. 'To silence her.'

'Silence her as to what?' asked McGuire, barely concealing his fatigue. 'Consider the facts, Pearl. You went and found Marris and questioned him about an incident that took place twenty years ago . . .'

'Concerning vulnerable underage girls,' she said pointedly. 'If nothing else, he should be properly investigated about that.'

'And I've told you, he's being questioned right now,' said McGuire. 'But there's nothing to link that with the death of this woman. The police have only just established her full name from some paperwork on the boat.'

'Which is?'

'Celia Finch.'

Pearl was silent on the end of the line. For a moment, McGuire allowed himself to believe he had finally got through to her. He spoke gently but firmly. 'I think it's time to back off and leave this to the police.'

'But it's my case,' Pearl argued. 'I have a responsibility to Christina.'

'And to your own safety,' said McGuire.' Think about Charlie . . .'

'Please let's not argue about this,' said Pearl softly.

'It's important,' said McGuire. '*You're* important, Pearl – to me.'

She closed her eyes, relieved to hear this, but equally torn. She paused for a moment, trying to organise her thoughts then said, 'Look, I know I don't have rank, or a salary, or even a proper office, but the work I do is important to me – and to everyone who comes to me for help. Charlie's right: I don't have any backup to rely on, and I don't even charge my clients very much for what I do – but I still give a good service. I work hard and I rely on my instincts to get results. I solve my cases because I don't give up – I keep going.'

'I know,' said McGuire. 'But you work alone, Pearl. Every good private investigator I've ever known has been the same – a lone wolf – but *I'm* not a PI and *you're* not a police officer. If you were, you'd have to respect the rules, as I do. That's the difference between us. As a police officer I have to work within the legal system to bring any kind of justice to victims.'

'I understand,' said Pearl calmly. 'So let's just talk about what connects us rather than what divides us? The need for justice. This isn't your patch – the investigation into Celia's death belongs to Swale Police and they'll deal with it with all the formality it requires – but you and I are witnesses, and there's no reason we can't continue to work together on Steven's disappearance, is there?'

McGuire tried to protest. 'Pearl—'

'Please, just hear me out for a second. Celia knew that I was investigating Steven's disappearance, so what she wanted to discuss with me last night must have been connected with that – but why now? Was there something she hadn't told me when we first met? Or had something happened *since* then? If so – why could it not have waited until the morning? She said to me on the phone that she'd spoken to someone last night – but she couldn't talk to me on the phone right then because she thought that person was still there. I didn't know what she meant at the time – because surely she would know for sure if they were, or they weren't there, but then I remembered that when she was talking to me, I could hear a sound in the background. I wasn't sure at the time what it was – it sounded like . . . cowbells. But when I was giving my account to the police last night, I remembered. A strong wind blowing through the rigging of sailboats has an eerie quality to it. Sometimes, at sea, it can sound almost heavenly, but last night when I arrived on the quay the wind was gusting and sending loose halyards clanking against the metal masts of sailing boats on their moorings.'

'Halyards . . .?'

'Part of the running rigging on a boat – the tackle that's used to hoist the sails – and that's what I heard on the phone when Celia called me. She wasn't *in* the boat, she must've been outside for me to have heard that, either on the deck of *The Seahorse*, or on the quay, but she told me she thought the person she had been talking to was still there.'

'So . . . why couldn't she see them?' asked McGuire.

'Because that person must have been hiding – maybe on one of the empty boats or perhaps . . . behind the restaurant building, I don't know, but something must have made Celia suspect that they hadn't left the quay last night.' She came to a sudden realisation. 'Perhaps because they live there—'

McGuire tried to interrupt. 'Pearl . . .'

Ignoring him, she went on: 'Jonathan Elliott,' she said. 'The house was in darkness last night. He'd told me he was going away for a few days.'

'When?'

'When he came to see me in the restaurant the other day. Perhaps he was preparing an alibi . . .'

'The police will check it,' said McGuire.

'But an alibi wouldn't be too difficult for him to manufacture . . . I'm sure he has a girlfriend or two. I've told you, he's a very attractive man. He's also wealthy – and wealth brings power.'

McGuire frowned at this. 'So what would his motive be?'

Pearl admitted: 'I don't know. But that's something I'm having to consider for everyone in this case. Sally Ferguson, for instance. She ran her husband's company and she's clearly not short of money – she helped Christina and Steven buy their house in Seasalter and she's sold her own at a good profit. Is it possible that some of her money may have gone to Steven to start a new life?'

McGuire asked with suspicion, 'What do you mean?'

Pearl explained: 'Sally loves her daughter but, I've told you, she's also very protective of her. She made it very clear to me that she'd do anything to keep Christina safe and happy, so perhaps that might have stretched to . . . getting rid of Steven.'

'Paying him off in some way?' said McGuire.

'I don't know, but it's something to bear in mind. And

then there's the whole business of the Chapel of the Wooden Cross. Christina told me Steven had been looking into the structure of the ministry because he'd become suspicious of his parents' dependence on it. Perhaps being married and about to become a father himself had highlighted for him his own parents' reliance on this chapel. Alan and Linda are in thrall to that minister and constantly having to do good work on its behalf. What if Steven really had found something substantial to be suspicious of?'

'Yes,' said McGuire. 'Or maybe he just resented the time his parents spent at chapel and away from him?'

'Well, there's also something called the Lazarus Group,' said Pearl. 'A kind of grief counselling group run by Minister Cameron. I asked a friend to infiltrate a meeting recently . . .'

'You did what?'

Pearl explained: 'I didn't want any alarm bells ringing for Cameron if I turned up in person. Steven's parents know I'm investigating their son's disappearance . . .'

'So you planted someone?'

'Yes,' said Pearl proudly. 'She was quite up for it.'

'And aware of the risks?'

Pearl steeled herself and responded defensively. 'Well, perhaps there wouldn't be any risks if the police had taken Steven Scott's disappearance more seriously seven years ago.'

McGuire failed to reply and Pearl calmed herself before admitting: 'Look, I'm sorry. You're right. We're both tired and we shouldn't be fighting about this. We're on the same side, aren't we?' She paused and then added: 'Please come to the carnival tomorrow afternoon? It begins around five.'

McGuire paused for longer than she liked but then replied: 'OK, Pearl. I'll see you there.'

Pearl gave a final sigh of relief.

An hour or so after McGuire's call, Pearl was firmly ensconced at The Whitstable Pearl, ensuring that the chef, Dean, had everything he needed for the post-carnival party at the restaurant the next day. Once satisfied that all was in place, she drove quickly on to Seasalter to meet her client. Sally Ferguson had taken Martin out on the beach for the afternoon, and Pearl was able to give Christina a full account of what had happened regarding Celia's death at Faversham Creek, while remaining guilty and frustrated, in equal measure, that she had failed to come up with further news regarding Steven.

Christina, looking wan and anxious, shook her head before commenting: 'Such an awful thing to have happened to that woman – and the day before the carnival too. It seems terrible that we should be continuing as if nothing has happened but . . . we're actually going to meet Linda and Alan there.' She looked at Pearl and admitted: 'In some ways this investigation has helped us all, I think. Mum seems to have found a nice property to move into and . . . if we really are never to find out what happened to Steven, then perhaps it's time for us to heal any breaches in our family – for Martin's sake.' She paused for a moment. 'I know I've had my difficulties with Linda, but my son still has her genes and she and Martin will always be connected.' She frowned. 'It's the chapel and the minister I have problems with but ... well, perhaps if we come together more as a family, Linda and Alan won't feel so dependent on them.'

Pearl took this in and said: 'You told me that Steven had been looking into the chapel. Did he ever find out anything in particular?'

Christina shrugged. 'Nothing you couldn't discover by doing some searches on the internet. But he didn't like the hold the minister always had over his parents – Linda, in particular, because she's so vulnerable. A child looks to a mother for their needs, but Linda has always been so needy, it's as though she requires parenting herself. She has Alan, of course, but he clearly wasn't enough to send her spiralling down after Mark's death, so I'm sure Steven could never really trust her with his own needs as a child. When Minister Cameron came along, Steven was sidelined even further, and that must have been so confusing for him because the minister arrived, as if out of nowhere, and just ... made himself indispensible. He has this tremendous confidence and he used it to go round the whole area, introducing himself, and managed to persuade business owners, and even the local MP, to help out with all his fundraising events. The congregation grew and we all know word of mouth is the best form of advertising.'

'He's a widower, I believe?' said Pearl.

'He's certainly single, and gets invited to all sorts of dinner parties across town and further afield.'

'And the fundraising for the sale last week was for . . .'

'Disadvantaged children. A holiday trip of some kind. It was one of the main reasons that I took Martin along. This might sound cynical, but I think the minister realises that events for children tend to be well supported by the community, so he's on to a winner.' She looked at Pearl guiltily. 'Does that sound awful?' she asked. 'I'm sorry but I can't help it, because the way I see it, so much of what he does seems to be less for the love of God and more for the love of Russell Cameron. I find him too controlling and, from what I've seen of how Linda is with him, he's never questioned about his motives or his opinions – and that surely can't be right? He's meant to be a very spiritual person who cares deeply about every single congregation member, but Steven always felt the basic message of his ministry was all wrong.'

'What message?'

'Well, that people should become independent of their friends and family and strike out to do God's work alone. The minister says they should do so according to their own "gifts" and "talents" and that his role is to help everyone with their own spiritual journey. But I don't believe Linda has "travelled" in the right direction at all,' said Christina sceptically. 'And so I've been thinking lately that perhaps if I keep in contact with her more, she might not feel the need of the Chapel of the Wooden Cross – *or* the minister.'

'Yes,' said Pearl, thoughtfully. 'Yes, you may well be right.'

*

Straight after the meeting with Christina, Pearl set off for Herne Bay, arriving at the front door of an Edwardian house on Mickleburgh Hill in the late afternoon. The exterior of the property sported an elegant porch, affording some shade from the strong afternoon sun and allowing Pearl to enjoy a panoramic view of the coastline.

The front door opened and Minister Russell Cameron looked quizzically at her as he attempted to fasten his clerical collar. 'Yes?'

Pearl showed him her business card before asking: 'Could I have a word?'

The minister frowned, unsure. 'Well I . . .'

'It's very important,' she said firmly.

Minister Russell Cameron opened the door wider for Pearl to enter and she waited in a spacious hallway before he gestured for her to go through one of three doors on the ground floor. Pearl found herself in a high-ceilinged sitting room filled with expensively upholstered furniture. An antique chandelier hung from the ceiling and in an alcove stood an attractive Victorian desk on which paperwork was stacked in neat piles.

The minister followed in directly behind her and invited Pearl to take a seat before sitting down himself. 'Could you please tell me what this is about?' His tone was gentle but there was a look of tension in his dark eyes.

Pearl turned to face him. 'Steven Scott,' she said boldly. 'His parents are members of your congregation?'

'That's right,' Minister Cameron said. 'I know Linda and Alan very well . . .'

'And they attend your Lazarus group.'

The minister hesitated. 'I'm still not sure what you—'

'Spiritual support for bereavement?'

Cameron nodded. 'Yes.' His eyes moved to a framed photograph on the top of an elegant mantelpiece. It featured a young couple on their wedding day. The woman was tall, slim and fair, smiling into the eyes of the man beside her – a young Russell Cameron dressed in a grey wedding morning suit. 'I lost my wife to cancer when she was only thirty-five,' he said. 'But I found God. So you could say I gained purpose – through suffering.'

'And you started up the charity known as the Chapel of the Wooden Cross,' said Pearl. 'All the . . . good work you do through it?'

The minister nodded. 'I try to play a useful role within our local community – as do many members of our congregation.' He placed his hands together as though he were about to pray, but his fingers suddenly interlaced and he grasped his palms tightly before his chest, his knuckles pale from the force.

'Helping young people?' Pearl asked.

'Certainly.' He nodded. 'They are our future. The way ahead. So we are actively involved in outreach . . . we aim to inspire young people. And to that end we try to engage wherever and whenever we can. We have a Bible Study Group, numerous activities . . .'

'To which girls from a local care home were once invited?'

The minister frowned, confused, before offering a charming smile. 'I'm not sure what you—'

'The Bay Care Home,' said Pearl, 'was responsible for several girls in local authority care, some twenty years ago – just about the time when your ministry began. Is it possible your "outreach" work extended to them? An invitation to take part in services?'

'We do work with a number of community groups and youth clubs.'

'Forming relationships with them?'

'The groups – yes,' he said pointedly. 'But no more than that. I can't say I have a clear recollection of the establishment you mention.'

'It was closed down,' Pearl said. 'There had been irregularities, failures in the duty of care. One young girl later died. Homeless. Pregnant.'

The minister frowned and looked away to compose himself.

'I'm deeply sorry to hear that,' he said softly. 'And I'm even more sorry that I wasn't personally able to assist. I do recall extending an offer of support to the local authority, but it was never taken up – which in my view was a great shame. We are currently fundraising for disadvantaged local children and teenagers to make a cultural exchange visit to France. Our town has a Twinning Association with the French town of Wimereux to promote friendship by organising various joint activities – and, as far as the chapel goes, its doors are open to all, including you.' He held Pearl's look. 'Now, if you'll excuse me, I have to go and conduct an evening service.' He got to his feet and opened the door for Pearl to leave. She moved as though to do so, then hesitated as she came face to face with him.

'Can I ask what you know about Steven Scott's disappearance?'

He frowned for a moment, then: 'Very little,' he said sparely.

'But you said you know his parents well – Linda and Alan? I saw Linda working hard at the chapel's summer charity market only the other day.'

'Our fundraising sale,' he said. 'Linda has helped a great deal with many of our chapel activities – Alan too.'

'Because they became involved in the chapel after losing their son, Mark.'

'As I've mentioned, grief can bring us closer to God.'

'And seven years ago, they lost their second son too – with Steven's disappearance.'

'That's true . . . but I don't see what any of this has to do with me.'

'Knowing them for all that time, you've formed absolutely no opinion as to what might have happened to him?'

The minister paused before he replied: 'If I had, it would be nothing more than opinion.'

'All the same, I'd like to hear it,' said Pearl.

He paused again, this time bracing himself before commenting. 'I understand the police have suggested Steven's disappearance may have been staged. And it's my personal belief that some of us are destined to encounter a time in the wilderness. Not literally – I mean, of course, a time of adversity; a time during which we might need to . . . endure a trial, a spiritual or emotional test, a struggle which comes when we might least expect it – and ironically when we think we have everything we need. In the Bible, the Israelites came through the miracle of the parting of the Red Sea only to endure a long journey through the desert. Job, too, was tested, and Christ experienced the wilderness for forty days and forty nights. But we should not forget that the Bible tells us how, throughout all that time, "angels attended Him". The Lord created the Garden of Eden but he also created the wilderness. In time, we can all emerge from it.'

'Even Steven Scott?'

'With sufficient faith – yes.' He fixed Pearl with a confident look. 'And now, if you'll excuse me, I really do have a service to get ready for.'

Pearl passed by him into the hall. As she reached the front door, the minister spoke again. 'I will pray for you.'

Pearl looked back at him – and left.

Late that night, back at Seaspray Cottage, Pearl tried to work on her laptop, making a search for the owner of a boat called *The Seahorse* – a woman called Celia Finch. But she could find little information and certainly nothing that cross-referenced with Minister Russell Cameron. When her phone rang she braced herself to answer the call but instantly softened when she found it was Charlie on the line.

'How did it go at the restaurant tonight?' she asked. 'Did you cope OK?'

'Fine,' he said. 'No problems in the kitchen; all Dean's new specials went down well – *and* I got plenty of tips.'

Pearl smiled. 'Well done.' Then her smile began to fade as she thought about all that had happened the night before – an evening she had been looking forward to, but one which had ended in tragedy.

A silence followed on the line, then: 'Listen, Mum, I . . . really wish you weren't on this case,' he said. 'I don't like the idea of you having to tidy up all the loose ends of everyone else's lives. The death of that woman last night—'

'Will be investigated by the local Swale Police,' said Pearl. 'Even McGuire won't have a part in the case. He was merely a witness – like me.'

'Right,' said Charlie, only half satisfied with her response. 'Well, I just want you to know that if you don't feel up to coming along tomorrow, to the carnival, Gran and I understand, OK? We'll be there with the float—'

'And I'll be there to support you,' said Pearl. 'We're a family, OK? Charlie, whatever happens, I'll be there.'

Chapter Eighteen

Early the next morning, Pearl was in the kitchen of The Whitstable Pearl, listening to the distant clamour of beating drums and whistles sounding from somewhere on the beach – a foretaste of what was to come with the Carnival Parade scheduled for later that Saturday afternoon. The rain that had been promised in an early forecast had failed to materialise, and the sky, though streaked with ominous cloud, showed patches of blue, but nevertheless Pearl sensed what Norwegian customers had once described to her as '*lummert*' – a feeling of heaviness in the air that arrives just before a storm is due.

The weather still hadn't broken by the time she left the restaurant – a hopeful sign that lifted her spirits, along with the fact that she knew everything was in place for a post-carnival celebration at the restaurant as soon as the parade had made its way through town. It was due to set off from the castle on the border of Whitstable and the neighbouring town of Tankerton, and then wend its way past the old almshouses on Tower Hill and into the centre of town where crowds had already begun to mill. The heat seemed to be compounded by the wall of people now lining the High Street, and the fact that the tide had retreated – taking with it a certain freshness from the air – but, nevertheless, the afternoon was still filled with expectation. Carnival merchants had ignored the cordons at the pavement and were strolling up and down the road selling flags, balloons, and fabric snakes on sticks, to anyone who could afford them. A burger van chugged out the smell of fried onions but a greater number of customers seemed to have been attracted by the treats on offer from a traditional ice-cream vendor on a tricycle, complete with sunshade, bearing the name Lickett & Smyle. It was true that in spite of all the recent changes in the town, the abundance of holiday lets and the appearance of coffee chains and shops to satisfy the tastes of the DFLs, there were still some things that would always remain the same. Even at Chambers Wharf, Jonathan Elliott's towering Oyster House still over-shadowed every other new development on the creek – even the new Quayside restaurant, over which there had been as much resistance as there was in Whitstable to any risk of the town losing its character. In spite of the influx of DFLs and holiday homes, the carnival remained as much a part of Whitstable's cultural heritage as the annual Oyster Festival, and with the sound of clashing cymbals, and trumpets sounding a fanfare, its parade was just about to begin . . .

Pearl jostled her way down to the front of the pavement, where local stewards were clearing the road for the passage of members of the local fire brigade, who traditionally led the parade with one of their own engines. As soon as they had passed, holding out buckets for charitable donations, the beating of a drum and tinkling of a glockenspiel signalled the imminent approach of the band of the sea cadets. The boys soon appeared, marching in time in their smart naval uniforms, followed by their own 'float' consisting of a trailer carrying their training boat.

As Pearl watched it pass, she couldn't help but think of Celia, wishing that McGuire had been in touch to let her know how the Swale Police investigation was progressing and what time he would be arriving but, disappointingly, she had heard nothing from him all day. The sea cadets' music began to fade as the boys moved on and various walking groups followed on behind: members of local charities dressed in eye-catching costumes to raise awareness of their causes, including the staff of a local animal rescue centre who appeared in turn as a moth-eaten lion and a pantomime horse, with a number of supporters dressed in animal 'onesies' – a panda, a rabbit, and a cat recognisable only by the face-painted whiskers of the suit's owner, as its ears had relaxed in the wash. Vehicles streamed by, some merely commercial vans with their rear doors open to reveal tableaux of various company employees in fancy dress, then a large float approached, blasting salsa music, to which a number of attractive young women were dancing, sporting colourful cha-cha dresses and turbans made of tropical fruit.

On the same float, Pearl spotted her old suitor, Marty Smith, owner of the Cornucopia fruit and vegetable store in the High Street, which had recently taken over its adjoining building to open a juice and smoothie café. Marty was wearing tight black velvet trousers and a scarlet silk shirt with ruffle sleeves, its neckline split open to the waist, exposing a suntanned six-pack of muscles and a gold medallion. On seeing Pearl in the crowd, he waved and began enthusiastically shaking his maracas to the music – but out of time. Pearl waved back, and as he passed on out of sight she felt the same sense of relief that she always did when Marty finally left the restaurant after personally delivering her fruit and vegetable orders. Though Marty was an attractive man, Pearl had long ago recognised, over a few dinner dates, that it would take more than his business acumen, and his passion for obscure fruit, to hold her attention. In fact, only one man had seriously managed to do so for any reasonable length of time – McGuire – and though she knew full well the tension created between them by this case, she still hoped he would arrive at the carnival.

At precisely that moment, a troupe of young majorettes began to approach, and the smiling girls, ranging from small children to early teens, led Pearl to think again about Alice Weston and the young girls at the Bay Care Home. If Alice had lived, she would now be in her thirties and a mother herself, so it seemed all too poignant for Pearl that her death had meant the loss of two lives – that of Alice herself and her unborn child. Had that child been a girl, she might have been one of the proud majorettes passing by at that very moment, or perhaps even Miss Whitstable herself, who was soon destined to appear aboard her own float accompanied by her Carnival Princesses.

Pearl turned away from the procession and wandered further along the crowded street. The stewards had relaxed now that the carnival was under way without mishap and were allowing children to sit on the pavement kerbs for a better view of the proceedings. Men in drag, dressed as housewives with rolling pins, carried plastic buckets for cash donations to charities, while the float for a local bar called the Pyramid showed Cleopatra on her throne, surrounded by beautiful young girls, fanning her with giant palm fronds. A cheer went up as a mobility scooter display team followed on, renowned as they were for their charity fundraising, and Pearl thought again of Minister Cameron's words to her: 'I try to play a useful role within our local community – as do many members of our congregation . . .'

It was in the very next moment that Pearl suddenly caught sight of a few familiar faces in the crowd: Christina Scott stood with her mother, Sally, on the pavement. Alan and Linda were there too – young Martin Scott being held aloft by his grandfather to watch the procession; but the surprise for Pearl was that Minister Cameron also appeared to be part of the family group. As Pearl took in this scene along with the passing floats, she began to realise that, if nothing else, a family breach might have been healed in the course of her investigation, and she finally considered that McGuire had been right and police procedure would take over. It might even decide that the death of Celia

Finch had been nothing more sinister than the result of a tragic accident – though Pearl's instinct told her otherwise. She thought again about the first day she had encountered her at the quayside in Faversham, painting the name of her boat: *The Seahorse*. Celia, the 'live-aboard', had enjoyed the freedom of life upon the water – and perhaps she had also needed to escape something, as Steven Scott had done, and even Dolly had once thought of doing.

Looking around at the many families lining the carnival route, Pearl realised that, at forty-one years old, it was unlikely, though not impossible, that she would ever have another child herself. Over the last twenty years, she had never seriously considered it – until now, with the sense of time passing. But she also knew that the ticking of a biological clock was not sufficient reason in itself to bring a child into the world. As a single mother, Pearl had been lucky to have her own family's support in her decision to give up her police training and bring up Charlie alone – something she had needed to do because Charlie's father, Carl, had disappeared from Pearl's life as completely as Steven Scott had done from Christina's. She still had McGuire, even though the detective was sadly missing from the celebration. When her phone suddenly sounded, her spirits rose with the thought that it could finally be him. Taking her mobile from her bag she saw instead that the caller was someone she hadn't heard from in a few days ...

'How's the carnival?' Dee Poulton's voice sounded bright on the line.

'As colourful as ever,' Pearl replied. 'I arrived late but are you here now?'

'No,' said Dee. 'That's why I'm calling. I was hoping to make it down but . . . I have something of a distraction here.'

At that moment, Pearl heard a sound at the end of the line – a loud yap. 'Is that what I think it is?'

'I'm afraid so,' said Dee. 'A charming little mongrel puppy by the name of Dorothy. I've just picked her up from the rescue centre.'

'Why "afraid"?'

'Well, she's part poodle, part terrier – and rather a handful, so I'm thinking of renaming her Dolly.'

Pearl smiled to herself. 'I'm sure Mum will be honoured.'

'I thought so too. So, although I wanted to come today, I shan't be able to. But I did wonder how things were going on with your case?'

'They're not,' Pearl admitted bluntly. 'To be perfectly honest, I'm stuck. I feel like I have everything before me but I just can't make sense of any of it.'

'I'm sorry to hear that,' said Dee. 'Sometimes you just need a bit of inspiration to set you thinking properly. In any case, I wanted to let you know that I did thoroughly enjoy being recruited by Nolan's Detective Agency. If you hadn't done that, I'd never have gone along to the Lazarus Group, and if I hadn't gone there, I might never have plucked up the courage to move on and get myself a new companion.' Another yap sounded.

'I'm really pleased you have,' said Pearl truthfully,

breaking off as she caught sight of Dolly's ancient convertible Morris Minor, a spectacle in itself, pulling a long trailer behind it. 'Dee,' said Pearl, 'I think our Whitstable Pearl float is about to appear.'

'What was that?' asked Dee as the new puppy began to bark insistently in the background. Pearl said nothing for a moment but gave her attention fully to the restaurant float that was approaching. It was a tour de force: an emerald green seabed covering the entire float's structure, the sides studded with papier mâché branches of coral through which enormous exotic angel fish and sea caterpillars appeared to be swimming. Charlie was at the head of the float, dressed as Neptune, in white robes with a blue toga thrown over his shoulder and secured by a silver belt. He made for a handsome sea god in spite of a silver headdress threaded with trailing dried seaweed. Seeing Pearl in the crowd, Charlie raised the trident in his left hand while rattling a charity bucket in the other. Pearl tossed some money into it; Charlie gave his mother a wink and continued with his regal performance, as a large squid now came into view on the same float, trailing far more than the usual number of arms and tentacles beneath a head fashioned from a white umbrella.

'What do you think?' cried Dolly as she raised the umbrella to reveal herself, then pointed it towards the main feature of the float, a spectacular oyster throne on which Pearl's young waitress, Ruby, sat – a Seahorse Queen, her pretty face framed by the tines of a bright yellow crown. The creature's head was above her own, with a high gold crest curving down the length of her back into a curling tail. The front of her golden taffeta bodice was studded with what appeared to be gigantic pearls, the whole ensemble earning gasps from the assembled crowds.

'Are you still there?'

Pearl suddenly heard Dee's voice still on the end of her phone.

'Sorry, Dee,' said Pearl. 'I lost you there for a moment.'

'No problem,' Dee continued. 'I just wanted to say that if you ever need help with another case, please don't hesitate to call me. I shan't be far away, just over here on the "other side", as Dolly always calls it.' She paused for a moment. 'I do hope we meet again, Pearl.'

'I'm sure we shall,' said Pearl. Another yap sounded and Dee quickly left the line, while Pearl continued to wave at The Whitstable Pearl float, which had became stuck in the general movement of traffic along the High Street. Pearl's arm was still raised but her attention was now drawn to the sight of Christina with her family and Minister Cameron across the street from the float. In the next moment, her phone rang again. This time it was McGuire. 'Where are you?' Pearl asked urgently. 'You're missing the parade. Everyone's here . . .'

McGuire spoke quickly: 'Celia Finch changed her name.'

'What?' Pearl was still finding it hard to hear above the carnival music.

'By deed poll when she was twenty-one.'

'Why would she do that?'

'Perhaps to make a clean break from her past.'

'What do you mean?'

'Her real name was Kim Roberts. She was brought up by foster parents – a couple in a village called Newnham. The father was a pilot on Faversham Creek.'

'Foster care . . .' said Pearl, trying to compute something.

'That's right,' said McGuire. 'She went to the couple as a teenager. Before that she was at the Bay Care Home.'

McGuire waited for Pearl's response but at that same moment The Whitstable Pearl float began to move on and the next appeared, carrying the court of Miss Whitstable and her Carnival Princesses. The young girls were all in their early teens, waving at the crowds from white thrones pulled by a pair of cardboard swans. As they glided by, Pearl considered something.

'Pearl?' said McGuire. 'Are you still there?'

'Yes,' she said, her voice a mere whisper. 'I've been so stupid . . .'

'About?'

'Let me get to a landline,' she said. 'I need to talk to you – urgently – before the party begins at the restaurant.'

Chapter Nineteen

The post-carnival party took place at The Whitstable
Pearl with a full complement of staff, including
Dolly and Ruby serving drinks and a selection of
delicious canapés that had been specially prepared by
Dean and Charlie. Pearl was dressed smartly for the
occasion, wearing black trousers, a white silk blouse –
and her new pearl earrings. As she circulated, chatting
to her customers, she felt someone's eyes upon her and
finally turned to see her old suitor, Marty Smith, still in
his rumba shirt, watching her from the seafood bar. He
flashed her a beaming smile and raised his glass to her.
Pearl came across, waiting until he had selected a canapé
from the tray that Ruby offered him, before she leaned
in and allowed him to kiss her cheek. As usual, whenever
offered such an opportunity, Marty lingered over the kiss
for longer than might be expected, and Pearl found herself
enveloped in a miasma of musky aftershave. Hitting the
back of her throat, it caused her to cough, which freed her

from Marty's wet kiss. He looked at the smoked salmon blini still in his hand then popped it into his mouth and downed it with a swig of Prosecco. 'Very nice spread, Pearl,' he said. 'As ever.'

'Thank you, Marty. I'm glad you could make it.' She smiled politely and started to move off, but Marty took hold of her arm and asked: 'Notice anything different?' He flashed another smile for her, exposing brilliant white teeth, then leaned in closer and explained: 'Bleached. Got to be careful though – no coffee, red wine, soy sauce or fruit juice for a good few days.'

Pearl gave a nod. 'Well, you should be OK with the blinis,' she commented, for want of something else to say. Marty bridged the awkward silence that followed, having taken in Pearl's appearance. 'Nice earrings,' he said. 'They go with your eyes.'

Pearl's hand moved automatically to one of the freshwater pearls and she thought instantly of McGuire and how much she would have liked him to be there. Marty seemed to read her mind and asked: 'Is he not coming, then? Your copper?' He used the word he always reserved for McGuire, though Pearl suspected he had a more pejorative term in his vocabulary for his rival. He sipped his drink and waited for Pearl's response. She shook her head. 'He's very busy with a case.'

'Shame,' said Marty. He moved a little closer, expanding his tanned pectorals beneath his open-necked shirt. His medallion rose with his expectations but Pearl suddenly saw rescue in sight. 'Excuse me, Marty, I've just got to welcome someone.' She moved off quickly to greet the guests who had just entered The Whitstable Pearl.

Christina Scott was looking around the restaurant, her anxious frown disappearing as soon as she saw Pearl approaching. 'Thanks for your invitation,' she said. 'We were just about to leave for home when your text came through.'

'Glad I caught you,' said Pearl, giving her attention now to the rest of the family. 'Come in,' she said. She indicated a large table in the window to Sally Ferguson, who was followed in by Linda and Alan. 'I've saved you a nice spot.' Young Martin Scott was holding his grandfather's hand as he looked up at Pearl and asked: 'Do you really have crabs here?'

Pearl smiled. 'I do indeed.' She looked to Ruby who had just come across. 'Would you like to show this young man one of our best Cromer crabs?'

Ruby smiled and led Martin off towards the seafood bar. Pearl watched them go then turned to see Minister Cameron had entered. He summoned an efficient smile for Pearl, but it was Linda Scott who explained: 'Alan and I thought it would be nice if we brought the minister to see the parade.'

He held Pearl's gaze as he said: 'There's a possibility our Chapel of the Wooden Cross may take up a charity float next year.'

Sally Ferguson looked far from impressed, and as though she had taken up Pearl's invitation under sufferance. She checked that her grandson was being entertained by

Ruby at the seafood bar before she asked: 'Have you any news at all?'

Pearl gave a nod and replied: 'Swale Police are still holding in custody a man they arrested for questioning last night.'

Christina frowned. 'About the murder of the young woman at the creek?'

Before Pearl could respond, Minister Cameron added: 'Do you know for sure if she *was* murdered?'

Pearl was careful in her response. 'The police are still waiting for autopsy results, and they can only keep this man, Leon Marris, in custody for a limited amount of time without sufficient evidence to charge him.'

'But he *could* be guilty? Is that what you're saying?' asked Alan.

Christina looked confused and shook her head. 'I'm sorry . . . but this has got nothing at all to do with Steven's disappearance and . . .' She looked at Pearl in frustration. 'That's what I asked you to investigate.'

'And that's what I've been doing . . .' Pearl tried to explain, but at that point she broke off as the door to the restaurant opened and Jonathan Elliott appeared. 'I got your message,' he said. Pearl smiled. 'And I'm glad you could make it.' Looking back at the family, Pearl introduced him and explained: 'I haven't yet had a chance to tell you, but Jonathan has an idea to put to you, Christina. It's about a possible new exhibition. But first let me get you all a drink and some food.' She moved off to the seafood bar, where Martin Scott was still being shown some of Pearl's finest Cromer crabs by Ruby, while Dolly handed the boy a small sandwich cut into neat triangles. 'See what you think of that, young man.'

Martin looked down at it and then up at Dolly. 'Crab?'

Dolly nodded. Martin tentatively picked up a sandwich and tried it. After a moment of suspense, he smiled and nodded his approval. Pearl asked Ruby to take the boy back to the table and handed her a tray of drinks. Dolly looked across at the guests then back at her daughter. 'Is that the woman whose husband's gone missing?'

Pearl nodded.

'Shame you haven't been able to find him,' she said, genuinely. 'But you can't win 'em all.' As she moved off into the kitchen to fetch more canapés, Pearl reflected on what her mother had just said.

The party went on for another half an hour, during which time Pearl tried to keep a keen eye on Christina's table, though she suspected the topics of conversation were limited due to young Martin's presence. Dean was keen to get some feedback on his new menu items before the evening service began and, after several more Proseccos, Marty indicated he was shuffling off, flashing Pearl a final tipsy smile and threatening a farewell kiss, but Christina offered another welcome interruption. 'It's been lovely, Pearl, but I really have to get Martin back.'

Pearl smiled. 'I understand.' She waved a quick farewell to Marty at the door, then looked across to see the Scott family waiting with Minister Cameron and Jonathan Elliott to say goodbye. 'Let me see you out.'

She moved with Christina to the door, where Alan Scott gave her a warm smile.

'Thank you for inviting us,' he said. Beside him, Linda and the minister nodded their polite agreement.

'Yes,' Sally said briskly. 'It's made for a welcome break and the food was delicious.'

Jonathan offered his hand. 'I'm glad you called, Pearl.'

Outside on the street, Christina helped her son into a jacket, zipping it up efficiently, and running a hand through his hair as Pearl said: 'Thank you all so much for coming. I was thinking, it would be really nice if—'

But before she could finish her sentence, an incoming text sounded on her mobile phone. She took it quickly from her pocket. 'I'm so sorry . . .'

She checked the message quickly and her smile suddenly faded. Christina noted her expression and asked with concern: 'Is something wrong?'

Pearl looked up from her phone. 'No. In fact . . .' She paused to gather her thoughts. 'It looks like I might finally have some information.'

Christina asked urgently: 'About Steven?'

Pearl nodded. 'I talked to a senior police officer earlier today and received some help with distributing more posters around the area at Oare. I think they may have finally come up trumps because . . .' She indicated her phone. 'It appears a witness has remembered seeing something – or someone – on the slipway the morning Steven's car was found.' Looks were exchanged, but before anyone could respond, Pearl began tapping out a reply on her phone.

'Well,' frowned Sally. 'What're you going to do about it?'

'I'm suggesting I meet the person there right now.' Pearl sent the text.

'At Oare?' asked the minister.

Pearl nodded. 'You never know, being there on that slipway might just help jog some more memories.'

Jonathan Elliott frowned at this. 'Hadn't you better let the police know?'

Pearl looked at him and quickly shook her head. 'No, I think it's best if I meet this witness alone. I don't want to go scaring them off.'

Minister Cameron exchanged a look with Pearl. 'Then I'll pray the person has good news for you,' he said.

'You will let me know?' asked Christina anxiously.

'Of course,' said Pearl. 'And straight away. Because I'm heading to Oare right now.' She looked down again at the phone in her hand, then slipped it quickly into her pocket.

Forty minutes later, a lone figure stood on the slipway at Oare. It was Pearl, who was staring across the Swale towards Harty Ferry. The tide was high and the light fading fast. There were no boats to be seen and the pathway of the Saxon Shore Way was deserted. She looked back towards the old boathouse, some twenty metres from the slipway, its wooden doors closed and its windows shuttered. A cold wind blew in from across the river, stirring blades of grass, as if trying to awaken the marshlands. The first drops of rain began to fall, pattering on the stone slipway. At that moment, Pearl fought doubts that anyone might come at all, and instead clung to an abiding hope that her instincts were sound and she would finally be rewarded with the truth.

An old upturned skiff lay abandoned on the path close to the slipway and, as rain began to fall harder, she moved to it to find shelter. She waited for some time. Eventually, she saw two pale circles – car headlights – approaching in the distance. Pearl viewed the vehicle's progress along the winding road, then saw the headlights disappear into the rain and the fast approaching night. Crouching down out of sight, she pressed her cheek against the damp wood of the old skiff and kept her gaze on the road. Nothing. Perhaps, she thought, the car had simply ferried a birder or twitcher to one of the many hides on the marshes. She took a deep breath and tried to relax. Then she heard the sound of footsteps crunching on the track. A shape appeared in the gloom, nothing more than a ghostly shadow; then finally something more substantial – a figure, looking east towards the Saxon Shore Way then west towards the old boathouse. With nothing to identify the person, Pearl felt her heartbeat quickening, her mouth dry as she summoned up courage and called out, 'I'm over here!'

The figure turned quickly but then remained immobile, rooted to the spot, hands thrust deep into the pockets of a bulky anorak. Pearl slowly emerged from behind the boat. Seeing her, the figure now walked across to meet her, standing in front of her before finally pushing back the anorak hood and asking: 'Are they here yet?'

Alan Scott offered a warm smile, then scoured the scene once more before looking back at Pearl for an answer.

'No,' she said. She came a little closer, still keeping a distance between them so she was forced to raise her voice. 'But there's only one person I was expecting.' She paused for a moment. 'You.'

Alan's smile remained in place, but it now seemed frozen on his face. He gave a half-laugh. 'I'm . . . not sure what you . . .'

Pearl went on in a calm tone: 'It was you who brought Steven's car here that morning seven years ago. And that's why you're here now.'

Confusion flashed across Alan's face but he said nothing. Pearl took another step closer and said: 'I always knew there was something wrong about the note, the one Steven was meant to have left in the car? Two lines written lengthways across the page . . .' She frowned. 'And why would he go missing just before an important exhibition – something that would surely have helped solve some of his financial problems, and any others he might have had with Christina?'

At this, Alan looked away for a moment, then back at Pearl as he began to slowly shake his head. 'No,' he said starkly. 'She would never have been satisfied. Christina was turning out just like her mother; trying to manage him, boss him around? Stevie wanted to be free, don't you see? ' He looked at Pearl in all innocence, then turned away again as though needing to concentrate on something. 'If only she'd left things . . . instead of trying to dig up the past.'

'Alice and Kim?'

At this, Alan looked quickly back at her. Pearl went on. 'Kim Roberts, who became Celia Finch, perhaps in an effort to erase her own past – a girl who had been at the Bay Care Home. Just like Alice Weston . . .'

'No,' said Alan firmly. 'She *wasn't* "like Alice". *No one* . . . was like my Alice.' He fixed his gaze on Pearl but went on in a gentler tone: 'Alice was innocent, special.' Then his voice suddenly hardened. 'And I told her not to tell anyone . . . about us.' His words trailed off into a painful silence.

Pearl took another step closer. 'She was fourteen years old . . .'

'But I didn't know,' he said, helplessly. 'Not until it was . . . too late.' He looked back at her. 'When I found out, I broke it off. Straightaway. I didn't want to get involved with anyone. I loved my wife, my boys . . .' His face began to crumple. 'But it was a terrible time. We'd lost our Mark. And my Linda, she . . . she turned away from me. I had no purpose any more.' He broke off, and stared away across the Swale, as though looking back into the past. 'I'd go for a drive at night. I couldn't sleep. Stopped for petrol one night on the way home and went to the café next door. Alice was there. She . . . just got talking to me. A little ray of sunshine. She asked me for a lift and, suddenly, I was caught up, I . . . couldn't get free.' He looked back at Pearl and his expression froze. 'I *told* her not to tell anyone.'

'But she did,' said Pearl. 'Teenage girls can never keep quiet about their first love.'

With a pained expression, Alan stared down at the wet

slipway beneath his feet, covered in moss and weed. Pearl continued, 'She must have been so proud of the man she'd fallen in love with – a man who said he was taking her away to build a real home for her, a castle, where she could live like a princess. That's what happened, isn't it, Alan? You said you'd take care of her because . . . that's what you do. You took care of everyone: Mark, Linda, Steven . . .'

'And I would've taken care of Alice too,' he said almost in a whisper. 'But . . . she was too young. They all were. That's why the home was closed . . .'

'And that's why you had to let her go.'

He frowned. 'I told you. I *had* to break it off. Alice had told me her real age and I . . . couldn't let my Linda find out. She was going to chapel by then, finding her way. So, I started going too. And I began to pray – to ask forgiveness for my mistake. I became a good person.' He nodded at this, as though to convince himself.

'And you tried to forget all about Alice Weston,' said Pearl. 'But Alice couldn't forget about you.' She came closer. 'And one person knew that. Someone who cared about her – her friend, Kim Roberts.' Alan said nothing but Pearl went on. 'There are times for synchronicity and coincidence, but a meeting on the pier between two teenagers one day never happened by chance, did it? Kim planned it. *She* took Steven away to that caravan park on purpose. *"Young girls will do a lot of things for love."* And while Alice may have forgiven you for breaking her young heart, Kim hadn't. So she struck up a conversation with young Steven on the pier at Herne Bay and persuaded him to run away with her – first to the amusement arcade and finally to the caravan in Reculver. Perhaps she'd decided she would tell him what had happened between you and Alice? But if so, something got in the way. Maybe she heard Steven's story first – of a boy who hadn't been able to save his twin brother in the currents off the Street of Stones in Whitstable ... Whatever Steven told her that night, it was enough to prevent Kim telling him the truth about his beloved stepfather, Alan Scott – the man who had taken advantage of an underaged girl from a local care home.'

Alan shook his head furiously, as though trying to shake off the truth as he recited a Bible passage like a mantra: '*Blessed are ye, when men shall revile you, and persecute you, and shall say all manner of evil against you falsely . . .*'

'But this isn't false. It's true,' said Pearl. 'If Kim learned that night about a twin brother drowned and a boy who felt blamed forever by his mother for that death, Steven must surely also have told her how he relied upon one person – you.' She paused, gathering her thoughts. 'And if Kim *had* decided to betray you that night, she failed to do so. Because when the police arrived the next morning, she said nothing, and may never have said another word had she not had reason to return so many years later to Faversham Creek, where she met a young man painting on the quay ...' Pearl trailed off, then frowned as she realised something. 'You had to tell me about Steven running away to the caravan park because Linda had told the police seven years earlier, and so you couldn't risk me finding out another way, or it might have looked as though you were hiding something. But you also knew that the incident had sown a seed in everyone's minds that Steven was capable of running away again – much later – as a grown man. What you couldn't know was that the same seed also caused me to question what had happened to those girls – and what had happened to Alice Weston. I suspected it was Leon Marris she had been in love with – and I went off to confront him. When he tried to scare me off the island, I thought he must also be the one who was making hoax calls to me – but it wasn't Marris. It was you – covering up for the murder of your son.'

'No!' Alan cried. 'I didn't murder Stevie. I loved him. And he loved me. I did everything for him. Ask anyone!'

'And he was so grateful he would thank you in his own way – with a drawing, like the cartoon he did for you a few nights before he went missing?'

Alan nodded slowly. 'That was his way. His special way of thanking me.'

'But then something happened. Just days later. And early on that last morning he came to see you at the workshop in Hollowshore. Why?'

Alan Scott turned from Pearl and walked out on to the slipway, clenching and unclenching his hands as though trying to compose himself before he finally spoke again.

'I was still working on the frames.' He frowned. 'A few more to go, that was all. As soon as Stevie arrived, I showed him, but . . . he didn't seem interested any more. He said he knew. About me and Alice. He'd met up with her, Kim – Celia, as she called herself. She'd told him everything, and how Alice had died – alone and pregnant.' His expression clouded. 'I told him straight . . . that wasn't my fault. It wasn't my child. I'd finished with her long ago. I tried to explain that she'd been . . . temptation put in my way – and I'd been weak . . . unable to resist, but I'd spent years repenting, atoning for my sin. I told him the truth. He was still my boy, but he was looking at me as though I was a stranger . . . As though I meant nothing to him, after all these years – after everything we had been through, everything I'd done for him. I told him I'd asked for forgiveness and I'd received it. I was reborn.' Alan nodded at this, but his expression began to dissolve into sorrow before he responded in fury. 'He *was* my boy. I told him that, but he denied me. Like Peter in the Bible. *He* denied *me*. He said what I'd done was a crime and I'd have to . . . admit to it, own up to it . . . and to Linda – or he'd do that for me.'

Alan Scott looked to Pearl for understanding. 'It wasn't *my* boy any more,' he said in a whisper. 'The look in his eyes that day was . . . heartless, dead. I couldn't bear it. He turned away from me and I . . . just tried to pull him back . . . to face me. But I'd been working on the frames with a hammer. I still had it in my hand. I didn't mean to hurt him but he fell. At my feet.'

Alan lifted trembling fingers to his lips and continued like a dam finally broken: 'I turned him over. Saw blood. I put my face close to his. But he . . . wasn't breathing.' He slowly shook his head, trying to make sense of this memory. 'I kept thinking how he looked just like our Mark when I had to identify him. Drowned. Dead.' Alan looked to Pearl, helpless. 'I covered our Stevie with an old tarpaulin. Then I felt like I couldn't breathe so I went outside. Took a big gasp of air, and then I saw the car parked out on the road. Stevie's car. There was no one around and he'd left the keys, so I started it up and I drove . . . out on the road through the marshes. I didn't know where I was going – to get help, to tell the police . . .' He broke off suddenly, as though experiencing a familiar sense of panic, then he closed his eyes. 'But when I reached the road to Faversham, I thought of Linda, and the minister, and young Martin . . . I just couldn't do it.' He lowered his head in shame. 'I turned the car round at the crossroads and kept driving back through the marshes till the road ran out – right here. Then I saw our Stevie's jacket on the seat beside me and I . . . just broke down. I got out and looked at the river. The tide was rising just like now, and I thought I'd walk into it and be gone for ever.' He wiped his face with his hand. 'There seemed to be no other way. But then how would Linda manage knowing what I'd done? So instead I . . . asked for help, the only way I knew. I stood here, on this spot, and I prayed. I asked for forgiveness and a path to follow. I swore to God I would follow it. And I suddenly felt calmer. I reached into my pocket for my phone. I was going to call Linda, just to hear the sound of her voice, but then I realised there was something else . . . in my pocket.' He looked at Pearl. 'Stevie's drawing. The cartoon he'd given to me just a few nights before. He'd written a few lines on it too.' He paused. 'They're etched on my memory.' He began to recite: "'Dear Dad . . . I really appreciate everything you've done with the frames. I never thought what I did was of value – but Jonathan does – so I really can't go on like this any more – letting you do this at your own expense. After the exhibition I want to repay you properly.'" Alan was silent for a moment, blinking a few times before he went on. 'He'd drawn the cartoon just below those lines, and when I read them again, I felt like my heart was bursting. But I looked out over there towards Harty Ferry then down at the note and . . . suddenly, I could only see part of it, two lines that were left when I folded back the edges.'

Pearl spoke. 'So . . . you tore off some of the words to make a suicide note.'

He nodded slowly. 'Well, don't you see? I had to. That was the path that had been shown to me. It was the way.' He offered an empty smile and continued. 'By the time I'd walked back to the workshop, it was light. I knew people would be around soon so I . . . couldn't move Stevie. I couldn't risk being seen so . . .' He paused for some time before going on. 'I pulled up two panels of the plywood flooring and I started digging.'

Pearl closed her eyes for a moment but Alan went on. 'It took me three hours to dig deep enough. But I buried my boy.' His voice became strangely casual as he looked at Pearl. 'And he's been there. With me. Ever since.'

Alan took a deep breath, as though he had just been relieved of a great burden.

'And Kim?'

His face suddenly hardened at Pearl's question and he looked back at her. 'You had to go and find her, didn't you? With her new name? Just a few more days and she'd have been gone but *you* had to show her that poster. *You* told her Steven had never been found and then she came looking for me! She got suspicious, asked me what had happened to Stevie. She was worried he might have killed himself, so she told me to go to the police and tell them all about me and Alice . . . She said she'd give me some time so I could tell Linda, but I knew she'd never do that because I stayed on the quay that night and heard her on the phone to you. I came out from where I'd been hiding. I only wanted to talk to her again, but . . . she got angry, maybe she was scared, but I just put my hand out towards her and she pulled away and fell back. Her head hit the shelf in the dry dock.' He looked back at Pearl and said in a calm voice. 'And all because of you.'

Pearl shook her head. 'No. All these years you allowed Christina to believe she could have been the cause of Steven leaving? Taking his own life?' Her eyes narrowed. 'When all the time you'd made a widow of her – and robbed a boy of his father, and Linda of her son.'

Alan Scott's voice became a raw cry. 'He was my son too! But I lost him because of those girls.'

'No,' said Pearl. 'You lost him because of what you did.' She paused, summoning an efficient tone as she went on: 'You need to confess to the police about Steven and Kim. You'll be arrested and—'

'No.' Alan was firm. 'They have no evidence. And

neither do you. That's why you had to bring me here tonight – to trick me into thinking you were meeting someone? But you're the only one who knows. And that's why I can't let you go.'

His hand reached into his pocket and he moved slowly towards her. Pearl instantly retreated, knowing her escape route would be the marshland in front of the old boathouse. She tried to make a run for it but suddenly lost her footing on the wet moss, and in the next instant she fell down hard on the stone slipway. Winded, she had barely caught her breath when she saw Alan Scott looming above her. His hand withdrew from the deep pocket of his anorak and with it came a heavy iron wrench. He raised it high above his head and Pearl kicked out hard against his shin, using the movement to push herself further away. But as she did so, she felt herself sinking into the wet marsh beneath her. A lone bell buoy on the Swale began to toll and Pearl realised it was too late to escape. The cold mire had begun to swallow her up. Alan's arm fell like a guillotine.

Pearl braced herself but in the next instant the wrench suddenly clattered to the slipway beside her. A cry went out like that of a wounded animal. A tall figure was standing behind Alan Scott, a strong forearm held tight across the man's neck as he tugged Scott's right arm firmly behind his back. Silhouettes were streaming from the direction of the old boathouse. They took hold of Alan Scott, leading him roughly away as McGuire leaned down close to Pearl, drawing her towards him before he framed her face with his hand. 'Are you OK?'

Pearl saw the deep concern written on his face and quickly nodded but said only: 'Did you get it?'

'Every word,' said McGuire.

Chapter Twenty

Two figures stood on the beach at Seasalter – a woman in her fifties and a young boy – collecting shells left behind on the beach after a retreating tide.

At a distance from this scene, behind an old dilapidated chalet, Pearl and Christina Scott observed Sally Ferguson as she took her grandson's hand and walked further along the beach with him. Christina turned to Pearl and said: 'You put yourself in such danger for us.'

'No,' Pearl shook her head. 'I knew DCI McGuire wouldn't let me down. It was the only way we could be sure of getting the truth.'

'But you suspected Alan when you invited us to the restaurant yesterday?'

'Yes,' said Pearl. 'For some time I had all the clues I needed but I . . . just couldn't see things properly – not until the carnival brought everything together for me right before my eyes: the seahorse on our own restaurant float and the two Carnival Princesses in the parade – reminding me that there had been more than one girl at the care home. At the same time, I got a phone call from DCI McGuire about Celia Finch having been at the Bay Care Home. "A new name can often make for a new start" – that's what she'd told me on the day we met. She'd been referring to her boat at the time, but she'd actually made a new start for herself many years ago with a different name and a new hair colour. And while Celia may have had reason to leave her past behind as Kim Roberts, the new name she had chosen for herself was an anagram of Alice – the friend she had never forgotten.' She paused to reflect. 'It had been Inspector McGuire who had suggested that Steven had written lengthways across the page because he was an artist, but then it finally dawned on me that the words could easily have come from one of Steven's drawings – the cartoon he gave to Alan? But there was no way of proving any of this, no firm evidence and no sign of foul play. It was all just conjecture. That landscape at Oare is mysterious, riddled with gulleys where a body might never be found, so what we needed was a confession.'

Christina took this in. 'And Alan gave that to you,' she said, 'by turning up at Oare after the text you received.'

'The text was from Inspector McGuire,' said Pearl. 'Letting me know that everything was in place at the boat-house. He heard every word through the wire I was wearing.'

Christina frowned at this and shook her head. 'I trusted Alan implicitly. I didn't think for a minute he could possibly be capable of such a thing. Those girls . . . Steven . . .' She turned for an answer to Pearl, who thought carefully before she gave it. 'Ordinary people can be driven to make the most terrible moral choices when they're placed under extraordinary pressure. Minister Cameron told me that he had found God following the loss of his wife, but a child's death led Alan to the Black Spider Café. If he had only been honest with Linda about the relationship with Alice Weston, perhaps everything would have been different. Instead, he tried to live a lie, and nothing he did afterwards could put that right.' A pause followed during which Christina heaved a sigh. Pearl said gently: 'I'm so sorry.'

Christina looked back at her. 'No. It's been seven long years of not knowing, but at least we can now move on,' she said determinedly. 'Linda has the minister,' she said. 'And I have the truth, finally – thanks to you.' The words sounded like a punctuation mark in themselves and Christina paused to look out to sea. The afternoon sky was a leaden mass of grey, though Pearl hoped that a brighter day might yet follow tomorrow. Christina spoke again. 'I talked to Jonathan this morning.'

'Jonathan?'

'Mr Elliott. I've given permission for an exhibition to go ahead in the gallery space at the Oyster House.'

'Of Steven's work?'

Christina nodded. 'He says he doesn't want a share of any sales and that every penny of the proceeds must go to Martin.' She looked at Pearl. 'He's a kind man.'

'Yes,' agreed Pearl. 'I do believe he is.' She gave Christina a warm smile, comforted to know that Steven's widow and the man who had so loved his paintings would be partnered in this venture, but she said nothing more as Christina now looked towards the beach to see Sally and Martin waving to them. She turned back to Pearl. 'Will you come and say goodbye?'

Pearl shook her head. 'I have to get back,' she said. 'But come to the restaurant – all of you – when you're ready.' She held out her hand, and as Christina took it in her own, Pearl sensed none of the tension she had felt on their first meeting. Then she watched Christina move off towards the beach, to her mother and son on the shoreline – part of a landscape that would one day be utterly changed by the encroaching tide but which, in that single moment, remained timeless and secure, as Pearl dared to hope that someone in the near future would join them to complete their family.

It took only ten minutes for Pearl to drive home, but after a long day and with a tide of adrenaline finally ebbing from her system, she began to feel exhausted. Getting out of her car, she walked slowly to a lamppost on which she had placed a poster only days before. For the very last time, she stared up at Steven Scott's face, and the word MISSING above it, then she took down the poster and slipped it into her pocket and moved on towards her home. Daylight had begun to fade as she entered Seaspray Cottage, so she reached automatically for the light switch – but stopped in her tracks as she heard something. Closing the door silently behind her, she listened carefully, and knew she hadn't been mistaken. Someone else was in the house. She picked up a heavy torch she kept by the front door and tiptoed across the living room. Mustering courage, she threw open the kitchen door – and found McGuire.

'What are you doing . . .?' Pearl asked, breaking off as McGuire turned quickly, looking both flushed and shocked.

'What am I doing?' he echoed. He picked up a note from the counter top and read it out to her. 'Sicilian salt-baked sea bass,' he announced, 'with roasted vegetables and Trapanese pesto.' He looked back at her, adding, 'That's almond and tomato . . .'

'I know,' said Pearl. 'But how did you get in?'

McGuire looked awkward and set the note down while he picked up a tea towel from the counter. 'Charlie let me in,' he explained. 'This was all meant to be a surprise. But I've only just put the fish in the oven and there's still another forty minutes to go.'

Pearl moved closer and took a peek through the glass oven door. She pointed to the baking tray inside containing the salt-encrusted fish. 'You mean *you* made this?' She looked back at him, impressed.

'Actually no,' McGuire confessed. 'Dean did.'

'Dean . . .?' said Pearl, increasingly confused.

'Your new chef,' he said quickly. 'He's keen to get your opinion of this recipe.'

McGuire quickly tossed the tea towel over his shoulder, grabbed a pile of cutlery and set off into the other room, admitting in frustration: 'Look, I . . . haven't even had time to lay the table.'

Pearl followed him in. 'So I see.'

'But it shouldn't take long.' He began quickly laying the table and then suddenly turned to her, concerned. 'You're . . . not angry about me being here like this, are you? I know it's your home, your space but . . . well, I just thought you deserved something special.'

She came closer to him. 'For?'

'For being such a good detective,' he said. 'And solving this case.'

Pearl smiled. 'Well, maybe that's because I have a good partner.'

She was standing very close to him now, her beautiful grey eyes locking with his.

'Partner?'

'Yes. That's what we are, isn't it?' she said. 'Partners in crime?'

She smiled now and slowly pulled the tea towel from McGuire's shoulder, tossing it to one side so that it landed on an armchair. Slipping her arms up and around McGuire's neck, she continued to hold his gaze as she asked: 'How long did you say dinner would be?'

McGuire returned her slow smile and said softly: 'Long enough.'

He leaned in now and kissed her, pushing her gently back on to the sofa as the sea breeze beyond the open window brought the fresh salt tang of a high tide to mingle with the aroma of Dean's new dish – another treat in store for Pearl and McGuire – and for all at The Whitstable Pearl.

Acknowledgements

I would very much like to thank the following people for their kindness in helping me with research: Maureen Chapple and Mike Canty for all their boating expertise (and a cup of tea on the deck of their lovely Humber Keel, *Olga*); Marie Tilley and her husband, Rob, for 'birding' research at Oare; Reverend Peter Doodes for help with clerical matters; Amy Narain for clarifying some legal issues, and everyone at the charity Catching Lives, for all the work they do for those who are homeless or rough-sleeping in Canterbury.

Thanks also to Sally and Maureen Moesgaard-Kjeldsen for their kind permission to quote the lyrics from 'Disappearing', and to Simon J. Dunn for providing an excellent photo of Oare for the book's cover.

I'm also extremely grateful to Brian Pain for being so helpful and hospitable to me on my visit to Faversham, and showing me around his beautiful home, which served as inspiration for the Oyster House. Huge thanks also go to Louise Bareham for inviting me to the meeting of the Doddington Book Club, at which the idea of using Oare as a location was first suggested.

My continued thanks go to Liz Waller at Harbour Books in Whitstable, and Ruth Frost at Waterstones in Canterbury, as well as to Dominic King at BBC Radio Kent, Amanda Dackombe and Louise Frith of the Faversham Literary Festival, and Victoria Falconer of WhitLit – for all their support.

And finally, I remain indebted to Krystyna Green and the team at Little, Brown Book Group and to all at Michelle Kass Associates for making this series possible.

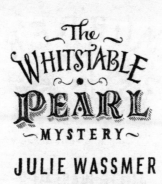

THE WHITSTABLE PEARL MYSTERY

JULIE WASSMER

Pearl Nolan always wanted to be a detective but life, and a teenage pregnancy, got in the way of a police career and instead she built up a successful seafood restaurant in her coastal home town of Whitstable – famous for its native oysters.

Now, at 39, and with son Charlie away at university, Pearl finds herself suffering from empty nest syndrome . . . until she discovers the drowned body of local oyster fisherman Vinnie Rowe, weighted down with an anchor chain, on the eve of Whitstable's annual oyster festival.

Is it a tragic accident, suicide – or murder?

Pearl seizes the opportunity to prove her detection skills and discover the truth but she soon finds herself in conflict with Canterbury city police detective, Chief Inspector Mike McGuire. Then another body is discovered – and Pearl finds herself trawling the past for clues, triggering memories of another emotional summer more than twenty years ago . . .

Available to buy in paperback and ebook

A Whitstable Pearl Mystery

JULIE WASSMER

In the lead-up to Christmas, Pearl is rushed off her feet trying to run her restaurant, plan a family get-together and organise a church fundraiser. However, things become even more complicated when Christmas cards begin arriving all over town filled with spiteful messages from an anonymous writer.

Having pledged not to take on a case before Christmas, Pearl reluctantly agrees that DCI Mike McGuire should take charge; after all, poisoned pen cards are a matter for the police.

But Pearl is embroiled once again when, in a packed hall at the church fundraiser, a guest suddenly collapses. Too much of Pearl's delicious mulled wine – or something more sinister?

Soon the bodies are piling up. Can Pearl possibly solve the mystery in time for the 25th December – or will the murderer contrive to ensure that her goose is well and truly cooked before then?

Available to buy in paperback and ebook

MAY DAY MURDER

A Whitstable Pearl Mystery

JULIE WASSMER

With things relatively quiet at the restaurant and the detective agency, Pearl resolves to spend some time at the family allotment. But her best friend, Nathan, has managed to persuade one of his favourite actresses, Faye Marlow, to open the May Day festivities at Whitstable Castle, and Pearl finds herself in attendance along with the rest of the town.

However, things turn ominous when Faye is nowhere to be found on the morning of May Day. As 'Jack in the Green' puts on his costume to start leading the parade, the actress's body is discovered – tethered to the maypole on the castle grounds. All eyes are on Pearl and DCI Mike McGuire as they attempt to unravel the mystery of the May Day murder …

Available to buy in paperback and ebook

MURDER on the PILGRIMS WAY

A Whitstable Pearl Mystery

JULIE WASSMER

Pearl receives a surprise birthday present from her mother, Dolly – an early summer break at a riverside manor house that has bee recently transformed into an exclusive hotel – the newly named V. Pellegrini.

Pellegrini – the Italian word for pilgrims – reflects the fact that the building lies on the old Pilgrims Way into Canterbury, and Pearl is looking forward to the break, not least because DCI Mike McGuire has been neglecting her due to his work. But when she discovers that she's actually booked in for a cookery course from Italian celebrity chef Nico Caruso, she begins to think again . . .

Available to buy in paperback, ebook and audiobook